# I AM NOT A COP!

## RICHARD BELZER

### WITH MICHAEL BLACK

SIMON & SCHUSTER

New York   London   Toronto   Sydney

SIMON & SCHUSTER
1230 Avenue of the Americas
New York, NY 10020

First Simon & Schuster hardcover edition October 2008

SIMON & SCHUSTER and colophon are registered trademarks of Simon & Schuster, Inc.

For information about special discounts for bulk purchases, please contact Simon & Schuster Special Sales at 1-800-456-6798 or business@simonandschuster.com.

Designed by Suet Y. Chong

Manufactured in the United States of America

10   9   8   7   6   5   4   3   2   1

Library of Congress Cataloging-in-Publication Data:

Belzer, Richard.
  I am not a cop! : a novel / Richard Belzer.
     p. cm.
1. Television actors and actresses—Fiction. 2. New York (N.Y.)—Fiction. 3. Missing persons—Fiction. I. Title.
  PS3602.E6545I35 2008
  813'.6—dc22

                              2008009534

ISBN-13: 978-1-4165-7066-0
ISBN-10:     1-4165-7066-7

To my supportive and loving family:
Harlee, Jessica, and Timbo;
Bree and Franklin; Django and Bebe.
I greatly appreciate and will cherish you always.

Our principal writers have nearly all been
fortunate in escaping regular education.
—Hugh MacDiarmid

# CHAPTER 1

I am not a cop.

Really.

I've just been playing one on television so long that people get a little confused sometimes. It's understandable. I've been at this game for a bunch of years, looking at corpses and bruised runaways all over New York and Baltimore, trying to ask the right questions, trying to find the right bad guy. Or girl, if that's the case.

Of course, when I'm through studying the corpse, somebody yells "Cut," and the body gets up and joins the rest of us on the way to the catering tent for a lunch break.

But it isn't just the general public that gets my role and my life mixed up. Sometimes when I leave the set after a long week's shoot, I'll hit the street and hope to catch a cab. A lot of times, a patrol car will pull over instead and offer to take me where I want to go.

"Mr. Belzer, or should I say 'Detective'?" the cop will say. "Need a lift?"

And hey, I'm not too proud to take the guys up on it, especially when it's raining and cabs are hard to find. Sometimes I even do ride-alongs with the NYPD and sit around precinct houses to soak up the atmosphere, learn the vernacular, and get the moves right.

So, as a consequence, between the cops who consult on the series, the cops I talk with in my everyday life, and the people I work with who act like cops, I sometimes feel like I've slipped into some kind of law enforcement twilight zone—a place where the role I play and the person I am threaten to overlap. Poor old Rod Serling would be proud of me, though. I think I remember an episode like that from when I was a kid. I loved that show.

But I digress. Now, where was I? Oh, the twilight zone of law enforcement, where make-believe and reality overlap.

Take that whole thing that happened in Brighton Beach, for instance . . .

I left the set Friday night in late September to meet a friend for dinner. (Harlee, my lovely wife, was across the pond at our house in France with our adored dogs Django, a border collie–Beauceron mix, and Bebe, a poodle–fox terrier mix who rescued me in France. My wife is a master gardener who loves to toil in the soil, an interior decorator of supreme taste, and an astounding cook, among many other things for which I am eternally grateful.) Having some empty time to fill, I figured I might catch up with an old buddy.

The guy I was meeting was a soon-to-be former medical examiner, a Russian immigrant named Rudy Markovich. I'd met him a few years ago when he visited our set as a consultant for a morgue scene. He looked things over and promptly turned to this young director, who thought he was a hotshot, and said with a thick Russian accent, "Dat is not how ve do it."

I liked Rudy immediately.

He was rather short and had a squarish physique. Very European-looking. I figured him for his late forties, but his hair had gone totally gray. He wore it short and had bright blue eyes and a contagious smile. After the scene I walked up to him and said, *"Zdravstvujtye,"* one of the few Russian greetings I knew. I had had to learn them a few years ago for a part in a Commie spy movie that never got filmed. But the phrases stayed with me. I have a very good memory. Some people describe it as photographic, but I prefer the term *closet genius*, if asked.

Rudy was delighted and started rattling off sentences so fast I had to hold up my hands and say, "Whoa." I explained that I'd already just about exhausted my entire Russian vocabulary, and he said, "Never mind, I speak five languages. That's enough for both of us."

He proceeded to prove it too, as I took him over to the tent for a cup of coffee.

I got a thumbnail sketch of Rudy's life. He'd emigrated from the then Soviet Union as a young doctor and found work cutting open the dead in the Big Apple, then worked his way up in the medical examiner's office; he started listing some of the famous cases he'd handled. In his day, Rudy had autopsied lots of high-profile dead guys for the City of New York. Everybody from politicians to Broadway royalty to business tycoons. His work had helped New York's finest, for whom I have nothing but respect, crack some really tough cases. As we had coffee that day, he told me some real amusing stories about the good old days, and some even better ones about the bad ones. His depth of knowledge about so many more subjects than medicine made him a great conversationalist. We became fast friends, and I got the impression he was a man on the move, so it didn't surprise me when I later read that he had been considered the front-runner to replace the current chief medical examiner. I know he sure helped our actors sound better and made our scenes much more realistic.

But apparently some things in his life had recently changed. Rudy had sworn off dead people and announced his resignation two days before that Friday in September. It was effective at month's end, and he'd told the reporters he was going into private practice. I guessed that maybe he thought it might be easier when his patients could talk back, but hell, the dead ones could never disagree with a diagnosis or sue him for malpractice. It seemed a strange move to me—going from being a towering expert in one field of medicine in the Manhattan ME's office to possibly starting over as a general practitioner in someplace like a Brighton Beach strip mall. But I figured it was his call to make.

Still, I wondered how long his enthusiasm for patient/physician repartee was going to last. I had a sneaking suspicion the novelty would wear off soon enough. The dead may not talk, but they don't lie either. That's the big plus in having corpses as patients: the dead have no interest in hiding the truth.

Rudy called me right after the announcement and asked if we could meet up and talk about a few things.

I'd said sure, and he'd invited me over for dinner in his neighborhood—a little ethnic place called Dimitri's, where the menus are printed twice, once in Russian and once in English. It's a great place for borscht, not to mention fine Ossetra caviar on savory little blini with a dollop of sour cream. Man, I couldn't wait.

Dimitri Gromyko, the proprietor, grinned broadly at me as I walked in. The place was very, very Russian. Dark walls, scarlet drapes drooping to the floor, subdued lighting, closely spaced tables, and a musical group singing folk songs in the native tongue. He greeted me with *"Dobro pozhalovat, Richard."* I replied with my best attempt to sound Russian. Dimitri's bright teeth appeared underneath his bushy mustache. "Rudy is waiting at his usual table."

I walked back past the bar where bottles of fine vodka lined the shelves, past the little stage where the quartet was singing some song that sounded suspiciously like "Back in the USSR," and through the narrow aisles of tables, each covered with a nice white tablecloth. The place had a savory smell that was all its own.

Rudy looked deep in thought. His head jerked suddenly as I sat opposite him, then he nodded.

"Belz, good evening."

"You look like a man with a lot on his mind," I said. He'd already ordered two glasses of Stolichnaya for us. His was now empty. A waiter came by and filled it up. He looked at me, like he expected me to down it in one shot and get a refill, but I needed something in my stomach first. I'm not a whiskey-and-a-raw-egg-for-breakfast kind of guy.

"I'll wait a bit on that," I said. "In the meantime, give me some coffee."

He nodded, set a basket of bread down on the table, and left, taking the bottle of Stoli with him.

"And where is your beautiful wife?" Rudy asked.

"Harlee's in France at the moment," I said. "I'm on my own for a few weeks while we wrap up this round of shooting."

"Ah, the television show. It goes well?"

"You tell me. You haven't been watching it?"

"Of course I have. I wouldn't miss my dearest friend in action."

"Now I know you want something," I said, grinning, "laying a compliment like that on me before we've even decided who's going to pick up the check." I saw a hint of something in his eyes. A catch, a hesitation. "What's bothering you?"

He lifted his eyebrows and tried to cover. "No, no, I merely wanted to ask you something."

"Shoot."

His face twitched fractionally, as if my metaphor had slapped him. He recovered quickly. "I know you're very well schooled in police work, yes?"

I waited for him to continue.

"Then you must know quite a bit about police work."

"Yeah, I've done a few ride-alongs with the cops now and then. Why?"

He compressed his lips, looked at me for a hard five seconds, and said, "I have a somewhat delicate matter for which I may need some police advice."

"Hey, I am not a cop," I said with a grin. "I only play one on TV."

"I know you have some good friends on the force."

"As I'm sure you do. How many years did you spend with the ME's office?"

He took a deep breath, but just then our waiter showed up with my coffee and two menus. After he set everything in front of us, he said he'd be back.

"You were saying . . ."

His head shook, his mouth twisting slightly. "Nothing. It is not important. I had a matter about which I wished to get some advice, but I will tell you about it another time."

I figured it was best to wait until he was ready. Far be it from me to pry into someone else's problems. Eventually, they seem to always have a way of morphing into your own.

"And at the moment, I have something else of much greater import." Rudy held up two tickets of some kind. I tried to see what they were, but he kept them facedown as he handed me one and said, "Alexi's fight tomorrow night at the Garden. I know how much you love boxing matches."

Alexi Zotkin was the reigning heavyweight champ for one of the alphabet organizations that had splintered the boxing game for the past three decades. He'd been listed as the best of the growing numbers of Eastern European boxers who'd started their training in old Soviet-era Russia as young teenagers, and then turned pro after the fall and had come to America hoping to make the big bucks. Alexi had succeeded. The sports page had recently run a feature on him under the headline "The Russians Aren't Coming, They're Here." Not only was he one of the three current champs, he was also recognized by *Ring Magazine* as the number one heavyweight, which was almost as good as having your name engraved on the official *Ring* belt.

I started to hand the ticket back to him, but he made a little shooing gesture with his fingers. All I could think to say was "Wow."

Rudy grinned. "I have two tickets in the third row. I was hoping you'd be interested in accompanying me there so we can watch Alexi get one step closer to unifying the title."

"Even the old KGB couldn't stop me."

That one made him grimace. I should have known better. He'd told me once—after we'd pretty much polished off a bottle of old Stoli by ourselves— of his early youth under the Soviets. "It vas all secret police and terror," he'd said, his accent growing thicker under the influence of the booze. Tonight, as he sat across from me, his clear blue eyes hinted at his previous life under the oppressors. In his case, Big Brother did a lot more than just watch. "I still have a mistrust of police, even in this country. I remember how I could never bring myself to trust them completely." He shook his head again. "Power brings corruption, and absolute power . . ."

"Corrupts absolutely," I said.

"Let us hope," he said now, "that they don't try."

"Seriously, Rudy, what's going on? If there's anything I can do—"

He raised his hand. "You are a good friend, Richard, and that is enough for right now. I need a bit more time to collect my thoughts, perhaps write a few things down to clear my head. We will talk more at the match tomorrow night."

I knew that was all I'd get out of him on that subject. As friendly as he was, when Rudy didn't want to discuss something, he'd draw his own Iron

Curtain closed, and that was that. Instead, we ate and drank and talked about everything from boxing predictions to political ones. He'd been following the recent upheavals in his old homeland near Kiev and commented that he was afraid things would one day devolve to the way they used to be.

"It ain't New York," I said. "That's for sure."

I saw a sadness flicker across his eyes, so when he changed the subject back to boxing, I went along, figuring I'd let him decide if and when he wanted to bring up whatever it was that was bothering him. After a lengthy good-bye to Dimitri, we went outside and I waved to the cab he'd been kind enough to summon for me. All at once a guy popped up and a flash illuminated the night. Luckily, I was still wearing my sunglasses.

"You're Richard Belzer, the TV star, right?" the guy asked, and snapped another picture. "Who's your friend?"

"He's the guy who might do your autopsy if you don't knock it off with the camera," I said.

"Okay, sorry, man." He lowered his hands and retreated to a respectful distance, probably pondering the effects of a flash with a zoom lens.

"Who is he?" Rudy asked. "Paparazzi?"

"Probably," I said, giving the guy my best cold-eyed stare.

"Do you want me to drop you off?" he asked. "I have my car nearby."

"And take you out of your way to Manhattan?" I shook my head. The cab pulled forward and stopped by the curb. I opened the rear door and saw the guy had his hand on his meter already. Rudy stepped over and gave me a sudden embrace. Once again, very Russian.

"Hey," I said, "you're not going to try to kiss me, are you? Like that guy did to Bogey in *Casablanca*." Then I kissed him.

He laughed and shook his head. "Tomorrow night, then? At the Garden?"

"I wouldn't miss it." As I started to get in, I noticed the lines in his face deepening. "You okay?"

"Yes, fine."

He didn't look fine. Once again he looked like a guy with a lot on his mind. I decided to try drawing him out one last time. "What about that matter you wanted advice about? When you mention the cops, that does kinda get my attention."

"Sir," the cabbie said. "I am going to start the meter at this time, please."

Even though I only had one foot inside. You gotta love New York.

I felt like telling him not to get his khakis in a knot, and I started to extricate my foot. If Rudy needed to talk, I'd send this dude scurrying for another fare. But Rudy reached out and laid his palm on my shoulder.

"We will discuss it another time," he said, glancing over at the impudent photographer. "Tomorrow, at the fight. In the street you never know who might be listening."

"Now you're sounding *very* Russian," I said.

He started to say something more, then his hand slowly slipped from my shoulder and he looked down. "Good-bye, Richard."

At the time I thought he'd mistaken "Good-bye" for "Good night." I watched him walk slowly away into the darkness. I got all the way into the cab and gave my address, but just as we pulled away from the curb, a movement caught my eye. I tapped on the screen and told the driver to slow down.

Three dark figures struggled in an alleyway, and one of them was Rudy. I yelled for the cabbie to stop and jumped out the door, leaving the driver behind screaming for his fare.

One guy had Rudy's arms pinned behind his back while the other one stood in front, delivering some mean body blows. Their voices were low and guttural, speaking in some foreign tongue I thought sounded like Russian. The puncher turned in the midst of throwing another gut shot, saw me, and pivoted around, throwing it my way instead. I let the punch sail past my face, then smacked his temple with the heel of my hand, using his momentum to push him down. The other guy tossed Rudy aside like a rag doll and reached into his pants pocket. Seconds later a flash of silver glinted with an accompanying snick.

A switchblade. It'd been a long time since I'd seen one of those. A real one, anyway.

He lunged forward with the knife, trying to slash my face. I pivoted and grabbed his hand with both of mine. I pulled the arm forward, down, and then up and back as I stepped inside, shifting my weight. He was bigger than I was, but the momentum was just right, and his feet skidded out from under him as I slammed him down hard, maintaining control of the wrist until I saw the knife skitter to the pavement.

As I started to reach for it, I spotted movement out of the corner of my eye. The other guy was up and coming at me. I kicked the blade away from us and whirled around, executing one of the best sidekicks I'd thrown since I'd knocked out the heavy bag at the *dojang*. It caught him just where I'd aimed—right in the lower gut area, just below the belt and above the balls. A perfect spot for causing some real gastric disturbances.

Something else flashed and I saw Mr. Paparazzi was back, snapping more pictures. I hoped the idiot had had the presence of mind to call 911 first.

The thugs saw the flashes too. They struggled to their feet and stumbled off in a half-assed run.

I stooped down and plucked the switchblade off the ground just as another damn flash seared my retina. "One more of those, dickhead, and I'll shove this up your ass," I said, holding up the knife. That was a mistake, because the guy called my bluff and the flash popped again.

"Man, that was awesome," he said. "You know karate or something?"

"Or something," I said, turning and helping Rudy to his feet. "Are you all right?"

"Ah, yes . . ." His words came out in shallow gasps. "I am fine, thanks to you."

Another flash.

I turned. "Make yourself useful, and go call the cops, will you, butthead?"

"No," Rudy managed to say. "No police."

"What?" I said. "Those two guys tried to—"

"It is not important," he said, regaining his composure. "Just a couple of muggers. You dealt with them most effectively."

"Rudy—"

"No, Richard. Please." He finally managed to straighten himself all the way up, both hands pressing in on his stomach. "I am fine. Thanks to you." His voice sounded nervous and obviously strained. "I did not know you were so skilled. Was that sambo?"

"A kissing cousin." Sambo was the Russian martial art combining wrestling moves with joint locks. I'd never formally studied that one. "Sort of a hybrid combination of kung fu and hapkido, actually. Was that Russian those guys were speaking to you?"

Rudy shook his head. "Ukrainian."

Another flash illuminated the night. I glared at the guy, wondering if he'd gotten my good side, 'cause he was sure gonna see my bad one in about thirty seconds. I pulled out my cell phone but felt Rudy's hand on my arm.

"Richard, please. Let's leave."

I nodded and helped him to the still-waiting cab. "We'll give you a ride to your car," I said. I looked up and saw the driver with a relieved smile stretched across his swarthy features.

"I apologize for not recognizing you sooner, sir," he said. "You are Mr. Steven Seagal, are you not? I have seen all of your movies. Very nice disguise, sir."

Marvelous, I thought. But at least he wasn't commenting on my acting ability.

# CHAPTER 2

One of the benefits of working the weekend on a special Saturday shoot is traveling through the early morning streets when you're one of the few people around. Or so I thought. When I reported in for work at six thirty a.m., the security guard told me something had been dropped off for me.

"Fan mail from some flounder?" I asked, using one of my favorite lines from the old *Rocky and Bullwinkle* show. He looked too young and too perplexed to understand the reference. But it was still a classic. His loss.

"From somebody," he said, pointing to the metal cart, which had a manila envelope lying on it.

"As long as it's not ticking," I said with a grin, picking it up. The flap wasn't even sealed. I opened the clasp and looked inside. A neatly folded newspaper page with a Sticky Note attached. The note was signed, "For your scrapbook. Cyrus Gustafson."

Cyrus who? Didn't ring any bells. But on the other hand, it sure beat the messages with the bunch of scribbles, like Rocky and Bullwinkle used to get. Besides, being the cultured, suave man that I am, I was curious about the article. Until I unfolded it, that is. A full page of the good old

*New York Inquirer* had a row of several pictures of me in various stages of beating the crapola out of those two thugs last night. Rudy was prominently featured in two of them with a terrified expression on his face. The accompanying headline read, "TV Star in Brawl Outside Brighton Beach Restaurant." The paparazzi prick from last night hadn't wasted any time selling the fruits of his labor. But the photos weren't that bad. Shows what good equipment in the hands of an asshole can do.

I didn't read the copy below the pics because I knew what it would most likely say. The *Inquirer* was the kind of rag that gave honest, up-standing conspiracy theorists like me a bad name. A business card was paper-clipped to the page as well. "Cyrus Gustafson, Reporter" was splayed in bold black letters across the front with a phone number, and "Call me" scrawled on the back. A card and a Sticky Note—this guy wasn't taking any chances.

"Who dropped this off?" I asked, holding up the envelope.

The guard shrugged. "It came by special delivery about forty minutes ago."

I crushed the envelope, article, Sticky Note, and card into a nice ball and dropped it into the trash can. This was the last thing I needed before I'd had my morning coffee.

I'd gotten bad press before and usually just ignored it. That's the best policy. Don't let it get to you, as they say. Besides, in the grand scheme of things, this one really wasn't so bad, I told myself. After all, what kind of idiot reads the *New York Inquirer* anyway?

I found out when I got to my dressing room. Vernon Franker, one of the television show's assistant producers, was waiting, holding a copy in his hot little hands. From the look on his face, I knew he wasn't happy, and from the sweat gathering on his follicly challenged head, I also knew his hands weren't the only things that were hot. When Franker's pissed, he sweats bullets. Let me tell you about Franker and assistant producers in general: Most of them are to actors what hemorrhoids are to the rest of the general population. He knew I didn't particularly care for him, and he relished berating me for what he'd come to call "negative publicity."

"Morning, Vernie," I said, knowing he hated to be called by that nickname. "Doing some highbrow reading, I see."

His lips pursed, then transitioned into a full-fledged scowl. He held up the newspaper with one hand and tapped the row of pictures with the other. "Have you seen this?"

"Yes, sir."

His eyebrows rose, as if he thought he'd somehow scored a point. "And?"

"And I tossed it in the trash like any good New Yorker would, keeping the city beautiful and shit, you know." A couple of makeup girls were watching us, and I love playing to an audience.

Vern's frown reappeared. I wondered if he practiced that move in the mirror. "This is not, I repeat, not a laughing matter."

"Do I look like I'm laughing?"

The girls giggled.

He shot them an angry glance, then turned it toward me. "You're in another altercation, only this time in the street."

The last "altercation" I'd been in was on a talk show and was purely verbal. "This one was totally unavoidable. A couple of muggers jumped a friend of mine when we were coming out of a restaurant."

His mouth wiggled into a frown again, like he'd just tasted something very sour. "Need I remind you that you're playing a police officer on television?"

I tried to look deep in thought as I looked around, milking the pause for all it was worth. I wasn't a stand-up comic all those years for nothing. Finally, after several more seconds, I said, "No, I think I can remember that all by myself."

A redness started to work its way upward from his neck toward the dome, as we termed his extended forehead. By the time he opened his mouth, the flush was at his cheeks. "We've discussed this at the highest levels of production and management."

I resisted the temptation to say, That's nice.

"And," he continued, "we've come to the conclusion that certain preventative measures must be taken. Immediately."

I have a feeling I'm not going to like what's next, I thought. Maybe I should have been less antagonistic. But, what the hell, my stand-up routine needed the work. "That's reassuring."

His lips curled back as he played what he obviously felt was his trump card. "Thusly, we're assigning a person—call her an assistant, if you wish—but she will be watching you for us when you're away from the set. And let me make one thing perfectly clear."

Uh-oh, I thought. Where have I heard *that* phrase before?

He held up his index finger again. "You're to have no contact with the press, except through her, until further notice. Do you understand?"

Now my dander was getting up. Chewing me out in front of other personnel was a sign of poor managerial skills, but we all knew Vern was sorely lacking in this area anyway. However, telling me that I couldn't speak freely was stepping over the line. "You ever hear of the First Amendment? A little thing called freedom of speech? I don't know if you've read about it."

"And did you ever hear of how bad publicity killed a show?"

"I thought in show business, no publicity was bad publicity."

"It's bad when our cast members are photographed in street brawls," he shot back. "It's killed many a show. And many a career." He held up his fingers. "I can give you numerous examples."

It was like we were caught in a loop. "I'm sure you can."

He dropped his outstretched hands and took a deep breath. I guess that meant he felt he'd won. Fine, if that little victory meant I could get to the set and start rehearsing, all the better. I was thinking ahead to leaving early and getting to the fight tonight. But old Vern wasn't finished. He glanced behind me, raised his hand, and snapped his fingers.

I turned and saw a twentysomething black girl walking toward us. She looked like a young Michelle Obama, dressed conservatively in a blue pants suit, her hair straightened and pulled back in a short bun. The expression on her face said one word: *nervous.*

"This is Kalisha Carter," Vern said. The girl nodded shyly. "She's been working in publicity and is now your official liaison to the press."

"Look," I said, "I really don't need a press liaison."

"Call her a personal assistant, then." Vern showed me his palms, one of which still had the copy of the *Inquirer* tucked into it. "Call her whatever you want, but she's going to be keeping you on a short leash. And that's final."

"Is it, now?"

His nod was emphatic. "This is directly from the top."

Kalisha looked about as happy about this whole thing as I was. Glancing around, I saw our audience had increased a bit. I figured this was no dream assignment for her, playing babysitter to a "troubled TV star," and I didn't want to embarrass her in front of everybody the way Vern was doing to me. Besides, my martial arts training has taught me that sometimes you must bend like the willow in the face of a strong wind, knowing it will fade, and let your opponent exhaust himself. Or at least that's how my buddy, Sammo Lee, would put it. I wasn't sure if Vern qualified as a strong wind, though. A lot of hot air, definitely.

I extended my hand. "How about I call her Kali? That all right with you, Ms. Carter? Glad to meet you, by the way."

She smiled and took my hand in hers. Firm grip, but not overbearing. There might be hope for her yet, I thought. But right now, if I still harbored illusions of getting out of here early enough to catch the boxing match at the Garden, I had to forge ahead. That meant smooth rehearsals and flawless execution in front of the cameras. Certainly doable. A smart general picks his battles, I always say. I don't know who said it originally, but I'll have to take credit for that one at some future date.

After getting my wardrobe and getting fitted with my wireless mic for some outdoor shooting, I decided to retire to my dressing room to read the newspaper. I stopped by the craft services truck to grab a coffee and saw Kalisha following me at a discreet distance. I turned and smiled. "Want a coffee?"

We sat, and the first thing she did was tell me how surprised she was by this assignment. "They called me in as soon as I got here and told me I had to do it."

"That sounds like them." I took a sip of my brew. Tepid, as usual.

Someday I was going to have to buy them a coffee urn heater. "So tell me about yourself. You done a lot of press relations work?"

Kali shook her head. "Not really. I went to City College. Majored in journalism. I had dreams of becoming a reporter and someday breaking this real big story. Front page. The next Bob Woodward." The corners of her eyes tightened slightly. "Then my mom got sick, and I was lucky enough to land this job with the television production company."

"So you put the Pulitzer on hold?"

"Yeah. Sometimes life has a way of interfering with your dreams." Her voice was wistful, then she seemed to gather her resolve and looked directly at me. "Mr. Belzer, I know you don't really want me around, but like I told you, I do need this job. Bad."

I sipped my now cold coffee and nodded. Damn. Despite the circumstances, I was beginning to like this girl. She had pluck, or like the Duke said in *True Grit*, "Hot damn. She reminds me of me."

We had a full day's shooting scheduled, trying to wrap up a two-part episode in which I had several crucial scenes. I spent most of the rest of my free time in my dressing room going over the script changes that always come at the last minute. I begged the director, whatever he did, to please shoot me out in time to head over to the Garden for the fight. We ended up having to reshoot the last scene from three different angles. When we finally called it a wrap, I glanced at my watch and saw I didn't have time to change back into my own clothes, not if I wanted to grab a slice of cheese pizza from the guy on the next street before I caught a cab. I figured, given the exigency, wardrobe would forgive me. Kali and I parted company at the front gate, with me assuring her I was headed to Madison Square Garden to watch other people fight tonight.

"Okay, Mr. Belzer," she said. "Have fun and be good."

Mr. Belzer? I was starting to feel like a surrogate uncle.

I waved to her just as I headed out the gate. Chris, the security guard, said, "Hey, Belz."

"What's up?" I asked.

He cocked his head. I followed the gesture and saw a short, big-bellied guy standing off to the side puffing on a smoke and staring at me. At least half a dozen smashed cigarette butts littered the ground around his shoes. Obviously, he'd been waiting a while. Either that, or he had a very nasty habit of hot boxing. I pegged him at being in his early fifties, and he was wearing a plaid sport coat that must have looked great at his high school graduation. He grinned as he started toward me, showing me that his last visit to a dentist had probably been around that time too. But he was holding a paperback copy of my book, *UFOs, JFK, and Elvis: Conspiracies You Don't Have to Be Crazy to Believe.* I took a lot of heat for posing with the cigarette in my mouth for the cover of that one.

"I admire your taste in reading," I said.

"Yeah, you know, this ain't half bad."

"Actually, I do know. I wrote it."

"No shit. Why do you think I been standing here?" He held the book out to me with a pen and said, "How about signing it for me?"

Time was tight, but how long could a signature take? Besides, it was, after all, one of my favorite works of great literature.

"Certainly," I said, accepting the book. Something about this guy was making the hairs on the back of my neck stand up. I'd have to make this quick. Extra quick. And make sure I washed my hands before I ate. "How would you like this signed? To you or to eBay?"

The joke seemed to perplex him. This guy was no rocket scientist, that was for sure. His rotund face froze in what could have been a semipermanent sneer, his lips still curled around the smoking butt. Was this dude a fugitive from the funny farm, or what?

"Sir?" I asked after a few beats, figuring polite professionalism was the best course. It was going to be tight if I wanted to make it to the Garden on time.

"Huh?"

"How would you like this signed? To you?"

He snorted. "Why, shit, of course it's for me."

"Fine," I said, smiling and taking a surreptitious glance at my watch. Still time to make it, if traffic wasn't too bad. "What's your name?"

Instead of answering, he asked, "So how did you like the article?"

"Article?" I played dumb, even though I now had a good idea who this joker was.

"The one I had dropped off here this morning," he said. "I'm the guy who wrote it." He held out his hand. "Cyrus Gustafson, reporter. Glad to meetcha."

I scrawled something half legible on the title page of the book and handed it back to him. "Thank you. I hope you enjoy it."

"What was that fight about last night?" He took one last drag on his cigarette and tossed it into the gutter. "From the looks of it, you really beat the shit outta those two street punks."

"You decked some punks, Belz?" the security guard chimed in. Just what I needed. A sideline assist for prolonging the conversation with Cyrus, the knucklehead.

"Belz, huh? That your nickname or something?"

"Or something. Nice meeting you, but I got to get going." No way I wanted to say where.

"So what's your connection to Markovich?" Gustafson asked. "I know he's with the medical examiner's office. And he's quitting. I heard rumors that maybe he was on the take or something. You know anything about it?"

"Nothing that an ace journalist like yourself couldn't find out on your own." I saw a cab with its availability light on turn the corner toward me. I waved and the driver made a beeline for us. I covered the distance to the cab in three long strides. Right now, I had to get away from Oliver Stone Jr. here.

"Hey, Belz, wait." His short legs carried him toward the cab just as I opened the door and got inside. "There are some more things I got to ask you. And don't forget you owe me, big-time, for plastering your puss on the front page like that. Free publicity."

"Send a bill to the producer," I said, "and if he pays you, buy a new sport jacket there, Slappy."

The driver's dark eyes stared at me in the rearview mirror. "Is the other gentleman coming with?"

"Not if you pull away quickly enough," I said.

He did and we were off to the races. Or, I should say, the fights.

I caught a glance of Gustafson's beefy face as we roared away. It looked like a cross between unadulterated stupidity and the goofy-eyed conceit that that crazy guy must have had back when he beat the shit out of Dan Rather. *What was the frequency, Cyrus?*

By the time we worked through the typically dense New York traffic to Seventh Avenue and Thirty-second Street, I had made three unsuccessful attempts to get hold of Rudy on my cell phone. I kept getting his heavily accented, "If you vant to leaf a message . . ." I hung up as the bright lights of the most famous marquee in all of sports loomed ahead of me, advertising *Heavyweight Championship Title Fight—Zotkin vs. Taylor—Tonight.*

"This is good," I told my cabdriver as we arrived at the Garden. I gave him a generous tip and got out. I looked in vain for Rudy, scanning the front doors and the area next to the elevators.

He must have his cell off, I thought. Probably up in the arena already. After patting my pockets and finding the ticket he'd given me, I proceeded inside and took an elevator up to the fifth floor, munching pizza as I went. The place was filling up with a large contingent of local Eastern Euros holding up blue and yellow flags and yelling for Alexi. I hated to tell them that the main event was still at least two hours or so away, depending on how quickly the undercards went. By that time they'd probably be good and plastered, so I made a mental note to beware of flying beer cups in case by some fluke Alexi didn't win.

I was just glad the Garden didn't serve anything in a glass bottle. I sure didn't want to end up as collateral damage. But then again, I'd have a doctor with me.

The seats were great. Third row on the aisle. Close enough to catch all the action, but far enough away to avoid the splatterings. The only problem was that both seats were empty. I sat in mine and nudged the guy one seat over.

"I'm expecting a friend," I said, pointing to the empty seat next to me. "He shown up yet?"

The guy shook his head and stared at me. "Hey, ain't you that guy on TV?"

I raised my finger to my lips and said, "Actually, that's my talented twin brother."

"Oh, okay," he said, giving me a nod and a vacuous look. He punched the guy next to him and whispered something. He'd obviously gotten a head start on his late night drinking.

I told him I'd be right back, and if my friend showed up to mention that. The guy nodded again, slightly less stupidly this time.

I figured if Rudy was anywhere, he'd be back in Alexi's dressing room, wishing the big guy luck before his bout. The guy he was fighting tonight, Calvin Taylor, was no tomato can, but I had no doubt that Alexi would take him. At six seven, Alexi was one of the biggest guys I'd ever seen, among them, Hulk Hogan. But while Hogan had had that bloated steroid look in his heyday, Alexi had a streamlined, Superman physique. Combine that with the straightest, hardest right hand in the whole heavyweight division, and Mr. Taylor was probably in for a short night and a long nap.

I worked my way back up the arterial aisle and cut down the hallway that led to the dressing rooms. A security guard stopped me as I approached and said the area was restricted. Then he extended his hand with a grin. "Mr. Belzer. Wow. Sorry, sir. I guess I didn't recognize you." He began patting his pockets. "Say, will you autograph something for me? If I can find some paper."

"I want to wish Alexi luck," I told him, taking out one of my business cards and signing it. "I'm a personal friend of his."

I gave him the card and he grinned from ear to ear as he knocked softly on the door and spoke to Carmen Lovato, Alexi's manager. The door opened wider. Carmen's round face was split open with a wide smile.

"Belz," he said, "come on in. We're just taping up."

I slipped past the security guard and shook hands with Carmen. I glanced around the sterile room, but no Rudy.

Alexi sat on a metal table wearing a blue and yellow robe and holding his massive right fist outward. Under the watchful eye of Horatio Turner, Alexi's trainer, another guy spun a roll of white gauze around Alexi's hand, looping it over the back and circling over a padded section. A third man, who I assumed was from Taylor's camp, stood nearby, as did an official.

Hand wrapping required numerous witnesses ever since the very old days when Jack "Doc" Kearns, Jack Dempsey's manager, had been accused of sprinkling plaster of Paris on challenger Dempsey's hands before the Manassa Mauler beat the holy hell out of then champion Jess Willard. The match had ended so quickly, with the champ suffering a broken cheekbone, jaw, and several teeth, that Willard's manager complained that the alleged plaster on Dempsey's hands had hardened when his perspiration had moistened it, thus making the challenger's hands like rocks. I remembered my grandfather telling me about Dempsey, and how the man's fists were like miniature hams even without gloves. But ever since then, a person from the opposite camp was entitled to inspect the opponent's hands prior to the fight. Even so, unscrupulous promoters, like Panama Lewis, have occasionally been able to slip illegal things into fights, like gloves full of horsehair. Carmen wasn't about to let anything like that happen to Alexi, though.

The champ had the robe on to keep warm and loose. Once the hands were wrapped and initialed, he'd start shadowboxing to break a sweat. I knew I'd have to be long gone before then to give him the time to prepare in privacy.

"Richard," Alexi said. "*Goud* to see you." His accent was almost as heavy as Rudy's.

I waved and smiled. "Rudy been by yet?"

Alexi's smile turned to a frown. "No, I have not seen him. He told me he coming too. He always come wish me luck before fight."

The attendant finished placing some white adhesive tape between each of Alexi's fingers. The guy had the biggest hands I'd ever seen.

Horatio held up an open palm and Alexi smacked his clenched fist lightly against it.

"How's that feel, Champ?" Horatio asked.

"It feel good," Alexi said. "Richard, you are going to meet Rudy? Where are you sitting?"

I was about to answer when Horatio cut me off. "Look, Belz, I love you, man, but we got a fight to get ready for. Do you mind?"

I knew his loyalty to his fighter was matched only by his intensity, and he was right. What they needed now was privacy: mental focus was almost

as important as physical conditioning. I smiled and said, *"Udachi*, Champ,"
which was as close to "Good luck" in Russian as I could muster. The by-
product of my questionable pronunciation was that anybody listening most
likely mistook it for "You da champ," which worked almost as well.

Alexi grinned and said, *"Spasibo*, but I have to start teach you Ukrainian. I'm going back there, you know."

"Wait till after you knock Taylor on his ass tonight," I said, heading for
the door. "And then unify the title, while you're at it."

Maybe Rudy was ringside by now, I thought. I heard some yelling and
realized the preliminary bout must have started.

I stopped at the concession stand for a cup of red wine and made my
way back to my seat. The one next to me was still unoccupied. No Rudy. I
thought about trying him again on my cell phone, but a loud roar from the
raucous crowd eliminated that idea. I'd never be able to hear him even if
he did answer. I am not a texter.

I settled back and watched the fighters on the undercard beat the crap
out of each other, hoping somebody would take notice. Unfortunately,
while these poor bastards were up there putting it all on the line, the
bloodthirsty crowd was booing as if they weren't seeing enough action. I
guess most of them didn't quite understand that the essence of "the sweet
science" involved not getting hit when you didn't have to. Especially on an
undercard where the pay wasn't going to come anywhere near matching
the pain.

I made up my mind to go out and call Rudy again from the lobby,
where it was a little less noisy, if he didn't show up after the next fight.
That one wasn't bad either. As the cameraman was focusing on the cable
TV guys, who I assumed were discussing the current disarray of the heavyweight division in preparation for Alexi's appearance, I stood and saw a
uniformed cop standing next to me. He looked down at the empty seat
where Rudy was supposed to have been sitting, read something on his
notepad, and spoke into his shoulder mic.

I nodded to him. He nodded back, then asked, "Hey, Belz, you been
here all night?"

"Since the thing started, why?"

"You seen anybody sitting in that seat?"

"No, I've been waiting for him myself," I said. I didn't ask why he was asking. I figured I'd find out soon enough. And I wasn't sure I was going to like the answer.

"You know the guy?"

"Yeah, he's a good friend of mine. I was supposed to meet him here."

The cop said something I couldn't quite understand into his microphone again, listened, and then looked at me. His face was grim.

"Maybe you'd better come with me."

Uh-oh, I thought, fuck me, something's not good.

# CHAPTER 3

As we were walking up the aisle toward the lobby, the lights dimmed and I caught a riff of rap music coming over the speakers. Calvin Taylor was making his entrance. When he was done, Alexi, as champion, would follow, and then the Michael Buffer wannabe would do the introductions. Or maybe they'd actually gotten the Buff for this one. After all, it was a championship fight at the Garden with the number one–rated heavyweight in the world. HBO was here. So were numerous sports reporters and celebrities.

But I was more concerned about Rudy. From the copper's expression, I figured something was up. I'd played a cop on TV long enough to assume, and had enough life experience to know, that when the men in blue show up, it's not usually good news. I got my second surprise of the evening when we pushed through the double doors and into the lobby. Maxwell Kaminsky, a detective I've known for years, was there talking to a couple of people, at least one of whom I was sure was another detective. They were standing in between the wall pictures of Frank Sinatra and Elvis. Something was definitely up. Max looked a bit more shopworn than usual. He was a big guy with a barrel chest, carrying about thirty more pounds than he needed. His hair, which had once probably been curly, thick, and black, was now sparsely combed back over his scalp and sprinkled with gray.

"Belz," he said, looking as surprised as I felt, "what the hell you doing here?"

"Waiting for the main event," I said. "And for my friend, Rudy Markovich. He was supposed to meet me here."

Max's eyes were dark brown and deeply set, making it hard to read his expression. Whether this came naturally or from concealing his emotions for close to thirty years as a cop, I didn't know. "You seen him tonight at all?"

I shook my head. "The officer here asked me the same thing. Now what the hell's going on?"

Max shook his head, but I wasn't going to let this explanation slip away in a current of police business.

"Max, come on. It's me. Belz. Your buddy, remember?"

He smirked and I saw the corners of his eyes soften just a little. Or had I imagined it?

"Plus," I said, "we're talking about Rudy, our esteemed medical examiner. He gave me tickets for the fight tonight. He's my man."

"I heard he was resigning," Max said.

"Does that make this any less serious?"

Max blew out a slow breath. The other detective looked at him sharply, but Max shook his head. "We found his car down by the East River. Bullet hole in the door, and his coat's in there too. Covered in blood."

His words hit me like a gut punch. "Is he all right?"

Max shrugged. "We ain't found him yet. They're getting a dive team ready to start checking the river."

"Shit," I said. The image of the dark water closing over my head as I looked up at the fading lights of the city rushed through my mind. Sometimes a vivid imagination is a curse. In any case, no matter how I tossed this one, it wasn't coming back pretty.

"Anyhow," he continued, "we checked his coat and found half a fight ticket for the Garden in his pocket. Figured we'd backtrack a little bit, see if anybody'd seen him here earlier."

"What are you going to do now? Did you notify his family?"

He nodded. "Got a couple of uniforms going over there as we speak."

"Maybe I should go too," I said.

He shook his head. "Not a good idea. Plus, we still don't know what's what right now."

I was feeling totally left out. Desperate. "Can I at least go back to the crime scene with you?"

"You know better than that," Max said. "You're no cop."

"Yeah, I know, but Rudy and I go back a ways. Like I said, he was supposed to meet me here at the Garden so we could see Alexi fight."

"Alexi? That big Russkie dude?"

I nodded.

"Did he win?"

My turn to shrug. "It's probably just getting started now."

"Then go back in and watch it." Max reached into his shirt pocket and took out a card. "Here, I'll write my cell number on the back. Give me yours."

He scribbled a number on the back of the card and handed it to me. I gave him mine and looked at what he'd written. "I can barely read this chicken scratching. Or is that intentional?"

He grinned, but it was an expression devoid of mirth. "Of course it's intentional. You don't think I'd be giving out my cell number to some actor, even if he does play one of us on TV, do ya?"

"It's like trying to read a doctor's handwriting," the other homicide dick chimed in. "A doctor of bullshitting."

The other coppers all laughed. Police humor. There's them, and there's everybody else. I'd seen glimpses of the cop fraternity from my time observing at various precincts. The thin blue line was always present, and it turned solid and impenetrable when you tried to get too close. I watched them leave and debated what to do.

I could try to grab a cab over to Rudy's. His wife was a real sweetheart, but her English was sort of limited. His kids were small too, and I didn't want to upset them. I'd probably do more harm than good trying to tell them anything. Plus, I didn't really know what to say. They hadn't determined exactly what had happened to Rudy. I felt the mental urge to add "if anything" to that last sentence, but I knew in my gut something was up. Rudy wouldn't have made plans to meet me here and then not shown up unless something, or somebody, stopped him. I thought back to our dinner conversation. I remembered the uneasiness that had punctuated his statements and pauses. Rudy was one of the most precise men I'd ever met. He'd made his living by being precise. The hesitation should have clued to me that something was seriously wrong. I should have pressed him more when he dropped those hints, asking me what I knew about police work and if I had any friends on the force.

Yeah, I had friends, all right. Friends that gave me a scribble on the back of a card and called it a cell phone number.

And I couldn't go check out the crime scene on my own since Max had been pretty general about where it was. "Down by the East River" could mean anywhere from the Brooklyn Bridge to Long Island Sound. It would be like looking for an Indian head penny somewhere along the subway tracks.

I heard some yelling from inside the auditorium. The crowd was getting rowdy again. Maybe the fight had started. I didn't really want to go back inside, but what if Rudy somehow managed to show up here? What if somebody had snatched his car? And his coat. Something Max had said bothered me, but I couldn't quite place it. Then it came to me. I pulled out my fight ticket and looked at it. Torn in half. Just like the one they'd found in Rudy's coat. Maybe he had shown up here earlier. Maybe he was still here, lying next to a toilet, hurt or bleeding.

I grabbed one of the security guards with some chevrons on his shirt and told him I was supposed to meet a friend of mine and he hadn't shown up. "You had any incidents of anybody getting hurt or anything?"

The guard squinted. "Hey, I know you. You're Richard Belzer, ain't you?"

"The last time I checked."

He snorted good-naturedly. "I watch your show all the time."

"Great," I said. "Can you check on those incidents? My buddy's name is Rudy Markovich."

"Markovich," he repeated, and asked the rest of the crew about the sweep they'd done for the NYPD earlier.

"Yeah, it was for that Markovich guy," a voice said over his radio. "We didn't find nothing. Want us to do another one?"

"Negative," the guard said. He turned back to me. "We've just completed a sweep, sir, at the request of the police. Everything's fine."

Over his left shoulder I caught a glimpse of a gorgeous woman with strawberry blond hair watching us. How long she'd been standing there, I had no idea. That shows you how worried I was. I looked back to the guard and thanked him, and when I started back to my seat, the redhead had disappeared as well. Had she been listening in? Oh, God, I thought. Please don't be another reporter.

At least I knew for sure security had checked the washrooms, but the fact gave me little solace. I felt totally out of my element, and totally dependent on Max to call me back, if and when he found something. At least I hoped he would call.

Suddenly I found myself wishing I had a script for all this so I could jump ahead and read . . . I wanted a deus ex machina to suddenly descend and set everything right.

But that kind of stuff didn't happen in real life, did it?

All I could do was go back inside and wait. Like Max had said, I am not a cop.

# CHAPTER 4

I know what you're thinking. I should have gone back to my seat, watched the rest of the fight, and then gone home to my apartment to wait for any news and let the cops handle it. And actually, that is almost what I did.

I stuck around nurturing the slim hope that Rudy would somehow come waltzing in late, with some wild-ass excuse that he'd been mugged or something. But hadn't that happened last night? Something was strange here. Plus, I should have mentioned that incident to Max. I'd foolishly assumed he knew about it. But what if he didn't?

Anyway, without his legible cell number, I would have to wait. So I watched Alexi give Calvin Taylor five rounds of boxing lessons. The fight was so uneven that midway through the fifth, Taylor butted him in a clinch. It looked like a bad cut, and I figured that if they called it and went to the cards, Alexi would win by technical decision. But the doc let it go on, and after a picture-perfect jab, Alexi whistled home a straight right that ended the contest the best way: without relying on the judges. Taylor didn't even roll over at ten. He looked like he could've slept straight through till Christmas.

The cut obviously needed stitches, though, so I didn't get a chance to let Alexi know that Rudy was more than absent from fight night. But maybe it wasn't something I wanted spread around either. No sense in being an alarmist. For all I knew, Rudy could have been located in an ER somewhere. I needed to get more info before I told Alexi. Besides, they'd whisked the champ off to the hospital right after his postfight interview. I caught a cab home after making one more tour around the lobby, still hoping against hope that I'd see Rudy somewhere.

For the general hell of it, I tried calling Max back at his regular office number but only got his voice mail message advising me that he was unavailable and that if this was a real emergency, to "please hang up and dial nine-one-one." As if anyone needed a reminder.

That reminder didn't sound any better the next morning when I called him again. I left the same message I'd left last night: "Max, it's Belz. I'm calling to see if there's any news about Rudy. Give me a call back, since you have all my numbers."

I wondered if my last line would get results or just piss him off. His cop humor about not giving me his cell number still kind of irked me. Information is golden when you're worried about a friend. Hmm, maybe I should have used that as my ending line instead.

As I pondered my next move over my second cup of morning coffee, I tried to figure what I did and did not know. I knew that Rudy had given me the ticket to the fights, with the intention of meeting me there. I knew he hadn't shown, and the cops had found his car, with a bullet hole in the door, and his coat, covered with blood, down by the East River. *Somewhere* down by the East River. Thanks, Max. They'd also found half a ticket inside the coat. Why half? Had he been to the Garden before I got there, and then left? Something didn't smell right here.

The little voice of reason inside my head kept repeating, Let the police handle it. There's nothing you can do. It was a calm voice. Beatific, in its own way.

But if I had a nickel for every time I didn't listen to that little voice, I could maybe pay off the national debt and still have enough left over to blow at the craps tables in Vegas. Besides, there were three good reasons why I couldn't sit tight on the sidelines and let this matter play itself out.

First, I never sit tight. Or tightly, if you're a grammarian. It's damn uncomfortable either way.

Second, I'm a natural-born snoop. Whether it's JFK, UFOs, or Elvis sightings, I can't resist a mystery. As a kid, I'd go through a Hardy Boys book in a single afternoon, always staying one step ahead of the youthful detectives. I kept up that pace until I discovered Marlowe. Chandler's detective, not the Elizabethan playwright. Then I grew to savor the prose.

But anyway, I digress. You're probably wondering about the third reason, which was the most important one.

Rudy's my friend.

That's why about ten minutes later I was in a taxi heading over to West Fifty-fourth Street. Midtown North, where Max worked out of. MTN meant that he was in Division Three, and the only stretch of the East River in D-three was in the Seventeenth Precinct, between East Twenty-ninth Street and the Fifty-ninth Street Bridge. But that was still a lot of territory to cover if you didn't know where along the river you wanted to go. I was hoping someone at one of the precinct houses could give me a hint.

On the way I called MTN again, asking for Detective Kaminsky. I figured using his title and surname might make the call sound more official, but all I got was the same old voice mail greeting. This time I hung up without leaving a message. I decided on another tactic and told the driver to head over to Fifty-first Street, the Seventeenth Precinct. Maybe if Rudy's car had shown up somewhere in their area, I could weasel the info out of them.

I told the driver to keep the meter running and went inside. The guy squared his turban on his head and insisted on my giving him some "good faith money," in case I didn't come back. You figure dropping someone off in front of an NYPD precinct house would have been enough.

"What? I look that shifty?" I handed him a twenty.

"No, sir," he said. "You look like that actor on TV." His teeth showed white between his mustache and beard. "On *CSI: New York*, but I heard that one is really filmed in Los Angeles."

Everybody's a fucking comedian nowadays.

The precinct looked like something from an old *Kojak* show. The Telly Savalas version, not the one with Ving Rhames. Easy as pie to walk into, desk officer sitting behind a glass window, numerous citizens sitting on old battle-scarred benches that ran along the wall, perpendicular to the entrance.

The officer looked up from his paper and down at me, his reading glasses perched on the end of a long proboscis. I mean, this guy could hire out as an anteater in his spare time.

"What can I do for you?" he asked.

"I was supposed to meet Max Kaminsky over here," I said, trying to affect the right amount of insouciance and irritation. "Something about the car you guys found down by the river last night. With the bloody coat and bullet hole."

He slipped off the glasses and thought, pointing that nose at me. I didn't want to ask if it was loaded. I caught a glimpse of his name tag. It read *M. Beavers*. With a name like that, and a nose to match, the guy was wasting his time being a cop. He should have been a porn star.

Officer Beavers picked up a phone and punched in a couple of numbers. After what I estimated to be five rings, someone on the other end picked up. "Yeah," Beavers said into the phone. "Detective Kaminsky around?" He paused and his fingers went to his elongated nose. I could tell he was resisting an urge to explore.

"Okay," he said, exhaling. "You know where he might be?" More hesitation. His upper lip wiggled like a rabbit's. "Uh, where was that at?" He nodded at me, like we were sharing some inner communication, then he hung up. His head canted to the side slightly. "Who you with? Do I know you?"

I shot him back my best laconic smile. "You might have seen me on TV. You find him?"

He snorted, which with a nose that size could have been semilethal. It was entirely the reaction I was hoping for. "They're over dragging the river by the bridge." A moment later he'd slipped the half-glasses back on the end of his long nose and gone back to his reading. I was out the door and heading back to Abdul, the taxi-driving comic. If this kept up, I was going to have to consider contacting a limo service.

By "the bridge" I assumed he meant the Fifty-ninth Street Bridge, also known as the Queensboro Bridge, if you're Nick Carraway, looking for that first wild promise of all the mystery and beauty of the city. But today, as the cantilevered steel girders spanning the water came into view, I wasn't looking for beauty. I didn't even want to listen to "Feelin' Groovy." I just hoped that I hadn't outsmarted myself, rushing over to a crime scene where, in all probability, the news wasn't going to be good.

As we traveled up Third Avenue and over to Second, I saw a lane obstructed by a marked squad car, and a uniformed cop standing behind it directing traffic to keep moving under the bridge. Off to my right I saw a couple more emergency vehicles sitting on the little flat cement section that has a dead-end turnaround and a locked, fenced-off stairway leading down to the water. Maybe two more marked squads and a fire department truck. It took me another half a block to convince Abdul to pull over and let me out. When I shoved the fare plus tip into his hand, he looked relieved and pleased.

"You want I stay in the area, sir?" he asked. "You are going to walk the bridge?"

What I wanted was not to have to walk all the way back to the crime scene, but I told him to go. I could always catch another cab, and maybe if I showed up with no visible means of transportation, Max would take pity and give me a ride back. I should've stopped at Starbucks first so I could have brought him a cup of coffee. But then again, I didn't want him to think I was impersonating an officer.

Usually autumn in New York is one of my favorite seasons, but today was a bit overcast, and it looked like rain. A hint of winter's chill seemed to have seeped into the air as well, even though it was only late September. By the time I made it to the stairs that led down to the cement section under the bridge, I saw a small group of curiosity seekers standing on the civilian side of the yellow crime scene tape. About sixty feet beyond, four men in slick wet suits were standing smoking cigarettes, their masks and scuba gear on the ground next to them. A perimeter officer stood just inside the plastic yellow ribbon, which was flapping from the strong breeze coming off the water. It looked dark and murky, and even though I could see over to Roosevelt Island, I wondered how many secrets that water held beneath its roiling surface. Across the expanse, the quadruple smokestacks of the island's power station, with their red and white striping, looked like gigantic inverted candy canes. But there was no sweetness in the cop standing at the entrance to the descending stairway.

"Sir, you can't come in here," he said as I ducked under the tape and walked toward him. "Get back."

The small crowd of onlookers seemed totally shocked at the breach that had occurred. Maybe they thought the yellow tape was electrified.

"I just need to talk to Kaminsky," I said, affecting my best bored NYPD detective look. After all, I've had years of practice, and it had worked once this morning. Why not try for a double?

"Sorry, crime scene." He looked like he was going to grab me and slap the cuffs on. I stepped back and raised my arms, palms out. No way I wanted to be arrested this early in the day.

"Not a problem," I said, "but can you just tell Max I'd like to see him for a minute?"

Our conversation must have attracted someone's attention because down on the sloping shoreline, one of the other plainclothes dicks slapped Max's shoulder and pointed up to us. Max looked and I watched as his face contorted into a frown.

Nice to see you too, buddy, I thought, as he came marching over, his arms swinging like twin pendulums. He stopped at the base of the cement stairs and jammed his fists on his hips, arms akimbo.

"Belz, how in the hell . . . ," he started to say, then shook his head. "Aw, shit, I don't even want to know." He motioned to the uniformed copper that it was okay to admit me and stood there at the bottom with his arms crossed, giving me that one-eyed squint that he does so well when he's really pissed off. I took this as a good sign.

"I would've brought the doughnuts," I said, "but they'd just put a new batch in the grease."

The squint was still working overtime. Finally he dropped the crossed arms and looked at the ground, shaking his head slowly. "You got the tendisacity of a fucking pit bull, you know that?"

Max tends to murder multisyllabic words when he's trying to sound philosophical. I didn't correct him this time.

"Well, now that I'm here," I said, "can you tell me if you found anything?"

He sighed and shook his head. "We hooked the car last night. CSU is processing it along with the coat. If the blood on it turns out to be his, it's a good bet it was some kind of stickup gone bad."

That sounded grim. I nodded but said nothing, inviting him to continue. He did.

"The divers have been down there a bunch of times already, but nothing."

Beyond us, nearer to the water, some of the men in wet suits were coiling up a long rope.

"Mind if I stick around?" Since I was already here, I figured now was as good a time as any to ask permission.

He frowned again. "Suit yourself. The only reason I let you come down here was we're calling the search off."

"What? You're stopping without finding him?"

"Maybe there ain't nothing to find," Max said. "Shit, currents, tons of garbage on the bottom . . ." He shrugged. "Maybe he never even went in the water. We just don't know."

"Aw, Max, come on."

He shrugged again, his face taking on an almost pained expression. "Missing Persons will keep looking into it. We got to stop sometime."

The thought that they were giving up so quickly had my blood boiling. "Yeah, like before you happen upon another body, maybe?" Right after I said it, I regretted it, but it was too late.

Max's face darkened a shade and his scowl got worse. No good-natured chiding and one-eyed squint this time. No, this time it was a full-fledged "Go fuck yourself," before he stormed away. I watched him stamp over to the fire truck and say something to the divers. All four of them nodded, like they were discussing the outcome of a Yankees game. They started breaking down their gear, twisting dials, and stowing stuff in ditty bags.

I took a few steps closer and raised a finger toward Max. His nostrils flared, but he came over to me.

"What?" he asked.

"Sorry. I'm just a bit concerned about my friend. Didn't mean to imply—"

"Ah, can it." He made a dismissive wave in front of my face, and his voice had risen a few decibels. "You think I'm looking forward to getting out of here and grabbing a beer someplace? Now I gotta go tell the vic's family that we couldn't find shit."

"Hey, here's something that might be relevant," I said. "The night before last, Rudy and I had dinner together at Dimitri's. Afterwards, a couple of thugs jumped him."

His eyebrows rose. "You know who they were?"

I shook my head. "But they started working him over pretty good, and they were speaking Ukrainian."

"Ukrainian? How do you know that?"

"That's what Rudy told me. I ran them off, but if you check with the *New York Inquirer* newspaper, they should have pictures of them."

"The *Inquirer*?" His face soured like he'd just sucked on a lemon. "I wouldn't use that rag to pick up a pile of dog shit."

"Neither would I, but it might be a good lead."

"A lead." The way he said it I knew he'd taken umbrage at my suggestion. But shit, I thought, this was important. "You telling me what's a good fucking lead . . ."

"Yeah," I shot back, "a good fucking lead. You know one when you trip over one, right?"

He looked mad enough to punch me, but he didn't. "You know, why don't you do some real fucking work for a change, instead of just playing the supercop on TV?"

Before I could think of something to say, Max called up to the perimeter officer and told him I was leaving the crime scene area.

I guess by now you've realized that no one is going to ask me to write the sequel to *How to Win Friends and Influence People*. But I've always looked at my acerbic side as a rare gift. I muttered a half-assed apology and trudged up the hard stairs, figuring it was time to cut my losses.

When the officer ushered me through the gate with a rather truculent sneer, I smiled and nodded politely. I'd been pissing off way too many cops lately.

The crowd of onlookers had started to thin out. I figured they'd seen that the party was breaking up and if they wanted to catch a glimpse of a dead body they'd have to wait for another one on the six o'clock news.

Despite the mayor's bragging about the lowered crime rate, there was still no shortage of stiffs in New York.

As I was walking around the crowd, I noticed an exceptionally gorgeous woman checking me out. She had strawberry blond hair cut in a short but attractive style and the kind of regal cheekbones and pale skin that said Eastern Euro to me. Plus, I'd seen her someplace before. I just couldn't remember where, and I don't usually forget a pretty face. Seconds later I noticed she had something else that almost spoiled her looks: a copy of the *New York Inquirer* tucked under her arm. That rag had caused me enough trouble the past few days. I quickened my pace and started looking forlornly for a vacant cab. Then she was at my side, almost stepping in front of me to cut me off.

"Excuse me," she said, "but you are Richard Belzer?"

Her English was good but had a foreign tincture. "That depends. If you're a bill collector, a process server, or someone who wants me to autograph a copy of that scandal sheet you're holding that they try to pass off as a newspaper, I'm not."

She seemed slightly confused, then recovered, taking the *Inquirer* from under her arm and unfolding it. What was a girl with so much obvious class doing with a copy of that loser periodical? "This is you, yes?" She tapped the ignominious photo array from the other night of me running off the two street thugs.

"It's me, all right. I like to practice beating punks up so I can do most of my own stunts."

More confusion touched her face, like she had to give the wisecrack a veracity check. Lucky thing I wasn't booked for any stand-up gigs east of the Seine. They just didn't appreciate good old American ironic wit. Her full lips compressed inward. It looked like she might have had the same plastic surgeon as Sharon Stone. But comparisons aside, this gal was nervous. Uncertain about something. So I decided to drop the smart-ass routine and play straight man.

"Is there something I can do for you, miss?"

Her eyes, which were a greenish blue, sort of like the East River, flashed to the ground, then back to me. She held up the paper again, this time pointing to Rudy's picture. "And this man. You know him?"

She didn't seem like a reporter, and with her accent I wondered if she had some kind of connection to Rudy. Maybe a relative sent by his family. "I do. Why?"

A tear formed at the corner of her right eye, glistening but lingering in stasis along the edge of her bottom lid. I seized the initiative again.

"He's a very good friend of mine. You know him?"

Her head bowed slightly, and when she brought her gaze up to meet mine, the tear had begun to wind its way down her pale cheek.

"He was supposed to introduce us last night," she said. "At the boxing match."

Then it hit me. That's where I'd seen her. The Garden. So much for never forgetting a pretty face. "Introduce us? I don't understand."

She wiped the solitary tear away and recovered her composure. "Yes. He told me about you. And your friendship."

This was starting to edge into the realm of something I wasn't so sure I wanted to know about. Did Rudy have somebody on the side? And if so, did I really want to know? I'd met his wife and kids numerous times, and they'd seemed very happy. Plus, there was more than a little age difference between him and this chick, not that it means a hell of a lot nowadays.

"Our friendship?" I left it open-ended, hoping she'd follow suit and explain.

"You see," she said, "he was trying to work me back into his life, first by introducing me to you, Richard Belzer, his good friend. But he did not come."

"I'm not sure I'm following you."

She stared at me, giving me that same veracity-checking look as before, then blinked, as if she got it.

"So he did not tell you?" She straightened slightly. "I am Anna Katrina Doskeav. His daughter."

# CHAPTER 5

I took Anna Katrina Doskeav to the first joint we found, a small coffee-house on Second Avenue called Java Express. The place was an old converted store, with wooden floors and a counter running alongside where people in the neighborhood could stop in and buy a bagel and a cup of coffee. It also offered a secluded table away from the rest of the patrons—a pair of lost cyclists and a couple of college kids too self-absorbed to think twice about who we might be. I ordered another coffee for myself (just what I needed, since I was still feeling the residual caffeine buzz from the extra breakfast cups) and tea (in a mug and not in a glass) for her. I watched her pour in the sugar and let her get some of it down while I mentally assessed what she'd just told me.

It had hit me like a sucker punch. In all the time I'd known Rudy, and we're talking a couple of years, why hadn't the subject of a daughter from a previous marriage come up? Or maybe it wasn't from a marriage . . . She'd used a different last name when she'd introduced herself. Odd, but then possibly acceptable in her culture. Rudy's wife, Natalia, was younger than he by a decade or so, meaning she was probably in her late thirties. And his kids were young: six, eight, and ten. I pegged this gal for about twenty-five or -six. Maybe even a couple of years older. Doing the math, that meant she was probably born in the early eighties, when the Soviets were still marching in the streets on May Days. Rudy said little about his life under the Commies, other than that it was a combination of forced mediocrity and terror, but he would have been in his early twenties during that time, so he would have certainly been biologically capable of fathering a child. And if the mother looked anything like the daughter, who could blame him?

Anna set her mug down and looked at me. "Mr. Belzer, this must seem very strange to you, the things I have said."

You got to love what foreign syntax does when it hits American English. I gave her a reassuring smile before I answered. "Well, you did throw me a curveball with all this. But you can call me Richard, or just Belz, if you want."

The space between her brows creased ever so slightly, then released. "Ah, curveball—you are making a joke. A baseball joke, yes?"

"Yes." I waited for her to laugh, and when she didn't, I tried to ease into the subject. "It's just that Rudy never mentioned anything about another daughter."

She looked down at the table and toyed with her mug. "That is, perhaps, because he and my mother . . . never married."

Before I could offer any comment, she set her purse on the table and unsnapped it. Her hand went inside and plucked out an envelope. It had a bunch of Russian writing on it and an official-looking seal of some sort. She bent up a pair of folded metal clasps and withdrew a paper with more foreign printing. This one had the look of an official form of some sort.

"My birth certificate," she said, pointing to a name.

As if I could automatically decipher the Cyrillic alphabet in my spare time with some universal translator. Maybe she'd been watching too much *Star Trek*.

"But of course, this means nothing to you," she said. "You cannot read Russian."

I thought about saying something like, "Is that Russian? I thought it was footprints from a couple of chickens getting it on." But I remembered my early attempt at sarcastic wit. Better to remain silent and use the all-purpose nod. Besides, I wanted to find out what she had to say, not rub her the wrong way.

Her hand dug into the purse again, this time coming out with another envelope. "This, this is important. Very important." She opened the flap on this one and pulled out an old picture, laying it flat on the table between us. It was black-and-white and the edges were frayed, but the captured image was clear: a man and a woman dressed in simple clothes, staring blankly into the camera lens with a dreamy look in their almost-happy eyes. The woman had a classical beauty to her face. The guy was a very young-looking Rudy Markovich with dark hair. "You see?" Her finger tapped the photo's surface. "That is he. That is my father."

"Sure looks like him."

"They were students together at Moscow University."

I canted my head a little. "You said your last name was what?"

"Doskeav. I took the name of my stepfather. He and my mother married shortly after I was born." She picked up the picture and gently tucked it back into its paper holder. "I was raised as his own. By that time, Rudy had left for America. My mother told me he never knew about me."

How convenient, I thought. Still, the picture sure looked like him. But one picture could tell a thousand lies.

"Both my mother and my stepfather worked at the Chernobyl reactor," she said. "I was a child when the accident happened. We lived in Pripyat. They told us it was all right, that there was no danger, but my mother, she was educated. She knew. I was very young. They gave me iodine pills and sent me immediately to live with my stepfather's relatives in Moscow."

"That was in eighty-six," I said. "You must have been, what? Three or four?"

She smiled. "I was five."

"So that makes you . . . ?" I'd already done the math in my head, but I purposely asked to see what she would say. I'd done enough interrogations on the show to know that you have to lull people into a question-response interchange before hitting them with the things you really want them to answer.

"I am twenty-eight."

"Certainly young enough for a new start in America. I'm surprised Rudy never mentioned you to me."

She took a deep breath. "It was as I have said. He left for this country, and my mother married Yuri Doskeav, my stepfather. He was a good man. I went to a special school. Learned English. They wanted the best for me." Her eyes glistened again and drifted to the tabletop. "They were not working the day of the accident. Yuri was a technician, and they called him up. It was the middle of the night. He went in and stayed for eighteen hours trying to fix things, and then with the shell they put over it. They call it the sarcophagus. The exposure level was not an immediately lethal amount, but the cancer, from the radiation poisoning, came a few years later for him. For my mother, it stayed hidden longer, even though they still deny it in Moscow. She died two years ago. I was only allowed to go back to visit them one day every three months. Before she died, my mother told me she had mailed a package for me to my grandmother, her mother, many years ago. Right after the accident. She told me I must retrieve it. It would explain who I was, really." Twin tears rolled down her regal cheeks. She made no move to wipe them away. "I went to see my grandmother, who told me about Rudy and gave me these." She pointed to the photo and the birth certificate. "I applied for a visa to come here. Three weeks ago I managed to find Rudy and showed him this." Reaching just inside the collar of her blouse, she withdrew a thick pendant on a serpentine chain. The charm had a golden butterfly outlined over an opal background. "It was my mother's."

I just hoped it wasn't radioactive. She seemed to sense this.

"Do not be afraid. It is safe. It was with my grandmother in Moscow at the time of the accident."

"It's beautiful."

The tears had disappeared and she smiled. "When I showed it to him, he knew immediately who I was. But his wife did not know. And his family. He said he needed time to bring me into his life here. He spoke of you, and how smart you are. He wanted me to meet you last night. At the boxing match."

I considered this. It sounded plausible, but why hadn't Rudy mentioned her before? Or bought her a seat near us? "Where were you sitting last night?"

She looked confused for a moment, then nodded. "Oh, I understand. You wonder why I did not approach you there? Why I was not seated next to you, yes?"

"It did cross my mind."

"It was supposed to be so. When I arrived, an obnoxious man was in my seat. I wanted to ask him to move, but I was afraid. Since my father had not yet arrived, I waited where I could watch for him." Her eyes got a disappointed look in them. "I kept watching and waiting, but he did not arrive. Later, I saw you talking to the police and became more afraid, so I left."

Afraid of the cops? But a lot of people are these days. Especially foreigners. "And how did you find me this morning?"

Her perfect teeth captured her lower lip for a second. "I must tell you, when I saw you last night, at the boxing, I recognized you from the picture in the paper with my father, and I listened. Secretly. With Rudy missing, I did not know what else to do, so I followed your taxi in another to see where you lived. This morning, I was waiting near your building to talk to you. But you left so quickly, my taxi again followed. I waited outside the police because I was afraid. Then when you came outside, you walked with such purpose, I knew you had found some information, so I followed you to the bridge. But you were so far away this time, I could not hear." She leaned forward and placed tentative fingers on the back of my hand. "Please, Mr. Belzer . . . Richard, tell me. Did they find my father?"

That pretty much brought us up to the present, and I hated what I had to tell her next. "Not yet. But they're still looking."

She drew back slightly. "Are they? The way you looked, you seemed angry. I thought they had stopped."

Now it was my turn to check out the tabletop. I took a deep breath before I answered. "I'm sure they'll find him."

She compressed her lips again. "I have heard many things about the police in America." Her words came out in a halting, uncertain manner.

"The city is so large, like Moscow . . . How much do they really care about looking for one man? How hard will they look?"

I tried my most reassuring smile. "Don't worry, I intend to keep on them about this."

"Then you will help me find him?"

"Me?" I forced a quick laugh. "I am not a cop. I just play one on TV."

"But you have many friends on the police, do you not?"

"Well, that's debatable."

"And you are very intelligent. My father spoke of you to me. How smart you are. How you always want to find things out that are not true."

She knew how to stroke a man's ego, but I was trying to figure out a way to say no when she hit me with her best shot.

"Mr. Belzer, Richard, please. I must find what happened. You have many police contacts. Rudy is my father. He is now all the family I have left. You must know how it is to find someone, then to lose him, yes?"

I did.

What the hell, I thought. I wasn't sure I could let this drop anyway, so what would it hurt to keep her apprised? I took out one of my cards and wrote my cell phone info on the back. "I'll do what I can. Here's my card. How can I get in touch with you?"

She took out a pen and tore a blank sheet from her small address book, writing in clear English. "I am working as a waitress at this restaurant. And here is my cell phone number. I do not have a regular phone."

As I was tucking the paper in my shirt pocket, she touched my hand.

"Wait." She undid the clasp of the chain around her neck and let the opal pendant with the gold butterfly slide off its chain and handed it me. "It is the custom in my country to give a gift to someone who helps you." Her fingers brushed open my hand and she placed the pendant inside. "You keep it. For luck. I am, how do you say . . . superstitious."

"I couldn't," I said.

"Please." Her fingers tightened around my palm, pressing my fingers into the pendant. "My father will recognize it when you find him. Then you will know everything I have said is true."

I stared down at her hands clasping mine.

"You will keep it, yes? Carry it until you find him. Please."

I nodded and put the pendant into my pocket with the paper containing her info.

"I'll keep it close to my heart," I said, hoping I wasn't getting into something I was going to regret later.

But like I said, Rudy's my friend.

# CHAPTER 6

I fingered the pendant as I watched her walk down the block toward the subway. She had a model's walk and the legs to match. And I wasn't the only guy who was noticing. Still, that little voice of reason inside my head kept harping at me, Let the cops handle this. They're the ones with all the resources . . .

And while I knew full well the little voice had some really good points in his argument, I've always had this iconoclastic streak. I fingered the pendant one more time, admiring the fine and intricate Russian craftsmanship, before slipping it back inside my pocket. My pants pocket this time. It wouldn't be as close to my heart, but I'd stand less chance of losing it if I bent over. And I had a feeling if I kept looking into this, a lot of people were going to tell me to do just that.

My cell phone jangled me out of my reverie. When I answered, I heard the familiar Brooklyn accent of Jimmy Lee.

"Hey, Belz, what's up, man? You coming in for that lesson, or what?"

I'd totally forgotten that I'd reserved some special instruction time with Jimmy today.

"I'll be there shortly," I said as I waved to a cab.

The ride over to Canal Street gave me enough time to think about what to do about the Rudy/Anna situation. If nothing more turned up, I'd try to browbeat more info out of Max. Maybe even see if he'd light a fire under someone's ass in the Bureau of Missing Persons. The driver made a hard right onto Lafayette. Ordinarily, it would have been a soft one, but I think plastering his cell phone to his ear with his shoulder impinged on his manual dexterity. But the jarring motion served as a reality check. This wasn't TV or the movies. No happy ending was guaranteed.

I sat back and watched as we crawled through the snarl of traffic. When I saw a sprinkling of Asian features in the crowds and Chinese characters on the signs above the buildings, I knew we were getting close. When we pulled up in front of Jimmy's place a few minutes later, I unpeeled my pants from the back seat, paid the man, and stepped out to stretch.

The *dojang*, or school, was sandwiched between a souvenir shop and a jewelry store that sold fake brand-name watches. The perfect location. Solidly in Chinatown, but still close enough to the Bowery to strike fear into the hearts of the indigent, and also chic enough to pique the interest of the young gentrifiers intent on moving into the area. The place had gone through several incarnations since I'd been going there, the latest of which was the College of Martial Arts. *All Forms of Martial Arts Taught Here* was spelled out in block letters right below the aforementioned red, black, and gold sign. I liked the place for that reason. Whatever worked, Jimmy adopted and taught, much to the chagrin of his traditional-minded grandfather, Sammo. Jimmy's approach was like mine: totally eclectic.

I pulled open the front door and stepped inside. The waiting room and foyer had a comfortable sofa and several chairs where people could sit down and watch the ongoing classes through the glass partitions that separated this room from the main floor of the school. There was also a ceiling-to-floor curtain that Jimmy pulled when he taught his special classes, or when he had a celebrity student such as myself. I appreciated the privacy. I spend enough time in the public eye as it is. But as soon as I got a glimpse of Jimmy, I knew that curtain or no curtain, my reputation had preceded me today. He was slumped against the lower rung of a wooden kung fu practice dummy reading a newspaper. Well, actually, it was a copy of the infamous *New York Inquirer*. As soon as I stepped inside, he looked up and said, "Looks like your technique was a bit sloppy." His face puckered into a big grin and he held up the section showing me flipping one of the punks who'd attacked Rudy.

"Yeah, well, I didn't have much of a chance to warm up."

"We'll take care of that today." He went back to reading the article. "Hurry up and change."

I thought about slightly modifying the old-school warning to adolescents that too much of a bad thing, like the *New York Inquirer*, would make him go blind. But I was curious as to how he'd seen it in the first place. It's not like that rag would threaten the *Times*'s circulation. Moving down the narrow aisle next to the mat, I proceeded to the locker room. Another thing I liked about this place, besides the sauna room, was the private locker he afforded me.

Ever since that infamous incident a number of years ago, when Hulk Hogan dropped me on my head, I've been studying the martial arts. It added a bit of realism to my acting roles: a cop, even a detective, should know how to handle a suspect. Plus, I figured if it was good enough for Elvis . . .

I slipped into my *gi* and fastened the knotted strings through the slots, securing the jacket. It was a typical kung fu outfit, black top and trousers, with an inset white collar. Spiffy, to say the least. I also liked it because I didn't have to wear a belt with it. Jimmy wasn't big on giving them out. His famous words, when one prospective student asked him how long it would take to get a black belt, were, "Why? You think the belt's going to jump up and defend you if you get attacked on the street?"

Needless to say, the prospective student ran out the door, but I understood, and I stayed. More than once I've been glad I did, two nights ago being one of those times.

But I quickly found that the martial arts were not just about being able to beat somebody up. They helped you learn about yourself. The discipline has allowed me to reach a new plane of mental and emotional serenity. You can guess what Lenny Bruce would have said about that, so that's all the philosophizing I'm going to do in this chapter.

Plus, Jimmy had other plans for me. As soon as I got on the mat, he jumped up and we bowed. It's a sign of mutual respect. Sort of like a salute in the army, but one that's infinitely more natural.

"So show me exactly what happened," Jimmy said. "Did one of those punks have a knife, like the papers said?"

"Yeah. And my cabdriver mistook me for Steven Seagal."

"Not Chuck Norris?" He laughed and grabbed one of the rubber practice knives from the shelf and thrust it toward me. "Okay, you be the bad guy. Show me what he did."

I held the knife and looked at it. Somehow it didn't look half as menacing as the switchblade had. "First, how about telling me how you came across that copy of the paper."

"Why? They getting scarce?"

"I wish. It's been causing me a lot of headaches."

Jimmy laughed. "I can understand that. My grandfather picked it up when he saw your picture on the front page. He couldn't read it, though." He laughed again at his own joke, but I figured Sammo was the lucky one. "So, what techniques did you use to send those punks packing?"

Feigning as thoughtful an expression as I could muster, I said, "I thought about telling him I was Steven Seagal, just to strike fear into his heart, but I think he was Ukrainian."

Jimmy held out his hands, palms outward, and said, "Come on. Playtime's over. It's time to work."

And it was. In a move so fast I could barely follow it, he stripped the knife from my hand and grinned.

"Hey," I said, "that's the same move I used the other night, only slower."

"Yeah, right." He dropped the knife on the shelf. "Let's warm up. We'll get to that one later."

After he'd bounced me off the mat more times than a Wilson basketball, he took the knife and said it was my turn. Even though Jimmy's name is Lee, he's half Korean, and loves the arsenal of hapkido moves. I was covered with sweat after thirty minutes and ready for the showers. But Jimmy was having none of that.

"Uh-uh, Belz. I still owe you another fifteen."

"Put it on my account," I said, but I felt him grab my sleeve. I froze, not wanting him to demonstrate another bone-jarring throw to punctuate his sentence.

He led me back toward the shelves by the front of the mat where he'd put the rubber knife before. But instead of the knife, Jimmy picked up a plastic squirt gun and shook it next to his ear. "It's full."

"Of scotch, I hope."

"Belz, the idea is *not* to get shot. If I used anything but good old New York tap water, my students would be looking to take more hits than Schwarzenegger did in *The Terminator*."

"I don't think he's going to be in *Terminator Four*," I said. "He's too busy being the Governator right now."

"Maybe you got a shot at starring in that one, then." He motioned for me to take off my jacket. We'd done these pistol drills before, and they were almost fun, except when I was dragging from beating down the mat with my back and sides for half an hour. The object was to simulate being held at gunpoint and disarming your opponent. It's your reaction time against his, and if you lose, you get squirted, which means you got shot.

"My T-shirt's already soaked," I said. "How am I going to know if I beat you or not?"

"It's full of red-colored water," Jimmy said, giving my shoulder a squirt. "Supposed to look more like blood. Now come on. This could save your life someday."

Needless to say, I was a "bloody" mess inside of five minutes. But the exercise brought back memories of Rudy's bloody coat. Jimmy must have noticed that I was becoming distracted and slapped me on the shoulder.

"Let's call this one, Belz. You did good."

I stooped and picked up the jacket to my *gi*. As I straightened up, I heard another voice behind me, this one older and definitely more Asian-sounding.

"Belzer-*san*, you look troubled." It was Jimmy's grandfather, Sammo Lee. "What is wrong?"

"How do you know anything's wrong?" I resisted the urge to pronounce it as "wong." The urge was not toward disrespect or mimicry but for clearer communication. Just like I found myself wanting to add "yes" to every question I asked Anna when we'd been talking. I have a theory that humans have a natural tendency to mirror the speech they hear back to the other person in an unconscious desire to facilitate communication. There must be an old college linguistics paper lurking inside me somewhere.

The old guy smiled. A star in the Hong Kong kung fu movies of the sixties and seventies, he never missed a chance to unload some of his chop-socky philosophy on Jimmy's students. "It is just like I said in *The Fang of the Dragon*. Your chi is not in the proper balance." He stared at me with a serious look, before his face broke into a wide grin. "Have you seen that one?"

I shook my head.

He also never misses an opportunity to ask me to get him a part on the show. "I play Charlie Chan," he always says. When I remind him, quite respectfully, that good old Charlie was always played by a round-eyed actor, he changes his role of choice to Dr. Henry Lee, "the guy who got O. J. off. He is from Taiwan."

But this time he must have sensed something was upsetting me because all he said was, "What is wrong, my friend? As I say, you look troubled."

Sammo had a problem with the *el* sound, but his perception was right on. "I've got a lot on my mind, *sifu*."

He placed a hand on my shoulder as he guided me off the mat. "We talk, not as student to *sifu*, but as friend to friend."

I gave him a quick rundown of Rudy's disappearance, the police response (or lack thereof), and my meeting with Anna.

He nodded. "And this woman, the daughter, she is beautiful?"

Once again, he murdered the *el* on the end. "Yes, she is. Very."

He gave a knowing nod. "Then use caution. A beautiful woman can draw a man into much trouble."

I laughed. "I just agreed to look into things for her, not date her. I'm happily married, remember?"

Sammo nodded. "Just a general warning, like my movie, *Deadly*

*Blossom of the Lotus.*" He must have read my expression because he added, "Translation bad, I know, but movie number one."

"I'll bet it is," I said.

Sammo patted my arm and I knew it was time for another quotation from the cinema of kung fu. "Remember, Belzer-*san*, in the pursuit of wisdom and true enlightenment, sometimes you have to steal the fortune out of the other guy's cookie."

"*Fang of the Dragon* or *Deadly Blossom*?"

He shook his head. "From *The Way of the Tiger*. Number one movie. Comedy, like Jackie Chan's. One of my best, best."

I was thinking about reminding him that they were all "one of" his best, but I valued my health too much. Actually, I was touched by his concern and thanked him. I hit the showers, skipping the sauna, where I usually like to unwind after a workout. It was closing in on dinnertime, and I was seriously considering hitting one of the Mandarin joints on Mott Street for takeout. But then I thought getting hold of Max and offering to buy him dinner might serve as a peace offering for my unfortunate choice of quick retorts (euphemism for "smart-ass remark") earlier at the bridge. The last thing I wanted was to alienate the detective looking for Rudy. But when I checked my cell phone I found a message from the man.

"Belz, it's Max." Heavy sigh. "I just wanted to give you a heads-up. No trace of Rudy in the river or at any area hospitals. We're classifying him as missing at this point. Give me a call if you have a chance." He rattled off his direct line at the precinct.

I dialed it. "Kaminsky," I heard him say moments later.

"Hi, it's Belz. Just got your message. I appreciate your call."

"Yeah, like I said, just wanted to give you the heads-up, before it hits the news." His voice sounded heavy, disjointed. "We ain't saying he's dead, but we're presuming it. His family's down here at the precinct, in case you're interested."

I told him I was on the way and finished dressing in a hurry, hoping to find a cabdriver who thought he was Mario Andretti's long-lost cousin.

• • •

Midtown North Precinct looked typically busy when I walked in about twenty minutes later. The front benches were full of people waiting to make police reports about one thing or another. One lady had brought her kids and her mother. The women sat passively as the kids meandered back and forth in front of the big desk where the officer sat looking disgruntled. It wasn't Beavers, the guy who'd been at the Seventeenth, but this guy could have been his twin. He pushed his glasses back on his nose and asked if he could help me with something.

"Detective Kaminsky's expecting me," I said.

His head made a fractional movement and he picked up the phone. A few minutes later Max came strolling down the hallway and called my name. He actually looked a little bit pleased to see me. The hairs on the back of my neck began to stand up. That probably meant he wanted something. The question was, what?

"We got his family here," Max said over his shoulder. His voice was just above a whisper. "Wife and kids. Been trying to explore all the angles on this one. You know her well?"

"Just from a few parties. I know she's Russian."

Max frowned. "So's half the population of Brighton Beach, for Christ's sake. I figured inviting you over here might give me the edge." He stopped and turned around, staring me straight in the eyes. "Okay, Belz, level with me. Your buddy Rudy . . . was he a player, or what?"

"A player?" I didn't like the way this was going. "Of what?"

His face scrunched up and he made a little waggling motion with his head. Impatience personified, which was why I made no indication that I understood what he was asking. Still, he was a cop and he was just doing his job.

"You know what I mean," he said. "Was he screwing somebody on the side?"

Rather than ask, "On the side of what?" I merely shook my head. "Not that I'm aware of. Why? This starting to look like a crime of passion?"

Max sighed. "Like I said, we're trying to cover all the bases. Husband disappears, leaving wife and kids, we got to look at every possibility. She's telling us he was acting strange lately. Preoccupied, or something."

His use of "was" to describe Rudy's actions hit me like a gut punch. They were already assuming the worst. But their supposition that Rudy was a philanderer didn't ring true with me. Maybe he'd been hesitant about telling his wife about Anna, but that was understandable. *Honey, this is the grown daughter I sired back in Russia with another woman.* For the time being, I decided to keep that little tidbit for myself. "He mentioned something of the sort at our dinner the other night, but he didn't elaborate."

Max nodded. "How about you talking to the wife? She's in the interview room. I'll have one of the guys take her kids for some sodas outta the machine."

"While you watch our conversation." I frowned. "Is that the best idea you can come up with?"

"Hey, you're used to having an audience for your performances, ain't you?" He cocked his thumb, indicating for me to follow. "Just ask her if she knows of any friends, male or female, where he could be staying. Broach the subject gently."

"I get the picture," I said. "You find out anything about those two punks who roughed him up?"

He shook his head. "We're looking into it."

The room was your typical NYPD interrogation room. A metal table with a thousand cigarette burns, a couple of unmatched metal chairs, as uncomfortable as hell, and a big plate of one-way glass that looked just like a mirror from the inside. A smart science student would have known that a real mirror would set your reflection back a fraction of an inch if you held your finger up against it. One-way glass doesn't do that. But to an experienced criminal, every mirror looks suspicious anyway. Probably to those who grew up in the old Soviet Union they do as well.

Natalia, Rudy's wife, stood and embraced me as I entered. She was a pretty woman with brown hair and eyes. I figured her for around thirty-five or -six, but her young face was lined with worry.

"Richard, so good to see you. Have they told you anything about Rudy?"

Misha, his oldest boy, was ten. He stood and somberly held his hand out toward me. I shook it and brushed my fingers over his younger brother Boris's hair. The daughter, Olga, was six; she stood next to her mother's leg, her eyes looking forlorn and lost.

From the doorway behind me Max said, "How 'bout Detective Kelly takes you kids down to the machine for a couple of cold sodas? On me."

The boys looked to their mother and Natalia gave a slight nod. This was becoming an evening for understated gestures and facial expressions. Misha took his sister's hand in his and they all scampered out. Obviously the ordeal hadn't fully settled upon them yet. At this point, Daddy was just a bit later than usual. I watched the other dick take them down the hallway, then I stepped inside the room, knowing that Max would close the door behind me and set up his observation. I felt like a heel, and I was sure he was off base, but if it helped eliminate one possibility, it might free the cops up to look harder in another direction.

I sighed and shook my head. "Natalia, any idea where he might be?"

"Richard, no. Nothing." She looked up. "You have? I . . . I am . . ."— tears started to wind their way down her cheeks—"so worried." She began a long diatribe about how cruel this situation was, she and the children not knowing what had happened, how unfair it was. I could do little but listen to her melancholy rant, edging in occasionally with an encouraging monosyllable.

After several minutes, I heard a very slight, single tap on the window. It had to be Max urging me to snap it up. Maybe the other detective was getting antsy with the kids. I caught sight of my mirror image and didn't like what I saw. Still, I pressed on.

"Have you noticed any changes in his behavior lately?"

"Changes? What do you mean?"

"Has he seemed different in any way? Preoccupied? Worried? Depressed?"

She took a deep breath. "He has been distant. What was your word? Preoccupied. Yes, that. I asked him what bothers him, but he would not say."

"How have you been getting along?"

More tears. "Fine. We are fine together. No problems, if that is what you ask." Realization dawned a few seconds later as she wiped away a tear with a surge of defiance. "And how dare you ask me that?"

I felt like saying it wasn't my idea, but instead I offered an apology. "It's something the police will want to know. I thought coming from me, it might be easier."

"Easier?" She spit out the word, her dark eyes fixing me with what must have been the hex of all hexes. She shook her head and stared down at the table. "What kind of friend have you become?"

I licked my lips, trying to think of a way off this one-way street that Max had steered me onto. "I didn't mean anything. I just want to help find Rudy. Does he have any other family here, or back in Russia?"

She glanced up at me again with a look of pure contempt. "No. Why?" I was really batting a thousand this inning. This didn't seem like the right time to inquire if Rudy had perhaps mentioned Anna. It was like trying to reconstruct a train wreck. Before I could figure out something to say, the door opened, saving me from further embarrassment. The detective was ushering in the kids, who immediately noticed their mother's tearful state. She grabbed their necks and pulled the three of them to her in a quick embrace, then stood. Max sauntered in after them.

"Mrs. Markovich," he said, "I'll have some officers take you home. We have your numbers in case we need to get ahold of you, right?"

"We are going to stay with my sister upstate," Natalia said. "I will call you with her number."

With one more angry glance at me, she left the room.

Max walked over and plopped down in one of the chairs, his frown so expansive I thought he'd been sucking another lemon. "Aw, Christ, Belz, you blew the shit out of that one for me. Thanks a lot."

"You're very welcome, since you set me up to do your dirty work for you."

His head made that little waggling gesture I'd seen earlier. "You know, you're only here as a fucking courtesy. It's all at my discretion."

"I hope you don't want me to genuflect, because I don't do that. Now, how about that update?"

He snorted and slapped his open palm against the tabletop. "Well, it's like I told you. We didn't find shit when we searched the river, ditto at the area hospitals, and nothing at the morgues, so until something concrete pops up, we'll just have to classify him as missing."

"That's a great bit of detective work," I said, regretting it almost as soon as I'd said it. Again. It seemed like I couldn't open my mouth today without getting someone pissed off at me. But I was still kind of irked that Max had used me to try and pump Natalia, and it had backfired. So I couldn't resist adding, "Sherlock Holmes help you with that deduction?"

"You know,"—he slowly got to his feet—"I been at this since early this morning, and gave you the courtesy of a phone call update, like you asked." He stepped close to me so that our faces were only inches apart. "And all you can do is play the wiseass."

"What can I say? It's typecasting."

He snorted again, then shook his head. "I don't need this bullshit, and I don't need any shit from you either. Take a hike." He pointed toward the door.

I figured it was best to *git*, while the *gitting* was good.


As I walked away from the precinct house, I silently wondered if not telling Max or Natalia about Anna had been a good idea. I wasn't sorry I hadn't, although the opportunity had hardly presented itself. Still, if I expected Max to pull out all the stops, shouldn't I be leveling with him instead of holding back? But if it was something that Rudy had considered too private to tell his own wife, who was I to go blabbing? Anna would remain out of the equation for now.

I did, however, owe her an update.

My stomach was reminding me that I hadn't eaten since that late morning bagel, and now it was closing in on five. She'd mentioned that she had a job waiting tables in a Brighton Beach restaurant, so it sounded, as my old fifth grade teacher, Miss Whitherstick, used to say, like a set of fortuitous circumstances.

I'd always wanted to ask her what it was like going through life with a name like that.

• • •

"You have found something out, yes?" Anna's voice had a tremor of excitement as we stood in the alley behind the restaurant about forty minutes later. She was wearing a simple black top and slacks. The lady in black. She'd told the manager she needed to take a smoke break. I held up the lighter for her as she dipped the end of her cigarette into the flame. I had refused to discuss anything over my cell phone with her. Radio waves these days are about as secure as a silk negligee in a thunderstorm, not that I was into wearing silk negligees. Call me paranoid, but I'm a bit leery of discussing anything nowadays, with the heroes of homeland security using the Patriot Act as an excuse to listen in. George Orwell would have approved of my reticence.

"Yes and no," I said.

Her brow furrowed slightly. "I do not understand."

I gave her a quick briefing about what I'd found out and told her the police felt they'd exhausted all their leads at the moment.

The green eyes regarded me for a few seconds. She hadn't taken any more drags on her cigarette after that initial puff. "And do they know about me?"

I shook my head. "It didn't come up."

She nodded. "It is wise, you think, to keep my presence here a secret? I do not wish trouble with immigration. My visa is only good for ninety days more. And with my father being gone . . ."

"We can keep it between us for the time being," I said. "In the meantime, use your Russian contacts. Ask around. Rudy was"—I caught myself—"is pretty well known around Brighton Beach. Ask if anyone's heard anything."

Her eyes glistened. "You think my father is dead, do you not?"

Way to go, Belz, I told myself. You've made two women cry in one evening. Got to be a personal best for being an insensitive cad. "That's not what I'm saying. You can find out more than I can just by listening to what's on the street in Little Odessa. Report back to me and I'll ferry the info to the police."

"So you will continue to look for him, yes?"

I nodded. She dropped the cigarette, stepped on it, and reached over to squeeze my hand. "Thank you, Richard."

Anna tried to get me to go back into the restaurant for dinner, but after our alleyway conversation, and the sweet smells of rotting garbage wafting over from the Dumpsters, the thought of sitting down and eating some of that rich Russian food made my stomach curdle. Instead, I told her I had to go.

I replayed the last two days in my mind, trying to assess my last supper with Rudy. Ironic choice of words, I know. He'd hinted at something bothering him, and those two street punks attacking him . . . What if that had been a sign of things to come? *I have a somewhat delicate matter for which I may need some police advice,* he'd said.

And what had been my reply?

*I am not a cop. I only play one on TV.* And he'd clammed up after that.

Great comeback. Now I wish I'd spent more time offering to listen.

I needed some kind of break in order to get things moving. But I didn't have any script for this one. I'd have to keep poking around on the edges and hope for the best.

# CHAPTER 7

My sleep was troubled with a new anxiety dream to end all anxiety dreams: I was not only naked, but I found myself on the floor of the U.S. Senate ready to address Congress and suddenly realized that I'd forgotten my speech. You know, dreams were a lot more fun before everyone started explaining what the hell they meant. Another restless slumber had left me feeling more tired than if I'd pulled an all-nighter studying a script.

Speaking of scripts, the message on my answering machine was from Kali reminding me of our afternoon-night shoot today. There was an almost identical message from the assistant director too. I had an opportunity to get a few more hours' rest, but I got up and poured the water into the coffeemaker instead. No sense wasting time on sleep when I could be mulling over the causes of my anxiety dream.

As the cascade of droplets turned into a rapidly growing dark brown pool in the glass pot, I remembered that I'd been so dejected last night that I hadn't even checked my mailbox or picked up my morning copy of the *International Herald Tribune*. Our regular mailperson, who was cloaked in anonymity to such a degree that I didn't know whether he was male or female, usually hit our building before eleven, which stands as a testament to the stalwart individuals who deliver the U.S. mail. Besides, it wasn't like I was counting down the days until my winning entry from Publishers Clearing House arrived. However, to check the box meant braving the bright sunshine of the foyer, which faces east.

Unwilling to attempt such a daunting task without fortification, I waited until there was enough coffee in the pot to fill a couple more cups and then poured some into my solid-bottom, unspillable mug. In the old days, before they'd installed the safety device, you had to risk the switch-and-scald maneuver underneath the spout to get some quick java before the pot was completely filled. But nowadays, everything's safety-oriented. People seem to avoid taking risks whenever possible. Still, why make more than two cups anyway, when there's a Starbucks on every corner?

Winding breakfast up with the leftover remnants of my Subway sandwich from last night, I looked over the script for this afternoon's shoot.

I read it aloud and went through a solitary mini-rehearsal in front of the mirror. Unfortunately, the guy staring back at me reminded me of my dubious assistance in the interview room last night and threw me off my game. I didn't like being suckered into doing Max's dirty work for him.

Oh hell, it was time for a break. I wandered over to the windows to check on what kind of day it was turning out to be. The sun was holding its own, although I had a feeling rain clouds of some kind were lurking close by. Below, I saw the mail truck proceeding down the street and checked my watch. Ten twenty-four. The carrier was pretty much on time.

Just as I was heading downstairs, the phone rang. I picked it up.

"Hi, it's me," Harlee, my lovely wife, said over the phone. The connection was so clear it was hard to believe she was across the vastness of the ocean at our home in France. "I just had the feeling I should call you."

"Well, I'm delighted you did."

"Please tell me you're keeping out of trouble, Richard." Uh-oh. Had she somehow heard about my street encounter with those two punks? No, not possible. Must be woman's intuition.

"You know better than that," I said, which was more or less the truth. At least I didn't have to worry about the *New York Inquirer* showing up in Europe. Unless someone used it to line the bottom of a birdcage on a transatlantic flight. The guano might actually be an improvement.

We chatted about the girls, the new home remodeling she was supervising, her garden, and what we wanted to do as soon as she got back to New York. I spent most of the conversation listening, but my muddled vibes must have been transmitted by satellite.

"Is everything okay, honey?" she asked. Her voice suddenly sounded tight with concern.

"Sure," I said, not wanting to burden her with the Rudy situation or mention that I'd been involved in the street confrontation. There was no need to worry her, or the girls, with something that was way beyond their control. But I felt like a heel for keeping it all to myself. "Why do you ask?"

"It's just . . ." That tiny, echoing static of silence on transoceanic calls felt like someone gripping me in a *kimura* armlock. "I don't know. Your voice sounded funny, that's all."

She has an uncanny ability to see right through me, which is one reason I treasure her so much. However, now was not the time to burden her with my extraneous concerns. Or promises made to a missing friend's daughter.

We talked for a few more minutes, and I had her describe the pastoral scene she was looking at from our bedroom window. It was going on early evening over there. After our ending "good-byes" and "I-love-yous," I hung up and made the trek down to the lobby.

I grabbed the plastic-wrapped newspaper from the front porch. The mailbox was full. I could see the bright whiteness of the first envelope through the spaces in the box's circular grate. In these days of high-tech electronic communication, it's always a joy for me to receive a good old-fashioned letter. Sort of a reminder of things past. A rapidly evolving relic, right there in your hands. And when I opened the box, I found it right there among the bulk mailings and smattering of bills: a plain white envelope, no return address, Manhattan postmark, dated two days ago. Somebody had a penchant for conundrums. I handled the envelope gingerly out of habit. I have, upon occasion, received some less than desirable fan letters, and this one had some of the earmarks to make me suspicious. Holding it by the edges, I went back upstairs. I carefully set the envelope down on the table and assessed it.

Ordinarily, I try not to sweat the small stuff. But something told me, maybe that little voice again, that this letter had something to do with Rudy's disappearance.

Call it acting on instinct, but I used a pencil eraser and my plastic letter opener to slit the flap of the envelope and slowly upend it. It didn't explode, and no white granules fell out, both of which I took as good signs. I applied slight pressure to each end, causing the cut flap to bow outward. A piece of folded paper fell onto the table and sat tentlike in front of me. Normally, you can distinguish some printing through the translucence of the paper, unless it's got a really heavy bond. This was ordinary-looking typing paper and not much was visible on the other side. I could discern some writing, and something else. Small, dark-colored. Using the eraser and the letter opener so as not to touch the paper—Jim Rockford would have been proud—I stared at the neat, handwritten printing in black ink. Four sets of numbers, followed by "Tried and true, Four of a kind. Nyet five." The final, darker inclusion in the envelope had flipped down beneath the printing— the torn other half of Rudy's ticket for Alexi's fight the previous Saturday. This had to have been from him. He must have mailed it at the Garden, after he'd gone in. Or had he?

Something he'd said at the restaurant the other night came back to me like a beacon: *I need a bit more time to collect my thoughts, perhaps write a few things down to clear my head.* What had he meant? And what did this cipher of gibberish mean?

I looked at the sets of numbers. They were arranged in column fashion:

M03-418-05

M05-320-06

M06-719-06

M07-1314-07

The old *Thirty-nine Steps* routine. Rudy'd presented me with a riddle, knowing how I've always loved puzzles that tax the brain. Look for commonalities and the totality, I told myself. The first letter of each was *M*.

Significance?

Obviously some sort of labeling designation.

*M* is for . . . Murder?

Sue Grafton was already well past the thirteenth letter. I started mentally reviewing the other possibilities—Mayhem, Money, Mystery, Medical Examiner . . . Then it hit me. Manhattan.

Followed by numbers . . . What kinds of things have numerical designations? Dates, driver's license numbers, sweepstakes tickets . . .

But this was from Rudy. Totality, I thought again. Look for the whole picture.

M . . . Manhattan . . . Rudy . . .

I snapped my fingers. Each time the medical examiner got a body, the office opened a case. The letter designated which borough, followed by the number of the month, followed by the corpse number, and then the year.

*Tried and true, Four of a kind. Nyet five.*

What the hell did that mean? And why had Rudy written *nyet* instead of *not*? It wasn't like he'd written or spoken pigeon English. I recalled the lines from John Buchan's novel: *Thirty-nine steps. I counted them.* Rudy'd loved that book for some reason. Even conned me into reading it after we'd seen a re-release of the old Hitchcock movie at a film noir conference. One of the themes was that something seemingly out of place was important. *Nyet* was out of place.

After another five minutes of racking my already overtaxed and freshly caffeinated brain, I decided to give it a rest and get ready for work. I still found myself pondering my next move. Rudy had sent the info to me, but why? Maybe he trusted I'd turn it over to the cops if something happened to him. Maybe he thought I'd look into the matter.

But why do anything myself when I could hardly wait to present this new bit of evidence to Max, just so I could see his jaw drop? He wouldn't be able to blow this off. It was what they call a solid lead. One that he could check out ten times faster than I could, even with a couple of hot private eye–type secretaries helping me.

Or so I thought.

I stopped by Midtown North on my way to the set, carefully holding the properly bagged envelope, letter, and torn ticket in a transparent plastic bag, thinking, as I waited, how impressed he was going to be that I'd properly stored the evidence in such a way as to preserve any possible fingerprints or trace evidence. I was sure the letter would leave him champing at the bit, ready to renew the search efforts.

Like I said, or so I thought.

"Thanks," he said as he flipped the bag onto his desk.

I stared at him. "Well?"

"Well what?"

"Is that all you have to say about it?" I asked.

He frowned, made a half-assed shrug, and said, "I'll look into it when I have time."

"And when will that be? After Christmas?"

That caused the frown to deepen. "After Hanukkah. Your holiday lasts longer, don't it?"

"You're razzing me about Hanukkah? With a name like Maxwell Kaminsky? You do spell it with a *y*, don't you?"

"I'm half Polish, so I spell it any way I want, and I can celebrate both holidays if I want to."

"You must have cleaned up with presents as a kid, then," I said. "Either that, or you spent your formative years learning to pray in both Latin and Hebrew."

He rolled his eyes toward me, then back to the report he'd been reading. "Yeah, whatever."

"Come on, Max. I was thinking about those numbers. They've got to be ME cases, right?"

He glanced at the plastic bag on the desk. "So what if they are?"

"And the ticket. It's the other half of the one that was in his coat. Which means it had to have been sent by Rudy."

The half-assed shrug again. "Not necessarily."

I wondered if he could do that with his ass instead of his shoulders. "Aw, come on," I said, trying unsuccessfully to keep the anger out of my tone. "This is a solid lead."

"A lead to what?"

"To what happened to Rudy. It's got to be tied in somehow."

"And I said I'd look into it."

"And I can tell how hard." I smacked a copy of a folded *Daily News* sitting on his desk. "They only ran the story of Rudy's disappearance as a page two afterthought in that one."

"Hey, we don't tell them what to print, or how to print it."

I shook my head in frustration and muttered a curse under my breath.

"What did you say?" His voice sounded like a growl.

"Just commenting on how grateful you've been for all the leads I've been giving you."

"Like what?"

"Like that." I pointed to the envelope encased in the plastic bag. "And those two Ukrainian street punks I told you about. What about them?"

That made Max bristle. The next thing I knew his face was about an inch away from mine, his big index finger poised like a raptor's talon at eye level, punctuating every word.

"Belz, you just play a cop on TV, remember? I do it for real. So don't tell me how to do my fucking job, okay?"

"Okay, as long as somebody does it. This is more than just a simple disappearance."

He snorted a laugh, and in a tone laden with sarcasm he added, "Believe me, I'll keep my eyes open for any lurking *conspiracies*."

That was the last thing I wanted to hear. And to think I'd given him an autographed copy of *Another Lone Nut* on his last birthday.

Instead of going right to the set, I stopped in the corner coffee joint and ordered a small cup to go. The girl behind the counter stared at me with a look of innate dumbness, and then some flicker of realization touched her eyes. Just when I thought she was going to ask for my autograph, she asked, "What kind of coffee, mister?" and pointed to the charts behind her.

I settled on the house blend and grabbed a crudely fashioned little religious booklet from a stack sitting between me and the register. *Is It Too Late?* the front of the tract asked. I certainly hoped not. I grabbed the coffee-tasker's pen and scribbled down the first number I remembered from Rudy's letter, wishing I'd made a copy before turning it over to uninterested Maxie. I wrote down the second number. When I was in school, one of my math teachers, Mr. Cox, told me he thought I had a photographic memory. We used to joke about his name behind his back too. But he was right. I am good when it comes to remembering numbers. And promises to old friends.

As I was writing the last two numbers and the cryptic sentence, the girl set a paper cup down on the counter and rattled off the price. She glanced down at the tract and asked, "Are you the guy who leaves those things here all the time?"

"No," I said, pocketing the one I'd written on and handing her a new one. "But it's never too late." I paid her and got the hell out of there, hoping there wasn't something in the coffee that caused mental dullness. I took a quick sip as I walked, then resisted the urge to spit it out. Warm dishwater with a dash of Tabasco sauce would have been more appealing.

Two things were certain: the house blend really sucked, and Max couldn't be less interested, that was for sure. Only one option left—I'd have to run down these ME cases myself, but that was something that was going to take time. Unless I could con someone else into doing it.

Mike Hammer had Velda, Sam Spade had Effie, Marlowe had . . . well, Marlowe had Marlowe. But I had Kalisha Carter, a brand-new personal assistant, specially designated to keep me out of the crosshairs of controversy.

I smiled at the thought.


"Do what?" she asked as I gave her the *Is It Too Late?* booklet.

"Go to the medical examiner's office and get copies of those reports. The numbers are written in the margins. There's four of them."

"Where'd you get this thing?" She held up the tract. "Doesn't seem like something you'd be reading."

"I have very eclectic tastes, but you can skip what's printed inside and just concentrate on the case numbers, okay?"

"What's this?" Her finger traced over the cryptic sentence I'd rewritten from memory.

"That's not one of the numbers."

"I gathered that. So what is it?"

"It's a riddle wrapped in a mystery, inside of an enigma," I said. "Very Russian. Apologies to Winston Churchill, of course."

She looked at me. "I don't get it."

"You're not supposed to. It's a conundrum."

"Okay." She frowned. "And we're doing all of this for what reason?"

At least she'd said *we*. This was where I had to be a bit delicate. You always are when you're first explaining the unraveling of a conundrum. It's the most crucial time. You can easily lose your audience. "I need to do some research."

"Research? You see this?" She pointed to her head, which was doing a tremulous but controlled waggle. "This is my skeptical and I-am-not-amused black girl look. It's a precursor to telling you trouble's just around the corner."

I smiled. "You know, I always wondered what that particular type of quivering meant."

Frowning, she said, "I thought I was supposed to keep you out of trouble. Somehow this doesn't smell right to me."

"Must be something wafting over from Staten Island." I flashed her my most ingratiating smile. "You always wanted to be an investigative reporter, right? Well, look, here's your chance."

"And how am I supposed to get anything on these reports? I don't know anybody over there at the ME's office."

The smile wasn't working, so rather than up the wattage, I tried to be commiserative. "Nobody said it would be easy in journalism school, right? File a Freedom of Information Act request or something." I glanced at my watch. "Time for me to get to rehearsal."

Suspicion was still lurking in those almond-colored eyes. "Mr. Belzer, what's this really all about?"

"Call me Belz or Richard, but please, no more Mr. Belzer."

"Okay, *Belz*," she said, stressing the word, "what's this really all about?"

I thought about using the old *If I tell you, I'll have to kill you* line, but it didn't seem appropriate. Not with Rudy still missing and presumed dead. I shot her a lips-only, very subdued smile and said, "I promise I'll explain it all later. I know you can handle it."

As I walked toward the soundstage, I glanced back over my shoulder. She was studying the tract. I just hoped she was looking at the numbers.

After finishing the rehearsal and then going to hair and makeup, I settled in for the customary frustrating waiting period until such time as I finally got called on set. I spent the interval going over the script again and again, making sure I was totally familiar with all of it. Walking into a scene being filmed is like walking into the middle of a chemistry lecture. Nobody's sure what the hell is really going on.

The assistant director came over and briefed me and the other actors and we went to work. Unfortunately, my heart was in it but my mind was elsewhere. After I'd blown my lines for the third time, the director, Reggie Seals, yelled "Cut," and told everybody to take five. He approached me from an oblique angle, like he was afraid I was going to explode into a fury and start throwing set pieces.

"Richard, my man," he asked, "what's wrong with you today? You seem a bit off."

The truth was, I was burning with curiosity as to those damn ME numbers and wondering how Kali was doing.

"Sorry. Got a lot on my mind." I straightened up. "Let's try again."

In this case, the fourth time was the charm. Reggie was so pleased, he opted to break for an early dinner after checking on his headset. "The caterers have arrived," he said. The set closed down faster than quitting time at the hubcap factory, as people started marking places for the resumption and then moving toward the chow line. I took out my cell phone and called Kali. She answered on the second ring.

"I'm almost back," she said. "And I think you'll be pleased."

I told her to join me for dinner and got in line. I had just gotten back to my dressing room with two plates when she came sauntering up. From the way she walked, I could tell it had gone well. I invited her inside and we sat down.

"You want something to drink?" I asked, opening my refrigerator. "One of those plates is for you, by the way."

"Thanks." She looked at what I'd picked out. Macaroni and cheese, green beans, a tiny sampling of lettuce, and a chicken breast. Both plates were identical. "What you got in there?"

I gave her the list: bottled water, beer, assorted soft drinks, and more beer.

"I'll take a soda, I guess." I stepped back and let her look. She pointed to an Orange Crush and I retrieved it for her and water for myself. When I sat down, she pushed a large manila envelope across the table and smiled.

I was so excited, I couldn't even eat. "God bless Richard Milhous Nixon," I said, sitting down and opening the envelope.

Kali stared at me. "I didn't figure you for a Republican."

"I'm not, but if it wasn't for good old Tricky Dickie and his crew of Watergate bunglers, the Freedom of Information Act would have never been passed."

"Well, even old Tricky Dickie would have been extra proud of me, then, because the clerk at the ME's said an FOIA request takes forever."

I raised my eyebrows as I undid the metal clasp on the envelope. "I'm impressed. How did you manage that?"

"I told him I'd send him an autographed picture."

"Of me?" I felt my neck tighten. "Is he a fan?"

"Of the show? Yeah. And actually, the picture's of somebody else."

"Who?"

She winked as she told me. Figures, I thought. Everybody wanted an autographed picture of her. But what counted was the results.

"You're learning, kid." I started to peruse the first report. After the second or third line, I started skimming. Half of it used terminology I didn't quite understand, like "myrofractional" something or other, or "significant ventricular arrhythmia leading to coronary exclusionary activities." Wasn't that just a fancy way of saying a heart attack?

I skipped down to the bottom and saw that the name scrawled in the

"Reporting Medical Examiner" box looked familiar. The typewritten printing next to it confirmed it was who I'd thought it was: Dr. Rudy Markovich. I checked the boxes on the other three.

"He signed them all," Kali said, shoveling macaroni and cheese into her mouth.

I looked at my own congealing pile and set the reports aside. Few things are worse than cold macaroni and cheese. I thought about sticking it in the microwave but decided against it and picked up my plastic fork.

"Am I to take it that you've already gone over these?" I asked.

She was too much of a lady to respond with her mouth full, but she nodded. Finally, she finished chewing and said, "Four male Caucasians, all living in different parts of the city, all victims of a premature and unexpected death, apparently by heart attack." She loaded another forkful and held it poised. "And the ME who performed each of the autopsies was none other than Rudy Markovich. You know him, don't you?"

"I do." Maybe it was time to level with her. If she was going to be my Effie or Velda . . . "He's a good friend of mine, and . . ." I pondered a moment more. Did I really want to bring her into this? What if it turned out to be dangerous? But then again, if it turned out to be dangerous, I didn't much want to be involved either. Still, looking under a few rocks and reporting the findings to New York's finest shouldn't be too hazardous to anybody's health.

"And?" she asked.

"He's missing." I sighed and told her the story, all the way up to receiving the unsigned letter in the mail this morning.

"What did the cops say when you showed them the letter?"

"Not a hell of a lot. The detective working the case acted like he would rather be living in Philadelphia."

"Philadelphia?"

"Never mind," I said. "Someday I'll explain W. C. Fields to you. Right now, lunchtime's about over and we need to find the connections among these autopsies."

"Want me to do some more investigating?"

I grinned. "I was counting on it."

After another two hours of shooting, I was released. One of the benefits of starring in a show with an ensemble cast was that I didn't have to be in every shot. When I got back to my dressing room, Kali looked up from a notepad with a lot of writing on it. I saw she had raided my refrigerator for another Orange Crush. She smiled and tapped the can. "I hope you don't mind. I was thirsty."

"Kid, you could've taken a beer." I paused. "Ah, you *are* over twenty-one, right?"

She nodded.

"Good." I pulled back the chair opposite her and sat. "What more did you find out?"

"My one brother-in-law's a cop in the Eighteenth Precinct. I called him and he explained to me why they did autopsies." She drank some soda and started reading her notes. "All four men collapsed on busy streets in downtown Manhattan, and they were all relatively young. Because the causes of their deaths were undetermined, it's standard procedure to require an autopsy."

I already knew that, but I didn't tell her. She'd worked hard trying to help me out, and I appreciated it. Would Spade brush off Effie's hard work? Would Hammer dis Velda? Not on your life. I mentally calculated how much more info I'd have to get before I could stir Max out of his state of semipermanent indolence. It would take more, I thought. A lot more.

"All young, relatively speaking," she said, tracing an exquisitely painted fingernail on the page. "Two thirty-eights, forty-three, thirty-seven."

"I hope you weren't listing someone's measurements."

"No. Their ages."

"I'd figured as much, but I always like to keep in practice. I was a stand-up comic before I made it as an actor."

She looked at me over the rim of the soda can. When she'd finished her sip, she said, "I know."

"You do, huh?"

She got a serious look on her face. "It's my job to know, Mr. Belzer."

I sighed. "Belz, remember?"

"Belz," she said.

"Well, we're definitely on the right track. There's something rotten here and like I said, it ain't wafting over from Staten Island."

"So what's our next move?" She glanced at her watch and I wondered if I was keeping her from getting home.

"There's a saying in Spain," I said. *"Siempre hay mañana."*

Her almond-colored eyes focused on me.

"There's always tomorrow," I said.

"I didn't know you spoke Spanish."

"Just enough to get me in trouble," I said. "You ought to hear my French, though." I stood up and told her to call it a night. Suddenly, she looked a bit unsettled.

"You're not planning to go out and get into trouble tonight, are you?" she asked. "That's what I'm supposed to be on the lookout for, remember?"

"No, I've got a ton of rewritten script pages to go over. I'm heading for a soft chair and a cool drink."

She canted her head slightly, as if evaluating my answer. "For sure?"

"I promise. No getting in trouble tonight."

She nodded and smiled.

"But remember," I added, *"siempre hay mañana."*


I offered to share a cab with her, but she said the subway would be quicker and she was anxious to get the hell out of there. After hailing one for myself via 311, I got home and relaxed with the new script pages for tomorrow in one hand and the envelope of ME reports in the other. It was a given that I'd be burning the midnight oil. I wanted to go over those reports again, with the proverbial fine-toothed comb. The key would be looking for similarities. Kali'd found the obvious ones, but there had to be something more. What had Rudy been trying to tell me?

And once I figured that out, I could go back to Max with something solid. But it would have to be good. Otherwise, he'd just frown and stick it in a drawer somewhere, with all the rest of the "conspiracies."

# CHAPTER 8

I was dragging. It would have been different if I'd spent the night out on the town drinking red wine and having fun. Far from it. I'd been slaving over that blasted, hard-to-understand "medicalese," trying to make sense of it all. Made me wish I'd paid more attention in anatomy class. And the stuff I did understand seemed superfluous. Like it did me a lot of good to know that "in the upper extremities" the victim's "fingernails were short and clean," or that the abdomen was "moderately distended" and the "external genitalia" were that of a "normal adult male." Plus, getting up at five thirty in the morning when you didn't get to bed until almost three can be problematic. Especially when the script memorization had gotten the short end of the stick. But what the hell, they were always revising them up to the last minute anyway.

During rehearsals I kept mulling over the note from Rudy, with the damn cipher, as I tried to get the lines down, until I finally gave up and pored over the reports some more. But the lightbulb never illuminated for me with those either. Four seemingly unconnected men died suddenly of natural causes, on different days, at different locations in Manhattan. And Rudy performed all the autopsies. One name, Ivan Peters, sounded like it could perhaps be Russian, but the others certainly didn't. Glenn Perry,

Joshua Spaulding, and Arnold Wassler. And for that matter, Ivan might have been an Albanian or Serbian or something. It was clear I'd have to do a more in-depth investigation of each of these four. Which was why I collared Kali as soon as I saw her and gave her an assignment: check the obits of each.

"Obits? You mean obituaries?"

I nodded.

"Where am I going to find those?"

If I was going to make her into a halfway decent version of a private eye–type personal assistant, she was going to have to stop moaning every time I gave her an assignment. I decided on one of my famous pep-talk responses.

"A good administrative assistant like Effie Perrine would find a way."

"Who the hell is that?"

"Sam Spade's secretary in *The Maltese Falcon*. His girl Friday." I leaned back and did my best Bogart imitation. "How's your woman's intuition today, sweetheart?"

She canted her head, raised an eyebrow, and snatched the reports from my hand. "Good thing I brought my laptop with me. I can probably find something online."

"Check a few days after the dates of death," I called after her, dropping the Bogey accent. I watched her go, then headed to the set.

Except for the moveable walls, the interview room on the soundstage reminded me too much of the one Max had conned me into using on Natalia. I wondered about her, and Rudy's kids too. So after I'd blown more lines than the day before, the director called for another break and yelled for someone to get coffee for him and me. I don't think he planned on drinking his. I shook my head in self-disgust and plopped down in the suspect's chair and waited for my caffeine fix.

Maybe that will make it better, I thought.

Then I knew it wouldn't. As I looked up, the person entering the room was none other than Vernon Franker, or as we loved to call him, assistant to the assistant, abbreviated as the official double ass without the holes. The overhead light glared off his bald head. I held up my hand.

"If you're here to ask me why I'm wearing sunglasses inside," I said, "it's to reduce the glare."

It took him a couple of seconds to get it, then he frowned.

"Very funny."

At least he wasn't sweating today, which meant in the grand scheme of ass-chewings, this one would be relatively minor.

"Where's Ms. Carter?" he asked.

"Who?" I knew who he meant but figured why not take the offensive?

"Kalisha. The assistant I assigned to keep you out of trouble the other day."

"She's doing a good job too." I smiled up at him. "I'll bet you haven't had a bad report about me all week."

Franker pursed his lips. His features were small to begin with, and when he did that, his whole face looked pinched.

"That's not a very becoming expression on you," I said.

The pinch got tighter. "Now what are you saying?"

Before I could answer, one of the production assistants opened the door with a tray carrying two huge, steaming cups in one hand and a bunch of cream and sugar packets in the other.

"Ah," I said, "care to join me in a coffee, Vern?"

Franker glanced down at the drink with disdain, giving his head a little shake. "I asked you about Carter . . ."

I worked one of the cups gently out of its cardboard carrier and grabbed some additives. This was going to be a black, double sugar morning. The PA left to look for the director.

"I asked—"

"Careful," I said. "You definitely don't want to get blamed for my spilling hot coffee on myself. Look at how that old lady made out when she sued McDonald's back in the day."

He straightened up, his head bobbling like a gyroscope on a pencil.

After a hot sip that practically scalded my tongue, I had a weak moment and took pity on Franker. "Kali's in my dressing room. She's researching something for me."

"Researching?"

"Yeah." I took another sip. The jolt from the last one was still emanating upward from my stomach and this one met it halfway down. "Have you read this new script? It's going to take a bunch of research before we're comfortable enough to know how to react correctly."

Franker's chin quivered. He was starting to sweat now. "Does Reggie know about this?"

I held up the coffee and gave a deferential half bow. "It was his idea."

He processed this new info, let his lower lip encroach over his upper, and said, "Very well." He turned and left. I watched through the open back end of the soundstage as Franker's bald pate worked its way through the set, occasionally reflecting the lights like a big, errant lightbulb. As the last traces of his luminescence vanished, I drank some more java. Either it was cooling off or I was getting accustomed to the scalding liquid. But then again, my buddy Franker was doing his best to keep the heat turned up. I could see that if I wanted to keep my day job while I looked into Rudy's situation, I was going to have to get used to liking it hot.

Call it a caffeine buzz, call it the triumph of will over fatigue, call it incredible acting skills—please, call it incredible acting skills—but after rehearsal wrapped, I was able to affect the insouciance that had earlier eluded me throughout the takes. I was right on the money for the rest of the morning's actual shoot, and it had gone so well that Reggie was pleased. And when the director's pleased, everybody gets an early lunch. I walked over to Dale Treadmore, the scene supervisor. His job is to set up the sequence of the filming and assure continuity. For instance, if I'm talking to the DA in one scene, and we break for the day, when we come back, we'd better be dressed the same and not have our hair parted on the other side. Dale's great at his job. Plus, he and I are buds.

"Dale, my friend," I said, stepping up next to him and extending my hand.

He looked at me with a shrewd dubiousness. "What is it you're after, Belz?"

I grinned. "What scenes are on the schedule for after lunch?"

"Why?"

Now here's where it got ticklish. I couldn't remember if I'd used the old visiting my sick grandma routine one too many times with him this month. So I leveled with him. More or less.

"I've got to go out and look for a special anniversary present for Harlee," I said. "Don't dare miss this one."

Okay, so it was more on the "less" side.

He gave me a knowing nod as he paged through his book and told me what was on tap for the afternoon session.

I did some quick calculating. "And if I remember correctly, I'm not needed for any of those, right?"

He consulted the pages and said, "Right."

That meant I had a window of opportunity. I was free until dark. I headed to my dressing room with a feeling of exhilaration. Either the high-octane coffee was kicking into gear, or the thrill of the quest was getting to me. Or maybe the PA had dumped a bunch of Red Bull into the cup before he gave it to me.

Kali was sitting at my table drinking an Orange Crush and typing on her laptop.

"I take it you found what we were looking for?" I asked.

"I did, and I didn't use my woman's intuition either."

"Will you relax? It's just a line from the *Falcon*." I grabbed myself a bottle of water and sat opposite her. "What you got?"

She fixed me with a lopsided stare, one eyebrow slightly elevated, those light brown eyes scrutinizing me. "A line from the *Falcon*," she repeated. "The movie or the book?"

"Actually, both. There were three movie versions, but I'm talking about the last and best one." I twisted the cap on the water and took a long, slow drink, then sat the bottle down and pointed to her laptop. "You were saying . . ."

"Ivan Peters, age thirty-eight, dropped dead on the corner of Forty-seventh and Vanderbilt, apparently on his way to work. Heart attack. He had emigrated from Russia and was the president of Odessa Imports." She read off the address. "He left behind a wife and two children, was known for his charity work, yada, yada, yada."

"They say what part of Russia he came from?"

She shook her head. "The obits on all these guys were pretty generic, except Wassler's. I tried Googling the rest of them but didn't find much more. Looks like Peters changed his name from Petrovich, though."

"Petrovich." I grinned. "I wonder if he was any relation to Porfiry?"

"Who's that?"

"*Crime and Punishment.* You know, Dostoyevsky. The cop's named Petrovich."

"Oh."

Since my literary allusions were falling flat with her, I said, "Who's next?"

She tapped a couple of keys and read, "Glenn Perry, of Queens. Thirty-seven, no wife, no kids. That's about all his listing gave, other than his parents."

That was one we'd have to work on. "Okay." I rotated my hand for her to proceed.

"Joshua Spaulding, age forty-three, lived in Yonkers, worked in Manhattan, had six children, apparently with a couple of different wives." She paused. "Says here he was a gemologist and expert jeweler."

I nodded.

"And last, but not least, Arnold Wassler." Kali looked up from the keyboard. "There was quite a bit about him. He was a reporter."

"Now that's interesting. What paper?" I suddenly prayed she wouldn't say the *New York Inquirer.*

"Mostly for the *Times*, but there were a lot of articles in magazines listed too."

"And he was how old?"

"Thirty-eight." She sighed. "I guess the good, they die young."

"Sometimes." I considered where to start, then stood. "Feel up to some fieldwork?"

She closed the computer cover and stood up also. "I guess I don't have much choice if I'm to keep you out of trouble, do I? Oh, Mr. Franker came by to check on me. Asked how the task was going."

"And what did you tell him?"

"That you'd been behaving like a real gentleman." She smiled. "You have, haven't you?"

"Certainly," I said, holding the door for her. "After all, I am an actor."

As we approached the street, Chris, my favorite security guard, flashed me a cautionary hand signal, pointing to the tent that obscured the public's view. Kali and I stopped behind it.

"Belz," Chris said, "I just thought you should know that dude with the real bad plaid is waiting for you out there. He's got some guy with a camera with him."

I moved to a slight gap in the canvas and peered through. About thirty feet away good old Cyrus Gustafson was standing there with another guy who looked like he had an IQ well into the double digits. Although Gustafson had jettisoned his green plaid sport jacket for one with a black and white design, he still looked like a refugee from a seventies resale shop.

"Shit, it's that fucking reporter from the *Inquirer*," I said. "Next to Franker, he's about the last person I'd want to spend time with."

"Leave it to me, then," Kali said. "Wait here and follow my lead."

She walked out of the secured area and went to the curb. A taxi sat in the zone down the block and Kali waved to him. The driver immediately pulled up and she opened the back door but leaned down, talking to the driver through the open passenger side window. With her left hand, she waved me forward.

I did a quick trot across the space and slid into the backseat. Kali slipped in beside me and slammed the door. Too late, Gustafson and his photog friend had started a quick hustle toward the cab, but we whizzed past them. I couldn't resist the temptation to give them a little farewell wave.

"Elvis has left the building," I said as I settled into the seat. "You did good."

"Better than Effie could have?"

"Close."

"Where to, boss?" the driver asked.

I told the driver Forty-seventh Street and Sixth Avenue. Odessa Imports. It seemed like a logical place to start. I mean, the Russia factor seemed like a definite tie-in, and you couldn't get more Russian than Petrovich-turned-Peters. I also wondered what we'd find. This was uncharted territory for me, although at one time I worked as a census taker. But I also remembered Max's angry yet cautionary warning: *Belz, you are not a cop. You just play one on TV.*

On the outside, Odessa Imports was your typical building in the Diamond District: a couple of picture windows cutting back from the sidewalk to form a nice aisle where you could step into the enclave and admire the nice assortment of sparkly stuff in the windows. Lots of rings, necklaces, bracelets, and earrings artfully laid out in black velvet cases arranged on a white sheet. The door was mostly glass, and inside, it looked like more of the same.

I leaned over to Kali and told her I'd be right out.

"Are you telling me to wait in the cab?"

I sighed. "This could be tricky."

"I can be tricky."

"No doubt, but it could also be better if you waited in the cab." I told the cabbie to wait and got out. Kali jumped out the other door.

"No way I'm getting left behind on this, Mr. Belzer. My job's to keep you out of trouble, and I can't do that sitting in some taxi."

The taxi driver also got into the act. "Hey, what about my fare?"

"Just hold on," Kali said. She looked over her shoulder at Odessa Imports, then back to me. "You know, I'm not so sure this is such a good idea. How we going to handle it?"

"With the utmost aplomb." I could see where this one was going, and although I didn't like it, maybe taking her along would be best. If nothing else, it might serve to keep me subtle. I asked how much I owed and paid the guy. "Hang around the area, will you? We'll be out shortly."

"Yeah, sure." He took off so fast I thought his tires would catch fire.

I walked over next to Kali and stopped. I was actually trying to formulate a plan, which was smart. Never go into a place without one. After half a minute of coming up empty, I decided what the hell. We'd just wing it.

We opened the door and stepped inside. The wide floor had cases of jewelry on each side of the center aisle, which expanded back toward what looked to be an office area. An attractive woman behind the counter asked if she could help us, trying to keep from staring too much, obviously thinking we were a May-October romance. Well, maybe late September.

"Yes, I'm sure you can," I said, flashing my most ingratiating smile. "You have lots of great stuff here."

"We pride ourselves on stocking only the best." She eyed Kali, who was looking at the assortment of tennis bracelets in the case. "Is this a gift?"

"Yeah," I said, then to Kali, "see anything you like?"

"Lots I like," she said.

I raised my hand, extending my index finger as if I'd just thought of something. "You know, I've been here before, but it's been a while. I know somebody . . . Ivan somebody. Is he still here?"

Her face blanched. "Mr. Peters?"

I snapped my fingers. "Peters. That's it. He around?"

It took her a moment of compressing her lips, taking a breath, and considering a measured response. "I'm afraid he's no longer with the company."

"No? What happened? He was the boss, as I remember, wasn't he?"

She nodded her head. "He . . . died a few years ago."

I affected the appropriate shocked reaction. "Died? I can't believe it. He was so young. What happened? Accident?"

Again, she took her time formulating a response. "He had a heart attack."

"Damn, the old ticker, eh?" I shook my head. "Too bad. He was a super-nice guy. Did you know he changed his name from Petrovich to Peters?"

"I'm afraid I only knew him as Peters."

"Yeah, good old Ivan," I continued. "Do you know if he was related to Fyodor Dostoyevsky?"

She shook her head, her smile showing a forced amusement. "Would you like to see anything?"

"Yes," I said. "We would. Who took over after Ivan died?"

The woman looked surprised but recovered nicely. "Why, that would be Mr. Buteyko."

"Buteyko," I said. "Another Russkie, eh? Then he's the man we'd like to see." I just happened to still have my official-looking NYPD gold detective shield clipped to my belt, so I made a nonchalant gesture, placing my hand on my hip like I was reaching for my wallet, then moved forward pointing at a bracelet while saying to Kali, "That one's pretty, isn't it?"

"Extremely," she said. Our eyes locked and I felt she was warming to the task at hand.

Peripheral vision is a wonderful thing. I happened to catch the woman behind the counter's glance toward my belt as I flipped my jacket back into place. She'd seen the fake badge. No doubt about it. Now I had only to let nature take its course.

"May I ask what you wish to see Mr. Buteyko about?" she asked, her tone now sounding a bit more deferential.

Ah, I thought. The plot thickens.

"Yes," I said. "You may ask." I used a forced, irritating laugh to punctuate the punch line, like somebody who laughs at his own jokes not so much because he thinks he's funny, but more because it's a cue to the audience that he's just told a joke. "Hey, look at that one. Bet my wife would love that."

"Is this about a business transaction, then?" the woman asked.

"I'll discuss that with him."

"Of course I'll let Mr. Buteyko know you're here," she said, reaching for a phone. I continued my pseudoexamination of the glistening baubles behind the glass barrier, wondering how many laws I'd just broken, as I listened to her say, "It's the police, sir."

I'd noticed the dark half-oval bubble on the ceiling when we walked in. No doubt we were already on candid camera. Probably being videotaped too, but I doubted they'd be wired for sound. I pretended I hadn't heard the clerk's assumption that we were NYPD, although, all things considered, this wasn't turning out too badly. Certainly I could argue that I'd never identified myself as a cop. And if someone's mind was muscle-bound with erroneous assumptions because the only exercise it got was jumping to conclusions, was that my fault?

In any case, wearing a phony badge can open a lot of doors. You just have to make sure they're the kind that don't get locked behind you.

Kali must have been thinking along similar lines. She leaned close to me and whispered, "My alarm bell's going off again."

"Relax. It's standard procedure. In police vernacular it's called *tinning* your way in."

"Maybe for a real cop it is." Still sotto voce, she added, "Impersonating an officer is a serious offense in Manhattan."

"And in Poughkeepsie too," I whispered back. "That's why I usually take pains to avoid doing it."

The door at the end of the aisle opened and a big guy who looked like he could probably go ten rounds with Alexi waved to us. We moved through the door and I heard the distinctive click of a heavy dead-bolt lock behind us. Covert cameras, a huge security person, and dead-bolt locks . . . Maybe these were standard operating precautions in the Diamond District, but suddenly the hairs on the back of my neck were standing up. Finding myself behind a locked door to which I do not have a key does that to me. Plus, we were sort of sailing into uncharted waters here, and all I had were a couple of hundred questions and a fake badge. I longed for something more. Like a thirty-caliber carbine, especially walking into this with Kali next to me. I felt a twinge of responsibility and wished she'd agreed to stay in the cab. I could take care of myself, but having her along added to my stress level. Plus, I knew she was nervous too, although she was trying hard not to show it.

As if reading my thoughts, she glanced back at me and smiled. Maybe there was a future for her in showbiz after all. But that still didn't change the facts. The name was Belzer, not Rambo, and I was responsible for her. I made a mental note to tread carefully with Mr. Buteyko.

"This time follow *my* lead," I whispered. "Especially if it involves a hasty retreat."

The silent giant continued to lead us down the back hallway that looked so garishly lighted I wondered if they were causing a brownout somewhere else in the borough. We passed several doors with frosted glass, behind which I could discern definite movement and voices. And they weren't speaking English. Or Yiddish. Nope, I knew enough to recognize Russian when I heard it.

The big guy opened another frosted glass door with *Company President* spelled out in big block letters, etched with gold inlay. The office inside was a claustrophobe's nightmare: heavy wooden panels from floor to ceiling, no windows, and a desk that looked like it came right off the used furniture bus from Rikers. The man behind it stood up and offered me his hand. He was fiftyish, with a round, porcine face and slicked-back white hair. When he smiled, I felt like putting my hand on my wallet. I could see why he kept to the back room. The guy's stare was as cold and sinister as a Moscow winter. The triangular plaque on the front of his desk spelled out *Nikolai Buteyko, President* in fancy script letters. He said something in Russian and I heard the big guy leave and close the door behind him. I could see his hulking shadow standing right behind the frosted glass, though, like a big mean bear waiting for his cue to enter the main circus tent again. It did little to lift the uneasiness creeping up from my gut. Why the hell hadn't I insisted that Kali stay in the cab? Getting myself into this rather tricky situation was one thing, but drawing her in was another.

Still, it wasn't like we were going into the heart of Fallujah or anything. We were just a couple of citizens who stopped by to inquire about the untimely and premature death of good old Ivan. Hopefully, Buteyko was the type who spent his evenings drinking vodka and listening to opera rather than watching TV. Of course, there was still a chance he'd recognize me, but that had been going fifty-fifty lately, unless the person was a cop. And if Kali and I just happened to get mistaken for a pair of New York's finest, all the better. It was all a matter of keeping my cool. Acting in control, even if I was starting to feel a bit damp under the arms. And after all, acting is my business.

"And how may I help you?" he said. His voice dripped with an obsequiousness so forced he sounded like Peter Lorre trying to quote Shakespeare. He extended his hand across his desk, which was as tidy as a basic training bunk bed. "I am Nikolai Buteyko, at your service. Detective . . . ?"

As I shook his hand, I figured the situation was ambiguous enough that I could let the erroneous presumption about our official status ride for a while.

"Hey, just so there's no misunderstanding, you can call me Belz. And this is Kali. We'd like to talk to you about Ivan Peters. He used to be the president of Odessa Imports, right?"

"Ah, yes, poor Ivan," Buteyko said. A vein stood out in bas-relief along his temple. "He was very unlucky to die so young, no?"

"Did you know him well?"

He gave a portly shrug. "We were comrades. Business associates."

"And you took over once he was deceased?"

Buteyko bowed his head slightly. "Life, as they say, must proceed. Is that not the American way?"

"And the Russian way too." I had no idea where I was going with this, but I forged onward. "So why did he change his name from Petrovich to Peters?"

Buteyko's head jerked slightly, his eyes narrowing before he shrugged again. "He wanted to sound more, how do you say it? Americanized?"

"Did he have a heart problem?" I asked. "Or any other health concerns?"

"Apparently so." His face tightened into what I took for a real ugly smile. "After all, he died, did he not?"

"What else can you tell me about his death?" I asked. "I take it it was unexpected."

"Yes, it was. Very." Buteyko's smile broadened. His teeth were small and slanted inward; he resembled a feral animal trying to put on an air of domesticity. "As death often is."

"What was it? A heart attack?"

"Yes, yes, I believe it was." His eyes narrowed. "How rude I have been. Would you or your partner like some coffee?"

"No, thanks," I said.

"Miss?"

Kali shook her head. She was holding up quite well.

"As you wish." Buteyko lowered his chin and squinted. "In my country, a gentleman always makes the offer, no matter how short the visit."

A gentleman . . . This guy had about as much elegance as a fat announcer in a circus suit.

"And just why," he said, focusing his stare on me, "are the police so interested in Ivan's death?"

I had a hunch he was starting to see through my little faux dancing routine. We'd probably gotten all that we were going to get at this point, and once he realized we had no official standing, he'd probably clam up anyway. I said, "I don't know that they are, officially, that is."

"So what is it now you are saying?" His syntax was getting bad. A sure sign of mental confusion. Before I could formulate a proper response, he added, "You are with the police, are you not?"

"Actually," I said, "I am not a cop. Just an interested citizen. But I know plenty of NYPD."

That seemed to momentarily stun him. Buteyko squinted again and said, "You look very familiar. How do I know you?"

I shrugged, hoping the only channels he watched were Discovery and the Russian language news station. "I've got a common face, or so I've been told."

His squint was rapidly escalating to a glare, which he turned on Kali.

Suddenly Buteyko's scowl turned into a half smile. He raised his hand and pointed at me. "You look very much like somebody I have seen. Someone on television."

Uh-oh, I thought. Maybe it was my photochromic lenses.

He stroked his chin lightly. "That television show . . . What is the name?"

My gut had a feeling the other shoe was about to drop.

Buteyko snapped his fingers. "*CSI*. Grissom."

"That's William Petersen." I grinned. "People mistook me for him all the time until he grew the beard."

His smile vanished faster than spit on a hot iron. "Then there is no need to ask you for an autograph on your way out." He pressed a button on his intercom and barked something in Russian. The silent giant opened the door. "Wladimir will escort you, but before you go, you will need to show me some identification. I can have Wladimir go through your pockets, if necessary."

I was glad to see his English syntax was making a comeback. But there was still no way I was going to let him or his goon go through my wallet. Or Kali's purse. I found myself silently hoping that maybe she had a concealed carry permit and could pull out a Lady Smith & Wesson to facilitate our exit. But all she did was compress her lips in a way that signaled an escalating case of the nerves. It was up to me, and I wasn't relishing the thought of taking giant Wladimir on in a one-on-one office match, especially on the big guy's own turf. There's that old adage Sammo Lee always talks about: a tiger is fiercest on his home ground. And at the moment, I was feeling a bit disenfranchised. But remembering that a parry can sometimes be more effective than a strike, I reached in my shirt pocket and said, "Sure. Here you go." My fingers brushed against the card Max had given me the other night at the garden. The one with his official NYPD title and contact info on the front and his illegible cell phone number on the back. I handed it over with a grin. "That's a cell number on the back, by the way."

Buteyko accepted the card and squinted as he flipped it over.

I figured seeing the official logo would give him at least a moment's pause, and it did. I turned and grabbed Kali by the elbow, steering her toward the door. Unfortunately, big Wladimir was filling most of it.

"Excuse us," I said, wondering if I could risk trying a throw on the giant if I had to. It probably would have been easier to try to move the Flatiron Building.

Wladimir looked over my head toward Buteyko, then, apparently getting a signal, stepped aside and allowed us to pass. I positioned Kali in front of me and continued down the hallway. I could sense the giant's strides behind me, but he made no move to attack. Still, I didn't feel at ease until we were out the door and on the street again. Then I breathed a sigh of relief.

Kali did too. "Did you see the size of that one dude? Man, am I glad to be out of there."

"You and me both. See? I told you to wait in the cab."

"Well, we sure accomplished a lot." She flapped her arms. "About the only thing that proved was that my antiperspirant holds up."

Her sarcasm stung a bit. "Actually, we might have found out more than just that. I have a feeling that if we didn't upset the applecart, we made it hit a bump in the road."

"I'm not so sure I'm up to the task of keeping an eye on you," she said. "Remember, my job depends on my being able to keep you out of trouble."

"And trouble," I said, remembering that famous Raymond Chandler line, "is my business." I glanced around and thought fortune had smiled on us once more when I saw a cab sitting down the street, idling. "Come on. Let's get the hell out of here."

We walked down to the cab. At a distance, it had appeared to be empty, but as we got closer, I saw the roof light was off.

"Dammit," I said. "Occupied."

There was a flash of movement off to the side. Cyrus Gustafson was standing in the recess of a building still wearing his alternate loser plaid sport coat, the lapels so big a Cessna could have used them for a landing strip. It was a carbon copy of his green monstrosity.

"Where you been, Belz?" he said with a sly grin. "Looking for diamonds?"

"Cyrus," I said. "Is that a new jacket, or did you have the old one spray-painted?"

"Always the wiseass, huh? Well, listen. Like I said, you may not know it, but I'm a pretty damn good reporter, and I know there's a story here. You're mixed up in something, and I'm going to stick to you like white on rice."

"You're right. Tell Mrs. Hoffa Jimmy's body is near a large body of water."

His thick lips jerked back into a sneer. "Okay, why did you have your girlfriend here go down to the ME's office this afternoon?" I tried to keep my expression neutral. Acting training. But the thought that this little creep had been following Kali must have wormed its way close to the surface. I felt my cheek twitch. He smirked. "Yeah, like I said, I'm a good reporter, all right. I got connections all over this city. I know how to spread my juice around too."

"That must be why your fingers are so sticky." I turned and we began to walk away.

"Okay, run away if you want to," he yelled. His voice had taken on an agitated lilt. "But like I said, I'm going to be sticking to you . . ."

Figuring he was having trouble finding just the right metaphor, I stopped and said, "Like white on rice?"

His nostrils flared and the ends of his mouth curled up. "I was going to say like stink on shit."

I waved my hand in front of my nose, like I was expelling a foul odor. "And you would have been half right."

"Looking for a cab?" he said. "Come on, you can share mine."

"No, thanks," I said. Kali and I turned and began to walk again. I heard some scrambling behind us and suddenly smelled Gustafson's pungent BO right behind me.

"Hey, Belz, hold on, would you?"

"Only my friends call me that," I said, not slowing down, "so I don't expect I'll be hearing it from you again, will I?"

"Come on, I'm just doing my job."

"Then do it harder," I said, still walking. "And put in some overtime so you can update your wardrobe."

"Huh? What you talking about?"

"Never mind. It's above your head."

"Real smartass." He was starting to get a bit winded. "But like I said, I been following you two all day, and then some."

"Everybody needs a hobby." I scanned the street. Why wasn't there ever a cab around when you needed one?

"What were you two doing in Odessa Imports?" We quickened our pace and he was practically running to keep up. "I seen you going in there. Is this your girlfriend? You buying her off with some jewelry so your wife don't find out?" He gave what evidently was supposed to be a knowing grin. "Don't look surprised. I been shadowing you. I know about the red-head too."

I started to tell Kali to ignore him but caught an uncertainty in her expression. It suddenly occurred to me that this unscrupulous jerk might print some of his lascivious speculations in his scandal sheet just to make what he thought was a story. Perhaps it was better to put a damper on his overactive little imagination. I stopped and turned to face him, almost causing him to run into us.

"Gustafson, if you print one unsubstantiated little piece of your fabricated bullshit, I'll have my lawyer suing you so fast you and your paper will be lucky to be able to rent space in a Dumpster in the Bowery."

He smirked. "Hey, pal, it's called freedom of the press. Or ain't you heard of it?"

This little shitbag was starting to get under my skin.

Kali tugged at my sleeve. "Mr. Belzer, let's go."

"'Mr. Belzer,'" Gustafson said. "That's sweet. So if she ain't your squeeze, who exactly is brown sugar here?"

I felt Kali stiffen.

"She happens to be my personal assistant." I leaned closer to him. "Now read my lips. Watch your fucking mouth."

One side of his face pulled upward into a lopsided grin.

"First your shine girlfriend here is getting reports down at the ME's, then you two are going around asking questions in the Diamond District. What's the real story here?"

"I told you," I said, "watch your fucking mouth. This young lady is my personal assistant, not my girlfriend."

"Come on. What's the story? Give it to me."

"We're researching something for the show, sir," Kali interjected. I admired her restraint. "We do it all the time to add veracity to our episodes."

"Let me know if you need me to spell that for you," I added.

Kali suppressed a giggle. "He looks like he might have trouble with words with more than two syllables."

"The horse's ass." Gustafson reached over and grabbed Kali's bare upper arm, squeezing so I could see the flesh buckle. "You better level, ho."

She winced in pain. I'd had enough of this shitbird.

"Wrong move, dirtbag." I seized Gustafson's thumb, bending it up and out, away from Kali. As his fingers peeled off her arm, I brought my other hand in and laid my thumbs across the back of his hand, turning it into a forward wristlock.

"Hey, let go," supersleaze said. "You're breaking my fucking wrist!"

"If I wanted to break your fucking wrist, asshole, you'd be on the side-walk right now." I adjusted the amount of pressure I was applying to the hold, not exerting enough to cause a tear or break, but enough to ensure some decent pain compliance. "Now you're going to apologize to my personal assistant for your boorish behavior, and then you're going to make yourself scarce. Get it?"

Gustafson started to mutter something that sounded like a half-assed apology.

"Enunciate," I said, bearing down a fraction more and making the asshole dance up on his toes.

He squealed, then said, "I'm sorry, miss. Real sorry. Didn't mean nothing by it. Please."

Kali flashed an amused look. "'Brown sugar.' What's that, from the eighties?"

"No, I think that might be from the seventies," I said, doing my best Sylvester Stallone imitation.

Kali glanced at me and I said, "It's a line from *Rocky Balboa*. You know, Rocky Six?"

"Must've missed that one," she said.

"Yeah, you and most of the moviegoing audience. But it's destined to be a classic. And besides, Sly's not a bad guy."

Still dancing on his toes, Gustafson said, "Hey, listen. I know you're working on something. I can help you."

I looked at Kali. "Are we done here?"

"Most definitely."

I looked back to Gustafson as I released him. "We don't need any help from you, or the rag you work for."

"And speaking of that rag," Kali said, "we'd better not see one word about this conversation, or I'll be filing assault and battery charges against you so fast it'll make your head spin."

We watched him slink off, rubbing his wrist and occasionally glancing over his shoulder. I was tempted to take a couple of quick steps toward him to speed him on his way, but when he got to his reserved taxi, he jumped in and the ride took off. With impeccable timing, my cell phone rang.

I glanced at the caller ID screen and saw Anna's number. I answered, and after a profuse apology for bothering me, she asked if I'd found out anything yet.

"You at the restaurant?"

"Yes," she said.

I glanced at my watch. It would be a strain, but I figured that if we caught a few breaks, we had time enough for a quick stop before we were due back on the set. I told her I'd be over there shortly. When I hung up, Kali was looking at me. I remembered her questioning stare when Gustafson had mentioned "the redhead." I didn't want her to think I was holding something back. I owed her that much.

"Where we going now?"

"Back to the set," I said, "by way of Brighton Beach."

"Brighton Beach? That's way the hell over by Coney."

"Yeah, I know, but there's somebody I want you to meet."


When we finally got there, the restaurant was filling up with the usual borscht, pirozhki, and vodka crowd. It wasn't Primorski, but it had your typical Russian ambiance of huge mirrors, dangling chandeliers, and large panels of wood and red. A maitre d' bowed with courteous deference as we stepped inside.

"A table for two, sir?" he asked.

I glanced at my watch again. Time was running short if we wanted to be back on the set in time for my scenes.

"How about a rain check? I need to speak to Anna for a brief moment."

"Anna?"

I saw her in the back talking to a pair of men seated at a table. The men were laughing uproariously. Her strawberry blond hair seemed softer under the subdued lighting. I pointed discreetly. "That waitress."

"Ah, Luba," he said. Obviously some sort of affectionate nickname. "But she is very busy with customers. How about I give her a message. You are . . . ?"

"Andrew Jackson's cousin. Here's my card." I slipped a folded twenty into his palm with a bit of discretion. "And I assure you, we won't take her away from her duties for very long."

"I believe she is due a break," he said, smiling benevolently as he moved the hand with the folded twenty into his pants pocket. Slick move. Very unobtrusive. He strolled over to Anna and stopped next to her. Leaning in close, he whispered something. She turned, stared in our direction, and immediately started toward us, saying something over her shoulder toward the two patrons. I hoped it wouldn't affect her tip.

"Richard." Her voice had a breathless sound to it, like she had been surprised and was expecting the worst.

"We stopped by for a quick progress report," I said. "You got a minute?"

"Progress? Yes, for you, of course I have time." Saying something in Russian to the returning maitre d', she motioned for us to follow her outside. We went out to the same place by the Dumpsters where the detritus of cigarette butts lay scattered over the cement abutment.

"You going to light up a smoke?" I asked.

"A smoke?" Her brow furrowed, then she shook her head. "I don't smoke really. I only borrowed one last night to have an excuse to go out. But you have news, yes?"

"I do," I said, "but first, this is my personal assistant, Kalisha Carter." I introduced Anna to Kali and the two women exchanged acknowledgments.

"But where is my father? Have you found him yet?"

The last thing I wanted to do was dash whatever hopes she had left, but I knew better than to sugarcoat the questionable info that I did have. "We're working on it."

Her brow furrowed. "Working?"

"We have a few more leads to check out," I said. "Your father sent me a list of several suspicious cases he worked on in the medical examiner's office. It's a question of running them down to see where things lead."

"Running down?" The crease between her artfully arched eyebrows deepened. "I do not understand."

"Rudy sent me a letter," I said, speaking slowly. "I think it's somehow related to his disappearance. But I haven't been able to figure things out yet."

She sighed. "So . . . no news?"

I shook my head and caught a glimpse of her eyes glistening.

"Don't worry, we'll do our best to get to the bottom of it."

She nodded. "And you, Kalisha, you help Richard finding my father?"

"I'm his girl Friday," Kali said.

Anna looked confused again, so I explained, ending with, "She's helping me a lot."

After thanking Kali, Anna turned to me. "Richard, you will call me if you find anything, yes?"

I promised to call her as soon as I found out anything. We parted at the door, with Anna touching both our hands lightly and thanking us again.

As we left, Kali said, "So that's the redhead."

I nodded. She had a smile on her face that would have made the Cheshire cat proud.

"What?" I asked.

She gave me that I'm-not-amused black girl look again. "I just realized something, is all."

"Oh, yeah? Care to share?"

"Not really."

"Come on." I put my finger just under my nose. "I've had it up to here with riddles and ciphers lately."

She smiled. "I just realized that you're not such a tough guy after all, are you?"

# CHAPTER 9

After dropping Kali off in Brooklyn at her place, I arrived back at the set just as they started to look for me. Vern Franker, who had apparently taken on the new position of Belzer monitor, sidled up to me as I went in for a makeup reworking.

"And where were you?" He had the practiced strut of a schoolyard bully.

"Lunch was a walkaway," I said, meaning we were all free to eat at one of the neighborhood establishments. I feigned a modicum of irritability. "What, can't a guy visit a restaurant around here without Darth Franker sensing a disturbance in the Force?"

His small face seemed more scrunched than usual as he peered around. "Where's Carter?"

"Kalisha?" I sat down in the makeup chair and waited while the artist fastened a cloak around my collar. "She and I had something to eat, and I told her to take the rest of the night off."

His lower lip jutted outward. "What?"

"Relax," I said, closing my eyes and tilting my head back. "She had a rough day keeping tabs on me. You should be proud. In fact, give her a raise. I haven't been in any fistfights or gotten in trouble since she started."

"I'll be the judge of that." He made a little mini-snort, sounding a lot like an overweight goat. "At any rate, you had no right to do that."

"Do what?"

"Give her the night off. She was supposed to . . ."

"She was supposed to what?" I asked.

"Never mind."

"You know, I never much liked that answer."

He pursed his lips as he ran his index finger and thumb along his jawline. A most contemplative gesture for a man of his limited mental abilities.

"Come on, Vern," I said. "Spill it. I know you're dying to tell me."

The makeup artist was leaning over me, ready to start making me handsome and debonair for the camera, when I raised my hand. "Vern, you're holding things up. I won't be able to concentrate on my lines with that unfinished statement hanging out there."

He stood glaring down at me. I placed the back of my hand against my forehead. "Oh, the pain. And we've got a long night shoot ahead of us."

He stood there in brooding silence.

"Okay," I said. "How about I promise that afterward, I'll go right home and go to sleep?" His nose twitched. A crack in the armor. "Besides, what trouble could I get into around here? The set's closed, isn't it?"

I could hear his sonorous breathing for a few seconds. Obviously the cogs weren't turning at warp speed.

"Very well," he said. "She's supposed to report to me daily."

"Report? On what?"

This time he didn't answer. It only took me a couple of seconds. "Oh, I get it. She's supposed to report back to you on my activities each day, right?"

He still didn't answer, but he didn't have to. His face told me I was right.

"Vern, Vern, Vern." I shook my head in disgust. "That's so . . . Stalinesque."

I waved to the makeup woman to commence her task and reposed myself, closing my eyes again for effect. "If she didn't, it was probably because there was nothing to report."

"There'd better not be," he said. The schoolyard bully in him was flaring up again, searching for dominance. "Otherwise I'll go straight to George."

George was one of the producers and naturally higher up on the food chain than Vern. Thus, Vern figured he could strike fear into my heart with the mention of George's name.

I resisted the temptation to act like I'd been frightened by a symbolic peal of heavenly thunder. "Give him my regards when you do."

"Listen, I happen to know that your contract is coming up for renewal next year."

"Hey," I said, "glad you reminded me. I'll have my agent ask to double my salary because of all the stress you've been causing me. Oh, what was that line? I can't think. All I remember is Vern Fucker—I mean Franker—standing over me."

"You think you're untouchable, Belzer? Maybe you've got the protection of a contract, but Kalisha Carter can be fired at the drop of a hat." He snapped his fingers and said, "Just like *that*."

I opened my eyes and fixed him with a serious look. "Can I ask you a question?"

This seemed to stun him. His puckered lips parted and he nodded in assent.

"Good." I raised my hand and snapped my fingers in the general vicinity of his face. "Do you have to practice that, or is it a talent you come by naturally?"

Hildy, the makeup artist, suppressed a giggle. I leaned back and closed my eyes one more time. "And just for the record, don't even think about firing Kalisha Carter. If you do, my lawyer will personally escort her down to the EEOC, where she can file an unfair labor practice suit." I grinned. "She'll win it too."

I heard his footsteps storming away. Instead of opening my eyes, I asked, "Is he completely gone?"

Hildy chuckled slightly. "If he ain't, he's gonna be if you keep dissin' him."

• • •

Things have a way of not going right after the sun goes down, especially when you're trying to film some night sequences. I was still semiadrenalized from rattling the Russian bear's cage and my subsequent confrontations with slimy Cyrus and vituperative Vern, and the buzz seemed to give me the edge I needed. For a change, it was everybody else's turn to blow their dialogue. I stood there basking in the director's praise, letting the accolades flutter demurely around my feet, conscious the whole time of Franker standing just on the other side of the camera crews doing the slow burn. It did me good to think he got a case of the ass just because I was getting praised.

The guy was going to have to get a life.

It was after midnight when they called it a wrap; union rules gave us a twelve-hour turnaround between shoots. I enjoyed the neon-lighted streets and assortment of night folks as I made my way back home. Once upon a time, I would have stopped off for a couple of quick ones with some of the guys, but it had been such a long day, all I wanted to do was get some rest.

The next morning I awoke surprisingly refreshed and saw on my calendar that I had booked another lesson at the *dojang*. I packed my clean kung fu outfit along with a towel and underwear and headed for a workout. I was eager for it. There's something about intense physical activity that stimulates the brain. Thoughts about the possibilities of having to take on someone the size of Wladimir, Buteyko's silent giant, was another good motivator.

When I got there, I described the guy to Jimmy and asked him what the best way of dealing with someone that size might be.

"You say this guy was big?" he asked.

I nodded, holding my hand way above my head. It was a bit of an exaggeration. In reality, Wladi probably wasn't an inch over six seven or eight.

Jimmy smiled. "What's that old saying? The bigger they are, the harder they fall?"

"That was also the title of Bogey's last movie," I said. "And Max Baer's too."

"Who's Max Baer?"

"Didn't you see *Cinderella Man*? He was a heavyweight boxing champion in the nineteen thirties. The movie gave him a bad rap, though. He later went into showbiz."

"Say, that reminds me. How did your buddy do the other night in his fight? What's his name? Alex?"

"Alexi," I said. "KO in the fifth. It was practically a boxing exhibition."

"Boxing?" Sammo Lee said, walking over to us. "Chinese boxing?"

"Western-style," I said. "Or at least what the Marquess of Queensberry's original rulebook has morphed into."

Sammo frowned. "Belzer-*san*, I tell you many times, pure martial artist beat boxer every time. You know Bruce Lee, the original Little Dragon?"

I nodded, figuring I was in for another bit of Chinese movie history.

Sammo continued. "I knew him. When we were in high school, there was a large boxing tournament. All Hong Kong schools. Little Dragon enter, even though he never box before." He held his hands up in a fighter's stance. "But he have eight year training, *wing chun* kung fu." Sammo's left hand shot out in a strike so quick I didn't even have time to flinch, and his fingers tapped my forehead. "He win tournament. Beat every boxer in city."

"Grandfather," Jimmy said, "Richard's time is limited today."

The old man smiled, bowed, then shuffled to another section of the mat and started doing tai chi forms.

"How does he do that?" I asked. "I didn't even see it coming."

Jimmy grinned. "Yeah, and it's the one you don't see coming that gets you. Now, you asked about dealing with an opponent bigger than you?"

"A lot bigger."

"Then cut him down to size." He motioned for me to freeze, then delivered a snapping kick that stopped just short of the inside of my right knee. "Attack where your adversary is vulnerable," Jimmy said. "Be like water. Allow your form to adapt to your opponent, the same way water takes the form of whatever cup it's in."

"*Wing chun* wisdom?" I asked.

"Nope," he said. "It's from Bruce Lee. He wrote his own book about fighting called *The Tao of Jeet Kune Do*. That's what he named the style he taught. It means—"

"Way of the intercepting fist," Sammo finished for him. He seemed to appear as silently as a phantom. "Did I tell you I made a movie with him once?"

"Only once or twice a day, Grandfather," Jimmy said. He smiled and slapped me on my shoulder. "I've got to take off. I have an accounting class in an hour."

We bowed to each other and he said, "Why don't you stay for a while and work on some forms? Or punch the bags, if you'd rather. But next time I have to show you something important about that handgun-disarming technique. Remind me, okay?"

I assured him I would and faced the mirror. Doing forms is sort of like kung fu shadowboxing. You spend the time observing yourself in the mirror, if you can, and imagining battling multiple opponents. The best part is, none of them ever manage to hit you back. But as I went through my paces, thoughts of the riddle of Rudy's letter kept popping into my head. I worked through a few more forms and saw Sammo coming out of the locker room. When I stopped, he approached and stood next to me.

"Your chi shows much distraction," he said. "Something is bothering you."

"Yeah. I guess that doesn't say much for my acting ability, does it?"

His eyelids narrowed. "Acting in movie, not same real life. Real life sometime have much trouble, no can act. Your friend . . . still missing?"

Although his English left a lot to be desired, I appreciated his concern. "He is."

"And you look for him?"

I smiled. "I'm knocking on a few doors, but I wish I could say I'm getting close to something. I just seem to be pissing people off."

Sammo patted my shoulder and said, "It is just like I say in *The Blind Master*." He straightened up to deliver the line. "To seek a greater enlightenment is always a good thing."

"I thought that was from *Fang of the Dragon*."

Sammo shook his head and started to walk away, saying, "Not hardly, *pahdiner*." He stopped and grinned. "That was my John Wayne imitation. Pretty good, huh?"

"The Duke would have been honored," I said.

He grunted an approval, then raised his index finger. "One more thing, Belzer-*san*."

I was gearing up for another bit of chop-socky wisdom from one of his old movies, but he surprised me.

"For whom the bell tolls," he said.

"The novel by Ernest Hemingway?"

"No. In locker, your phone ringing. Perhaps, it is the bell of good fortune." He smiled again, but the look in his eyes told me he thought otherwise.

I went into the locker room feeling perpetually trapped in that old *Remo Williams* movie, where Joel Grey played Master Chiun, but I kept that to myself. I had a feeling if I told Sammo about another round-eye playing an Asian master, he'd make it a point to find the guy and chop-socky him in half. And he could probably do it without breaking a sweat.

I saw that my missed call had been from Kali. I dialed her back immediately.

"Where you at?" she asked. "I been calling and calling."

"I'm at the *dojang*. Why?"

"*Do* what?"

"*Dojang*. It's Chinese for kung fu school, or something."

"Oh, is that the stuff you used on that asshole Gustafson yesterday?"

"Yeah, but next time I'm thinking of just calling a pest exterminator." When she laughed, I said, "Now, what's up?"

"Spent the morning with my brother-in-law down at the precinct house. I've got a lead on that Glenn Perry dude. Can you meet me in Astoria right away?"

"Queens? I hope the address isn't 704 Hauser Street."

"What? No." I'd obviously confused her again. "Why? Who's on Hauser?"

"The Bunkers used to live there."

"Who?"

"The Bunkers. You know, Archie and Edith. Gloria and the Meathead."

"I know it's kind of early, but I got to ask you. You been drinking?"

"Never mind," I said. "I'll grab a quick shower and a taxi and be there shortly."

"And I'll be waiting."

After reiterating that that was all I wanted her to do until I got there, I grabbed my towel, soap, and shampoo and went to clean up, thinking that watching a few episodes of *All in the Family* should be mandatory for anyone between the ages of sixteen and twenty-nine.

The better part of an hour later I was mulling over everything as we hurtled in a northeasterly direction on the Long Island Expressway, making excellent time. It was still what could be classified as a reverse commute. As we rounded the curve getting on the Brooklyn/Queens Expressway, I saw the low-rise skyline giving way to the taller structures looming in the distance. In addition to being the place where Nathan Hale was captured, Queens was where, during the Revolutionary War, the occupying Brits used to quarter their soldiers in private residences. After the British got their asses kicked back to England, the Founding Fathers penned the Third Amendment clause prohibiting the generals in our own military from ever doing the same thing. Queens also has traditionally been one of the most ethnically diverse boroughs in the country, having a mixture of all nationalities and races. Astoria, besides being famous for Archie Bunker and family, has a large Greek population being offset by yuppie Manhattanites and their expanding gentrification circles.

"Glenn Perry," I said to myself. It didn't sound Greek. "I wonder if he knew Archie Bunker."

The taxi driver was staring at me in the rearview mirror. He looked like he just found out someone had put sandpaper in his turban.

"You were speaking to me, sir?" the worried driver asked.

"No, just to myself." I held up my hands, palms outward. "That's the only person who understands me."

He gave a quick little nod and I felt the car accelerate. We were exceeding the posted speed limit by a pretty good margin. I thought about telling

him I was seeking a greater enlightenment, but he might have miscon-
strued that as an urging to press the pedal to the metal a bit more. I just
wanted to get there, not get any more frequent-flier miles.

When we were coming in for a landing near Astoria, I called Kali on
my cell phone again and got her exact location. As we pulled to a stop in
the middle of a residential block with mostly single-family homes and a
smattering of town houses, I saw Kali walking down the sidewalk like a
door-to-door salesperson.

"This is good," I told the driver. He jolted to a stop and my head almost
collided with the Plexi screen. His medallion number showed his smiling
face and unpronounceable name, but when I shoved the currency in his
direction, he didn't look anything like his picture. I told him to keep the
change and he took off with an accompanying grunt and a squealing of
tires.

Kali watched him depart. "What was his problem?"

"I was chanting in Hindi and he thought I was listening in on his cell
phone conversation," I said. "Now, what you got?"

She smiled. "Well, Glenn Perry used to live right there." She pointed
to a modest two-story frame house with a high-peaked roof and the standard three cement steps leading up to the front door. Her expression spoke
volumes. "I've been talking to the neighbors on each side."

"And?"

"And, after Mr. Perry met his maker, the family stepped in and put the
place up for sale."

"The family?"

"His brother, according to the neighbors."

"Glenn was single, I take it?"

She nodded. "Sounds like it. I tried calling the Realtor but got a recording."

"I'm impressed," I said. "You found out a lot of information. People
must have really opened up to you, huh?"

She shrugged. "I told them I was gathering info for the census bureau.
Seemed like a good cover."

"Really? When I was a census taker, people used to threaten to throw
rocks at me if I bothered them."

that bit of police vernacular. I started walking toward the bisected
e, motioning for her to accompany me. "Just remember—"

I know. Follow your lead."

nodded. But it sounded a lot easier than I figured it would be. Gossipy
ladies generally like to talk, given the opportunity. I just had to figure
ght angle. We could always just tell her the truth . . . No, I decided to
that one back as a last-ditch resort. Telling the truth is always such a
Mary play.

considered another option. We could continue to use the same cen-
ureau story that Kali had been using, but that would probably get us
ck dismissal.

ow about a couple of cops inquiring about a dead neighbor? Nah. The
vas too old and not really overtly suspicious. She'd probably slam the
in our faces or just clam up. Especially if she was worried about a pos-
Peeping Thomas complaint. I shook my head. Binoculars.

Je could always say we were from a TV news station, which wouldn't
rrupting the final option too badly. After all, the news did come on
ly after my show concluded. So in a manner of speaking . . .

ut why not just level with her? Perhaps she had some suspicions of
wn and would welcome the chance to postulate about the late Mr.
's demise. Maybe it was time for that old Hail Mary play.

trotted up the stairs, still not sure how to handle it.

Vhat are we going to tell her?" Kali asked in a husky whisper.

was just about to answer when the door swung open and I saw a face
an as a bulldog's on the woman behind the screen door. Actually,
ose was more like a Doberman pinscher's: long and sinister-looking.
yes were dark, intense. Her visage was frozen in a perpetual scowl,
ng great determination, and probably impervious to anything below
on the Richter scale.

saw you two coming up the steps." Her heavy jaw jutted toward Kali.
've been watching this one for a while. What do you want, and what
u doing in this neighborhood? And if you're selling something, I
uying."

efore I could answer, she added, "And if you're some of those damn
ah's Witnesses, don't bother. Greek Orthodox till the day I die."

"They must have figured I'd throw 'em back. W
I found out?"

"Absolutely."

"Everybody I talked to mentioned one person
the neighborhood. Been here forever and knows all
everybody else's biz. Sort of like the Astoria Oracle."

I grinned. "Now, she sounds like someone we
Velda would be proud."

"Who?"

"Never mind. Which house is the Oracle's?"

She pointed to a double apartment structure a
ally, it wasn't really what you'd call a double. It wa:
been constructed as one big house and subsequently
or less right down the center. Two front doors sto
wondered if they'd put in a dividing wall from fro
who got the bathroom. Of course, maybe they share
looked faded, and dirty halos graced each of the fron

"Looks like someplace Hansel and Gretel might
the Oracle friendly?"

"The Oracle's name is Mrs. Sopkos," Kali said. "
an eye on everybody's comings and goings. With bin

"Binoculars? I take it subtlety is not her strong

"We'll find out when we talk to her."

"You've found out a lot waiting for me to get
haven't you?"

She shrugged. "I kept busy. Want to give it a sh

"Sure, why not? I'm just surprised you waited f

She smiled. "Well, once I heard the Oracle was
could use your charm on her."

"My charm? You must have me mixed up with s
mine up last night schmoozing Vern."

"Well, you'd better find some residuals real qui
try to 'tin' your way in again."

I rolled my eyes. I'd had a hunch yesterday tha

I tried one of my high-wattage smiles, guaranteed to melt ice on a frigid day. It fazed her about as much as spitting a wad of bubble gum at a brick wall.

"Well?" her voice thundered. "I asked you what you're here for."

"It's not to try to sell you a copy of *The Watchtower*," I managed to say. I was getting ready to try that Hail Mary. "We're—"

"Reporters," Kali said. "We're here to do a story."

I glanced at her and frowned slightly. Didn't she know that oracles seldom trust newspaper people?

"You are?" the Oracle said, flashing a coquettish smile in our direction. "You going to put my name in the papers, maybe?"

"Maybe," I said. Might as well pick up the ball and run with it. "We're—"

"What paper you from?" the Oracle asked.

"The *New York Inquirer*," Kali said. "I'm sure you've heard of us."

"Heard of you? I read you all the time." A simper had now replaced the scowl. "In fact, you, young man, look familiar. Is your picture by your column, by any chance?"

"Only in the Sunday edition," I said.

"Sunday? I didn't know you had a Sunday edition."

I smiled. "Actually, it's something new that we're planning on starting very soon."

"Would you be interested in subscribing if there were a Sunday edition, Mrs. . . ." Kali paused. The girl was showing a definite improvement in her thespian skills. Maybe I could get her a SAG card and have a new partner on the show. She finished off with, "What is your name, ma'am?"

"Sopkos. Lois Sopkos." She brushed back some errant hairs, as iron gray as steel wool.

"Oh, what a lovely name," my partner said. "Is it Greek?"

"Yeah. My husband's father changed it from Sopkanopherous at Ellis Island. Easier to spell." She unlatched the screen door and held it open. "You two might as well come in. No sense standing out there in the sun. Plus, people might be watching and wondering if you stand there too long." Her dark eyes narrowed as her aquiline, pinscher's nose shifted its aim to the right and then the left, checking out the block.

I grabbed the door and motioned for Kali to enter first, giving her a quick wink as she passed by. She winked back. My gallantry seemed to impress Mrs. Sopkos as well, because she commented how refreshing it was to see a gentleman hold a door for a lady. "Most of them got no manners today. My husband, Nikos, God rest his soul, he would always be the first one out the car to open the door for me."

Yeah, I thought. He probably knew if he didn't, he'd hear about it later.

Inside, a rigid center wall cut a swath right through the symmetry of the living room, making it look like John Denver's bedroom after he went through with the chain saw. The effect was a bit disconcerting, like being in one of those specially built rooms that make you feel small or off balance. Mrs. Sopkos had so much furniture stuffed into her living room, I wondered if she'd stolen some from the other side, though most of it looked like it had come with the house. Faded doilies were pinned on the arms of the sofa, but the shiny worn surfaces showed through in several spots, and the rows of folded blankets did little to offset the lugubrious sag of the middle. An end table held a framed picture of what had to be Lois and Mr. Sopkos on or shortly after their wedding. He apparently had been a big, robust man with a huge mustache sweeping upward over his smile. Mrs. Sopkos had the same dour look, minus a couple of deepened frown lines. Why did I think that mister wouldn't have been smiling if they'd taken the picture a few years later? I also noticed a set of aircraft carrier–sized binoculars sitting on a small end table next to the front window. An opaque shade had been pulled down, probably in an effort to obscure the view of anyone looking in from the street, but judging from her height, the position of the chair by the window, and the space between the bottom of the shade and the window frame, the Oracle had a slightly elevated street's eye view of everybody's comings and goings. She sat in the chair, probably out of habit. It also faced a twenty-four-inch television on a new wooden stand.

I glanced around, noticing that religious icons had been positioned on virtually every horizontal surface of the furnishings.

"We'd like to ask you about the man who lived across the street," Kali said. "Mr. Perry. Did you know him?"

"I did." Her lips turned downward as she said it. For a moment I wondered if she'd bitten into a lemon drop.

The curtness of her response must have stunned Kali too, but she recovered nicely. "Did you know him well?"

Mrs. Sopkos shook her head. "No. He wasn't the friendly sort. Not unless he was trying to sell me something. Wasn't much of a gentleman either. He'd think nothing of driving right by me in that fancy car of his when I'd be pulling my cart to and from the market." She gave another little shake of her head. "He'd toot the horn and wave, but do you think he'd stop?"

"You mean he'd just let you walk?" Kali actually sounded like she shared the outrage.

"Just like I wasn't even there."

Kali frowned in commiseration. "Had he lived there long?"

"A couple of years. When the yuppies started moving in. Most of them worked in Manhattan. They'd leave early in the morning, then come home after dark and never say two words to anybody. Not like the old days when neighbors all looked out for each other. Besides . . ."

Kali waited a beat before following up. "Besides?"

Mrs. Sopkos continued to squint at me. "Young man, did anyone ever tell you that you look like that actor on TV?"

"Which one?" I asked with a grin.

"The guy on that cops and lawyers show . . ."

Uh-oh, I thought. The price of fame seemed about to do me in. But maybe, with the right recovery, it'll gain us some purchase.

"Well, actually, I am not a cop," I said in as jovial a voice as I could muster. "I just play one on TV."

"No, no," Mrs. Sopkos said, shaking her head, which was massive. "He plays the DA. Played an Indian too, in a movie with the guy who used to play the president on *The West Wing*. I seen it on cable." She puffed up her cheeks, released a controlled exhale, then blurted out, "Sam Waterston. The district attorney. He's the best one we've had, even in the reruns, and Lord knows we could use a man like that in charge in real life too. I was hoping he'd run for president instead of the other fella."

"I certainly agree, ma'am," I replied.

"And you, young lady . . ." She turned to Kali. "You look a little like that pretty colored girl who won the Oscar a few years ago. At least I thought she was nice until I saw the movie on cable. *Monster's Balls*, or something. What's her name? Hally something. But I do remember that the movie was filthy. Just filthy."

I wondered how many times she'd watched it as Kali thanked her and artfully brought her back to Glenn, that late, unfriendly, inconsiderate young urban professional.

"Do you know anything about him?"

Mrs. Sopkos's mouth morphed into the now-familiar truculent scowl. "I know he lived alone, if you can call it that."

"Did he have many visitors?" I asked.

She shook her head. "None, except for a parade of other *men* I seen coming out of his house at all hours. Never any women, only men. It started me wondering until I figured it out one day when I happened to be looking out my window. Then I knew it. He was one of *those* people."

"Those people?" I asked.

She swiped her fingers under her nose, like she was flicking away a booger, and gave me a look that was both assessing and admonishing. "Like on that cable TV show. *Queer as Folk*. You know the one I'm talking about?"

I nodded, hoping she was going to save the deeper work until after we left. She rubbed the swiped fingers together down by the side of the chair. A real class act in Astoria. "You're saying he was gay?"

"Gay," she said with disparagement. "Back when I was young that meant fun-loving."

"*Queer as Folk*?" I asked.

"As a three-dollar bill," she said. "Not that I'm judgmental or anything."

"Of course not," I said, marveling at my own nonchalance. Her and Cyrus. Two bigots in two days. How did I get so lucky? But I wasn't about to get a wristlock on Mrs. Sopkos.

Kali asked if she knew where Perry had worked.

"He told me he done something with computers." She shook her head. "He was pleasant enough to talk to when I saw him out in his garden or collecting the mail. But he seldom talked about work. Although . . ." She held up her index finger and tried to rise laboriously from the sofa. She fell back down, causing a sudden creak from the springs that an anthropomorphist could have easily argued was a groan. I could see why it was sagging so badly in the middle. This broad was built like a barrel. She got up again, this time successfully, lumbered to the end table, and opened the drawer. It looked like an offshoot of Fibber McGee's closet. Maybe he'd run out of space and was renting some from the Oracle. After sorting through a collection of papers, she emitted a low grunt.

I took that to mean success.

Coming back, she handed Kali a business card.

"He gave me this in case I ever wanted to get my grandchildren's pictures made into paperweights. I asked him, why should I want to do that? He brought one over to show me and I looked at it and told him straight-out." She scrunched up her face into an almost feral snarl and held her hands out as if holding an imagined paperweight. "*This* is *shit*. Pardon my French."

Succinct and to the point, I thought, glancing over at the card. *Crystal Imaging* was spelled across the front in an artistic font. Underneath it was *Glenn F. Perry, Associate,* with an address and phone number.

"What kind of place was this?" Kali asked.

The Oracle shrugged and looked at her watch. "Beats me. I told you, he said something about paperweights, but I didn't pay much attention. Like I would let someone like him have pictures of my grandkids. I wouldn't let his kind near them." She shook her head and looked at the watch again, and then to the binoculars. Obviously it was getting close to some kind of regular neighborhood show. "You got any more questions? I got to start a stew pretty soon."

I stood, remembering the nose flick and not offering to shake hands. "We were just leaving. Thank you very much for your assistance."

At that moment it seemed to dawn on her that we'd been pumping her for info. The dark eyes flashed a look of suspicion and the frown lines deepened. "So are you going to put my picture in the *Inquirer*? Or quote me?"

"I'm sorry, all our sources are totally confidential," Kali said. "But we will send you a year's complimentary subscription."

The frown lines lessened as her cheeks untightened. "Oh, that'd be real nice."

Kali removed a small notebook from her purse and wrote down Mrs. Sopkos's info. We were able to move out the door with a little more fanfare and left the Oracle to her midafternoon peeping and picking.

As we walked down the block, I said, "I think she deserves a complimentary subscription."

"Yeah, I'll have to get her one."

"And when it arrives, she'll probably read it and say . . ." I couldn't help myself. I held my hands out and did my best mimic of the day: "*This is shit*."

Kali laughed. "Did you see her face?"

"Scary."

"This card lists a Manhattan address and phone number under Perry's name," she said. "We'll have to check that joint out."

I grinned. Everything was coming together, I thought. She's as into the investigation as I am.

# CHAPTER 10

The next morning, I began to regret Kali's growing exuberance when she called me at nine sharp. I'd spent the rest of the evening on set trying to get through several scenes that we needed to wrap up. We were behind, so that meant hurry up and wait. Till almost four in the morning. Most of the time I'd spent in my dressing room trying to sort out the Rudy conundrum when I wasn't going over the new script changes. On the way back to Manhattan, we'd called the number on the Crystal Imaging card only to hear it had been disconnected. Kali told me she would run down Perry's place of employment the next day, and true to her word, she had. And now she was raring to go when all I wanted to do was get another few hours' sleep.

"I didn't wake you up, did I?" she asked.

"You did, and it was just in the middle of a great dream where I was having a nice conversation with Angelina Jolie."

"For real? I'm sorry. Want to go back to it?"

"Nah, I don't want Brad Pitt on my tail." I stretched and managed to roll over in the bed and set my feet on the floor. "So what's so important that you felt compelled to rob me of what little beauty sleep I could get?"

Her laugh told me she got the joke. "I've been on the Internet doing a bit of research. The good news is I found out about Crystal Imaging Inc., the place where Perry worked. The bad news is, it's no longer in business."

"Lousy break."

"Yeah. It was one of those laser places where you can get a photo etched into a block of crystal."

"No doubt the paperweights that Mrs. Sopkos was referring to when she uttered her immortal line."

"But wait, there's more. We need to see Joshua Spaulding's family."

The world was still a bit out of sync for me. Sophocles may have been onto something when he said sleep is the only medicine that gives ease. I explored the carpet with my bare toes. "Who's that?"

"The third man on the list of dead men," she said. "Spaulding's obituary said he was a gemologist and expert jeweler for a large company in Manhattan. Isn't that great? One dead guy sold diamonds, and another one cut them. There's got to be some kind of connection here."

The excitement in her voice was like someone had passed me a shot of espresso. "How soon can you be over here?"

"Depends. Want me to take the subway or grab a cab?"

"Neither. I'm calling a limo service. We might as well be comfortable."

"Cool."

I looked at my bedside clock: 9:09. "Give me about forty-five minutes to get presentable and I'll buy you breakfast."

"At Tiffany's?"

"I was thinking more in the line of the local lox and bagel shop." I hung up and raised my window shade. Traces of sunshine were already working their way between the caverns of skyscrapers, and I felt renewed, despite the lack of sleep. I was more convinced than ever that we were on the right track to figuring out the mystery.


I was waiting on the street in front of my building when the limousine pulled up to the curb and beeped. Just out of habit, I checked to make sure it was Kali in the back and not our buddy Gustafson, although I figured he'd gotten the message yesterday. As I got in, Kali looked me over.

"You look tired. Did you get enough sleep?"

"It's a proven fact that the amount of sleep required by the average person is always five minutes more." I smiled. "I'm fine. I nuked some coffee from last night and I'm good to go."

"Last night? Oh, Lordy." She tapped on the screen behind the driver's head. "Stop at the next Starbucks we come to."

The driver, whose name was Mickey Schlitz, made an acknowledging wave.

"And then we're going out to the Island," she said.

"The Island? Coney, Staten, or Long?" I asked.

"Staten, of course."

"Ah, the forgotten borough. I wonder if Mr. Spaulding took the ferry in every morning."

"I can't swim, so we ain't taking no ferry. We're going by way of Jersey."

I noticed when she got excited her speech became more dialectical. I figured it was mostly for effect. Like the I'm-not-amused-black-girl-head-waggling thing.

She studied my face for a moment. "I hope you aren't doing a night shoot again tonight."

I shook my head. "Off until tomorrow evening." I felt the car slow as Mickey pulled over to the curb.

"Starbucks," he said.

Kali started to get out, but I raised a finger. "This is on me. Either of you want coffee or something?"

After taking their orders—one coffee-Boston for Kali and a medium house blend, black, for Mickey—I got out and stretched. Actually, I was doing a quick look-and-see up and down the block. It bothered me yesterday when that scrot, Gustafson, mentioned that he'd been shadowing me for a couple of days. I'd never seen him. All that good police tactical training I'd gone through, and I couldn't spot a simple tail. But I hadn't been expecting one either. Still, a man who values his conspiracies as much as I do should be more observant. *Scrot*, by the way, is an old Joseph Wambaugh term. (Go look it up.)

No fat reporters in garish plaid sport jackets were lurking in nearby doorway recesses. I figured we were safe enough. Plus, I thought if I had them add a shot of espresso to Mickey's cup, he'd be more than willing to leave anybody trying to tag us in a cloud of exhaust fumes.

We took the Lincoln Tunnel, and when we emerged into natural sunlight again, we were in good old Jersey—Weehawken, Union City, and Hoboken. Old Blue Eyes' hometown. I finished my bagel and cream cheese and washed it down with the remnants of my now cold coffee. But I felt surprisingly energized. "What part of the County of Richmond are we going to?"

She read off the address. "It's in the Great Kills area."

"You hear that, Mickey?" I asked.

"Got you covered, boss," he said. He held up the coffee I'd bought him. I guess that shot of espresso was doing the trick.

"You know," I said, "besides being kissin' cousin to tons of buried garbage, there's rumored to be a lot of Russians in Great Kills."

"Uh-huh," Kali said. "We're coming across a lot of coincidences, aren't we?"

"And you know what they say about coincidences." I settled back in the seat and watched the urban landscape shooting by. I wondered if Ivan Peters and Josh Spaulding could have known each other, both being in the diamond trade, so to speak. Glenn Perry was another matter. Perhaps there was no connection. But then why would Rudy have included them all in the letter?

I pondered these and other questions as Tonnelle Avenue turned into boulevards Hudson and finally Kennedy. I breathed a sigh of relief as we left New Jersey and crossed back into New York, even if we did have to pay a toll to do it. For years Staten Island had been famous for being the greatest producer of methane gas on the entire eastern seaboard. That infamous distinction faded when they closed down the Fresh Kills landfill in '01. The place, once the favorite dining spot of a million and a half seagulls, is slated to be a real nice park. Once they extinguish the last of the methane residuals, that is.

But the scenery soon transformed into magnificent green pastures and trees, emanating an almost bucolic sense of the serene. Great Kills was once all dairy land. Now it's rapidly transforming into a modified suburbia populated by those wishing to escape the confines of tall buildings by communing with nature and voting Republican. After all, it was easier than thinking.

"We're getting close," Mickey said. "You gonna want me to stick around?"

"Why don't you do that." I figured the convenience of having a quick exit ride might come in handy, especially if the ubiquitous Cyrus Gustafson had somehow managed to follow us. Trying to shake that guy was worse than scraping dog shit out of the grooves of your gym shoes. "I'm not sure how long we'll be, but I'll give you a retainer."

"Sounds good by me," he said, as we rounded a curve into a new-looking subdivision and slowed down. The houses, mostly a combination of brick and aluminum siding, sat off from the street behind a tree-lined parkway.

Not a bad place to live, I thought, if you could set aside the dubious distinction of having been the only borough in New York carried by George W. Bush in 2004.

"That's the place," Kali said, pointing to a nice single-family home. Brick on the bottom, aluminum siding on the second story, probably four bedrooms, two baths, a family room downstairs, and a two-and-a-half-car garage. A suburbanite's dream, and still in a borough of New York City. Who could ask for anything more?

Actually, it looked pretty much like all the rest of the houses on the street, except that it had a big sign in front of it that said *For Sale*. Printed on the upper half was *Cermack Realty, Incorporated*, with the name *Brad Sikes* and a phone number.

"This doesn't look too promising," I said. "We might be needing a ride back quicker than we thought."

"No sweat," Mickey said. "I'm at your disposal. I got a hankering to grab an early lunch down the street. Here's my card. My cell's on the bottom. Call me back when you're ready."

I looked at it and stuck it in my shirt pocket. "I got to ask you, what's it like growing up with a name like Mickey Schlitz?"

He shrugged. "Beats Herman Wizenstein. That was my real name before I changed it. Kids used to call me the Wiz."

I gave him a commiserating nod. "Hang in there."

The old guy with the hose in the yard next to the former Spaulding place
was making a show of watering his gardenias while he was watching us.
I walked up to the front door and rang the bell. A Realtor's lockbox hung
suspended from the doorknob. The chimes echoed inside, but no one answered. I leaned over and peered in the front picture window. Plenty of furniture was visible but covered with sheets. I turned back to Kali and gave
an exaggerated shrug.

"Nobody live there," the old guy called to us.

I looked over toward him and smiled. "How long's the place been on
the market?"

"Why? You want to buy?"

The cadence and inflections of his accent had a familiar sound.

*"Zdravstvujtye,"* I said, hoping I was right. The simper on his face told
me I was.

"Ah, you speak *Rusil*—Russian?"

"Not a lot," I said, shaking my head as he continued the conversation
in his native language. He swung back to pigeon when he realized I wasn't
understanding anything he said.

"They move out maybe one, one-half year now," he said. "Man die.
Woman, boy move. The bank owns now. You call number. They will show
you house."

"Why did they move?" I asked.

He shrugged.

"Did you know them well?" Kali asked.

The old man shook his head. "Not too much. Man, I talk to sometimes.
My son know him better."

"Is your son home now?" I asked.

The old guy shook his head. "Not here much lately." He resumed watering the plants. "You call that number. They show you."

I took his cue and dialed the number on my cell. A man answered after two rings with a crisp, "Brad Sikes."

"Brad," I said, "your name was recommended to me."

"Really." His tone warmed up. "May I ask by whom?"

"Cermack Realty. It's on their sign."

A slight pause told me that he was most likely not someone who appreciated wry humor, but with a salesman's acumen, he shot back a quick, forced laugh. It was enough to start me wondering if this guy was a run-of-the-mill jerk or only a desperate Realtor. "Okay, what can I do for you? Who am I talking to, by the way?"

"Call me Belz." I figured it was better than saying call me Ishmael.

"Is that B-E-L-L-S?"

"Close enough. A very pretty young lady and I are standing here on the lawn of a very nice-looking house at . . ."—I turned and gave him the address—"and we'd like to take a look inside."

"All right." The tone warmed up considerably, like the sun coming from behind a cloud. I could hear him shuffling something sounding like papers in the background. "I could be there in, say, forty minutes?"

"Forty minutes it is," I said, accentuating the positive. "We'll grab a fast bite and meet you back here."

After hanging up, I called Mickey and told him to swing back and get us.

"Damn," he said, "I just ordered my lunch."

"Tell 'em to keep it warm for you. In fact, lunch is on me, as long as it's quick."


For the quick lunch Mickey took us to McDonald's, where we hit the drive-up for the usual fastest of the fast food. Since I had hopes of getting some info out of this Brad dude, I told them to skip the onions on mine. We shot back in time to see a guy I figured was him pulling up in a gray Dodge Charger. If I'd had any doubts that he was a first-class knucklehead, they were erased as soon as he got out of the car. Brad Sikes had dark hair, flecked with a lot of gray, and an olive complexion. He looked to be on the far side of forty with an overbearing smile that must have made it hard for him to move his lips when he talked. He wore a brownish sport jacket and dark slacks. Tieless, he'd left his shirt collar displaying a swath of black chest hair just below a solid gold chain. A smoldering cigarette dangled from the corner of his mouth. If this dude was going to recognize me, it would only be from *The Groove Tube*. He would have been a real hit back when John Travolta was starring in *Saturday Night Fever*. He even moved with the jerkiness of someone endlessly playing a syncopated version of "Stayin' Alive" inside his head.

"Oh, my God," Kali said. "Is this dude for real?"

"Obviously he's a legend in his own mind, but remember, we're here for a purpose."

"I'm not sure it's gonna be worth it," she said.

Sikes took one last drag on the cigarette and flipped it across the street. I guess he figured it was biodegradable. With the crooked smile still plastered on his puss, he walked forward, his hand extended.

"Mr. Bells?" His voice had a raspy twang that came from too much smoke tweaking his vocal cords. "I'm Brad Sikes."

"I figured that," I said. "I could tell by the way you use your walk."

That caused a little stutter step, but he came back with, "You know, I like your name. Has a good ring to it." Sikes expelled a heavy breath that could be taken as a forced laugh or an extended precursor to a cough. I decided it was meant to be the former when the simper stretched his face again. "Get it? Bells . . . ring." There's something about a guy who laughs that hard at his own jokes and then feels compelled to explain the punch line to you that makes me want to yell, "Get the hook!"

I shook his hand and introduced Kali, not bothering to correct my name. What he didn't know wouldn't hurt me. His eyebrows rose fractionally when he looked toward the limo idling at the curb. "Hey, you like to ride in style, don't you?" I could almost see the little dollar signs dancing before his eyes.

"My Rolls is in the shop," I said.

Sikes gave me a half stare that lasted only long enough for him to assess if I was kidding or not, then expelled another heavy breath. "Good one, Bells, good one."

Jack Benny would have hired this dude in a minute for one of his audience stooges, except that his breath was bad. Very bad.

I shouldn't have worried about the onions.

"Say," he said, "anybody ever tell you that you look just like that guy on TV?"

"Most people tell me I look like a young Cary Grant." I tapped my sunglasses. "Except with photochromic lenses."

Sikes nodded in absolute agreement. "Yeah, yeah, you do."

As we walked up the sidewalk, Sikes paged through a booklet he had, quoting us all the attributes of the former Spaulding place, although he didn't call it that. He continually referred to them as "the previous owners."

He dialed the combo on the Realtor's lock, removed the key, then opened the front door. The house had a musty smell.

"Let me get those covers off the furniture," Sikes said, rushing forward. "You were early, otherwise I'd have had it a bit more presentable." He took a small canister of air freshener out of his pocket and sprayed a few blasts in the air.

"The place comes furnished?" Kali asked.

Sikes grinned. "Well, the previous owners left a good portion of their furnishings inside. We thought it makes it a little more homey to prospective buyers." His eyes darted between Kali and me. "Of course, the rooms don't seem quite as large that way, but believe me, this place is what they call capacious." He went on to quote the amount of square feet in each room as we strolled through the house. I studied the rooms but was getting very little in the way of a feel for anything or anybody.

"Brad," I said, "what about the former owners? Why'd they sell?"

"Well . . ." He drew the word out, obviously mentally calculating what he thought I'd want to hear. I hoped it didn't interfere with "Stayin' Alive."

"I heard the homeowner died," I said, interrupting his cogitative extrapolations. "Is that right?"

The smile drooped, leaving his mouth stuck open like an image frozen by a pause button. He barked another heavy breath, not quite intense enough to masquerade as his laugh, and said, "You know, I did hear something about that."

"His name was Joshua Spaulding, wasn't it?"

This time the barking breath became a laugh. "I can see you're a man who likes to do his homework."

"And the meter's running on our taxi," I said. "Did you know the Spauldings?"

"I . . ." He let the vowel drag on before he finally said, "No, not really. Mister died suddenly, and his widow got a big insurance settlement. Part of it guaranteed that the mortgage would be paid off upon the death of the principal wage earner." He allowed himself a noncommittal shrug. "When she got the money, she and their son took off for Arizona or someplace. Left everything here. Left everything on the property the way it was and hired us to sell it."

That sounded like a pretty fast exit from Staten Island. I began to wonder why. Maybe there was something here, after all. "Do you have a forwarding address for Mrs. Spaulding?"

"I can look into that." His eyes narrowed. "But let me assure you, there are no defects in this residence. Neither Cermack nor I would be involved in selling it if there was."

"That's good to know." I rotated my head, like I was surveying the place, and forced myself to smile. "I'd still like to speak to the previous owner though, before I make any decision."

"Well"—he was drawing out words again—"I'm sure the main office must have some contact info."

"Good," I said, taking out my pocket notebook. "Why don't you call them on your cell and get it for me while we wait."

The perpetual grin compressed and his eyebrows drew upward. "That might take time."

"Time? Time is money," I said. "I told you our taxi was waiting, right?"

Contemplative exhaling. "Ok—ay." He took a cell phone out of his jacket pocket. "Let me see what I can do."

Five minutes later he was following us out the door and toward the limo, trying to hand me one of his business cards and placing another cigarette between his lips. Made me glad I quit smoking. I opened the door for Kali and accepted the card as I slid in next to her.

"Mr. Bells," he said, trying to hold the lighter to the smoke as he spoke. Talking made it more tricky, and Brad was no Bogey. "Call me when you're ready to talk turkey."

Talk turkey? Maybe this guy had stepped out of a seventies time warp.

"Brad, I wouldn't call anybody else," I said, and did my best mimic of his irritating, halitosis laugh.

We left him standing at the curb, perpetual half grin still stuck in place.

"What time is it in Arizona?" I asked, looking at the number I'd gotten from Sikes as Mickey sped down the block.

"I don't know," Kali said. "Isn't that the state with one of those weird time zones where you can drive a few hundred feet and it jumps back an hour?"

"That's only if you cross Hoover Dam," I said. "Where you go from Nevada to Arizona on the other side."

It was twelve twenty here, which would make it around nine or ten out west, depending on which side of the Rockies the Widow Spaulding was. It might be better to call tonight, I thought, and stuck the notebook back in my pocket. But the elation I'd felt a few hours earlier when Kali had called was starting to ebb away. Aside from a few coincidences and four dead men, what did we have?

Not a whole hell of a lot, I told myself.

"What the hell, let's chance it." I started to dial the phone.

"Who you calling now?"

"The merry widow."

"Why?"

It was my turn to shrug. "You never know what you'll find, once you start turning over rocks and shaking the bushes."

"But what are you going to say?" Kali asked.

"I'll figure that out if she answers." A second later someone did. It was a woman.

"Hello," I said, doing my best imitation of Sikes's nasal intonations. "I'm calling from New York. I'm trying to reach a Mrs. Joshua Spaulding who used to live on Staten Island."

"This is she. Who's this?"

Now it was put-up or shut-up time. I could either level with her or delve into that quagmire of MSU—Making Shit Up.

"This is Rupert Cavell, Brad Sikes's assistant," I said. Why tell the truth when a slight prevarication might get you farther? "You know . . . Cermack Realty?"

"Is this about my old house?"

"Exactly."

"You've sold it?"

"Not quite yet," I said.

"I thought all that was settled. You weren't to call me until it was sold. Why are you bothering me now? You people have no reason to contact me about anything until the deal's done."

"You're absolutely right," I said, trying to think of a plausible inroad. "But we were just showing your old residence to a prospective couple this morning and," I paused, "the topic of your husband's untimely passing came up."

Silence.

"So," I continued, "it occurred to Brad and me that we really couldn't answer too many of the young couple's questions. I'm sure you under- stand. They've heard so much about houses with hidden radon gas deposits and the sort."

More silence. "What the hell are you talking about?"

"I just want to be able to assure them that your husband's tragic pass- ing wasn't related to something like that. I mean, were they sure it was a heart attack? Did he have any enemies?"

"Who the hell are you? Why did you call me?" Her voice was angry but had an undercurrent of something else. Suspicion? Or perhaps fear? "How did you get this number?"

"It's in our files, ma'am. Please, the last thing I wanted to do was upset you."

"The last thing you wanted to do." Even a continent away and over the phone, I could tell she spat out the words. "Don't call me again, you son of a bitch. Ever. Just contact my lawyer. I'm having my number changed."

She hung up.

Kali, who'd only heard half of the conversation but had been watching my reactions, did her head-waggling, I'm-not-amused black girl thing again. "Well, Rupert, that went really well."

"You should have heard what you missed," I said. "She called me a dirty name."

"Really?" she smiled. "I thought she didn't know you that well."

I smiled back. "Very funny. I used to do a stand-up routine too, you know."

"So I've heard. But we're back to square one?"

I closed my cell and stuck it back into my pocket. "Maybe, but I've played a cop on TV long enough to recognize a pattern when I see one."

"A pattern? What kind of pattern?"

"Well, I haven't seen it yet. But trust me, I will."

"Are we close to Jersey yet?" Kali asked Mickey. "I think the air's affecting him back here."

I snapped my fingers. Okay, so it was mostly for effect. But my snap put Vern Franker's to shame. "Commonalities."

"Commonalities?"

"Right. The pattern. There are certain commonalities in these four cases."

"Such as?"

I considered this. "Well, Russians and diamonds . . ."

"I already told you that."

"Yeah, I know. Let me know when you think of some more too."

She rolled her eyes. At least I knew what buttons to push.

I looked out the window and did a mental review. Four relatively young men, all dying on the streets of Manhattan of heart attacks. Rudy was the ME who did all four autopsies. A diamond merchant. Russkies. A gay guy who ran a laser-etching service and lived in Queens. And a dead gemologist/jeweler who had a house in Staten Island. With a Russian neighbor. And an irritated widow.

"Remember what I said about commonalities?"

"Yeah."

"There was something in that woman's voice," I said. "Anger, surprise, but mostly sort of an apprehension or dread."

"So? Her husband died, right? She has a right to be upset when people ask her about it."

"Yeah," I said, "but I noticed the same tone in someone else's voice not too long ago."

"Whose?"

"Rudy's."

The place that was Crystal Imaging was now a vacant store. Since we'd made great time getting back to Manhattan and the afternoon was still young, I had told Mickey to run us by Glenn Perry's last place of employment. He grinned from ear to ear when I handed him some bills and told him to grab a coffee and hang in the area for a while.

"So I gotta ask you," he said. "You're that guy on that TV show with the lawyers and the cops, ain't ya?"

I smiled. Finally, fame had preceded me. "Yeah, I am. But why didn't you bring this up before?"

"I'm used to dealing with celebrities and figured you valued your privacy, Mr. Woods. But I make sure I'm off so I can watch *Shark* every week."

"You know, most people don't recognize me with the sunglasses on." I tapped my right lens, wondering if it would be in poor taste to withdraw the tip at this point. Of course, if I did, he'd probably never watch James's show again.

He grinned. "But I gotta ask ya, what you doing in New York? I thought you were out in L.A."

"Actually, I'm doing some special location work."

"Oh, okay. I get you." He shot me an acknowledgment by pointing his index finger like a gun. "I'll be watching for them on the show."

"You do that," I said, returning his gun gesture.

His eyes narrowed. "One more thing."

I cocked my head toward him.

"I'm not positive," he said sotto voce, "but when we was coming back,

I thought a couple of times somebody might have been tailing us. I could be wrong, though."

Gustafson. It had to be him. That asshole doesn't know when to quit, I thought. Or what's good for him. I scanned the block looking for a telltale garish plaid sport jacket. He'd worn green and black. What color pattern was he due for? Red and yellow?

"So, you want me to stick close?" Mickey asked.

I was still looking around. Plenty of people, but no Gustafson. "What kind of car?"

"A black Chevy sedan. But maybe I was just imagining it. Lots of those in the Big Apple. So, you want me to hang real close?"

I shook my head. "Give us some space. I got a hunch I know who it might be, and if he gets close, I'll hear him."

Mickey gave us a quick wave as he pulled away, obviously going around the block to look for a temporary spot to park. Kali and I stood on the sidewalk looking at the dark windows. Even the sign had been removed. It was like Crystal Imaging had never existed.

"What now, Mr. Woods?" Kali asked.

"Well, what would Sebastian Shark do?" I held out my palm. "We go to some of the adjacent storeowners and ask if they remember anything about their erstwhile tenant and fellow merchant."

As we began walking, a burly guy with a big, crooked nose that would make a rhinoceros jealous stepped in front of us. As we adjusted to step around him, another equally meaty dude blocked the other half of the sidewalk. Together they could have given the New York Giants' offensive line a run for their money.

"Excuse us, gentlemen," I said.

"Hey, I know you," Rhino said. Maybe somebody had tried a rhinoplasty on him and botched it. I had to admit I was somewhat impressed that he could talk, even if his English was laced with a heavy European accent.

Before I could think of a witty retort, the second one opened his mouth and spoke as well.

"You that TV actor with big nose." He had a face full of scars and a crude tattoo of a web pattern edging upward on his neck and on his wrists, like snakes encroaching onto his hands. He had an accent too. Unless my ear was telling me a story, this guy was as Russian as a T-90S tank.

"No, but I've been told I look like him," I said. "Now excuse us."

"Hold it." Scarface put up his hand.

This was definitely not a good sign. I pushed Kali behind me.

"We got message for you about your big nose," the other guy said. Except for the scars, he could have been a clone of his partner. Well, his schnoz wasn't quite a match. "And for your girlfriend too."

Rhino began to shift his weight, and I knew he was winding up to throw a sucker punch. He would have been better off sending it Western Union. I sidestepped, slipping the punch as it sailed by, and grabbed Rhino's wrist. Using his momentum to pull it down, then back and over as I stepped with it, I executed a perfect hapkido throw. Rhino hit the pavement hard with his back, his face blanching as he struggled for breath. The wind had been knocked out of him.

Scarface withdrew something long and black out of his pocket and reared back. The blackjack started its descent, but I pivoted to the side and felt it whoosh by my face.

Shit, I thought. Almost.

He was carried forward from the force he'd sought to put behind the blow, so I pivoted again. Remembering Jimmy's coaching from yesterday, I shot a quick heel kick to the inside of his left leg, catching his knee. He stumbled forward and left his throat wide open. I jammed it with an open-handed palm strike. It sounded like I'd smacked a Wiffle ball a city block. Scarface immediately brought both his hands to his injured throat, gasping hoarsely, and let the sap fall to the sidewalk. I stepped in close and sent my right elbow into his nose. I felt the cartilage give with the blow. Now he and his buddy Rhino would be a matching set. As he went sprawling, I quickly grabbed the sap from the sidewalk and smacked Rhino right across the chops as he was attempting to rise. His lips fluttered and he spit out a couple of teeth in a spray of crimson.

I stepped back, ready to deliver a front snap kick, but both of them were in the process of scrambling away in the opposite direction as fast as they could, just like a couple of illuminated cockroaches.

I watched their progress as they half ran, half shuffled down the block, leaving a blood trail as they went. A few people had witnessed the event and one of them yelled, "Hey, mister, want me to call nine-one-one?"

"Does he look like he needs the cops?" the guy next to him said. He gave me a thumbs-up. "Way to go, buddy."

I turned back to Kali. "You all right?"

She nodded. "Wow, that was just like a Steven Seagal movie."

"Oh, puh-leese. I'd much rather be compared to Chuck Norris."

"You were doing the Dew, all right." She grinned. "But I ain't sure you were *that* good."

"You really ought to consider that stand-up routine." I sighed and slipped the blackjack into my pocket. Maybe it would come in handy the next time we ran into Gustafson. It might also go a long way toward convincing Max we were dealing with some serious baddies here. Of course I knew what his response would be: "Stay out of it. You're not a cop." The guy was starting to sound like a broken record, even though nobody even played vinyl much anymore.

# CHAPTER 11

I called Mickey's cell as I pondered our next move. From all appearances, Frick and Frack, otherwise known as Scarface and Rhino, were still beating a hasty retreat, but that old adage about not lingering at the scene of the crime was beginning to loom large. This time they'd tried to intimidate me with fists and a blackjack. If we remained here, maybe they'd be back with reinforcements who could up the ante. The limo swooped over to the curb and came to an abrupt stop.

"Where to, boss?" he asked.

The Russian accents of these two new assailants bothered me. Like déjà vu all over again. It was like I'd sidestepped into an old Sean Connery James Bond movie.

I looked at Kali. "We need to vacate the area here. Plus I want to talk with Max and let him know that another pair of foreign thugs tried to jump me. Even he's smart enough to catch the pattern."

"Max?"

"Oh, sorry. Max Kaminsky. A police buddy of mine." I told Mickey to take us to Midtown North on Fifty-fourth Street.

At the precinct I made my usual request for Detective Kaminsky. It was getting to be a habit. At least there was a different guy working the desk than I'd seen the last time, so he told us to have a seat on the bench and he'd see. After a fifteen-minute wait that seemed like an eternity, Max came ambling out from the back and nodded.

"Hey, Belz, how you doing?"

"Great, considering we've been waiting so long our feet are stuck to the floor."

"Well, pardon me all to hell," he said, bristling.

This wasn't starting out too well. "Look, Max, I didn't mean to sound cocky, but two thugs just tried to beat the hell out of us."

His heavy eyebrows almost knitted together. "Shit, you all right?"

"We're fine."

"Where'd this happen at?"

"Forty-third Street, over by Tenth."

"I hope you made out a report."

I smiled. "Actually, our first thought was to come over and talk to you."

"You keep saying 'our.' You mean you got a witness?"

I turned slightly and Kali stood up. "You should have seen him, Detective. He was great. Took out those two punks like," she canted her head and looked at me, "he was Chuck Norris or somebody."

"Thank you," I said, giving her a wink.

"I doubt he was that good." Max looked her up and down, with a hint of salaciousness in his eyes. "Say, who's your friend, Belz?"

"May I present Ms. Kalisha Carter, my personal assistant. And this is Max Kaminsky, the best detective on the NYPD."

"Aw, go on," Max said, guffawing at the compliment, and shook hands with Kali. "Anyway, this altercation sounds like something I'd like to hear about." Max motioned for us to follow him. He led us down a corridor and cut left, ushering us into a break room. Several plastic chairs were scattered around the room along with a couple of cheap Formica tables, a beat-up old TV mounted on the wall. The brackets looked ready to give way any minute from the dull greenish paint of the cinder block walls. The effect was rounded out by a host of vending machines lining one side. Max pointed to an empty table and told us to sit, asking over his shoulder how we liked our coffee.

He came back to the table with a cream and sugar for Kali, a black for me, and a cream only for himself. Some of the hot liquid spilled as he set the triangle of cups down and he swore.

"Hottest cup in town," he said.

"You ought to practice that the next time you go to a fast-food joint," I said. "You might be able to sue and get some money."

"Shit, then I'd have to get in bed with some lawyer." He took a shallow sip, shook his head, and set the cup down. "So how you been doing, Belz?"

"Outstanding," I said. "The reason we came by—"

"And you, miss," he said, interrupting me. "You in show business too?"

Kali smiled and shook her head. She braved a sip from her paper cup and pulled away. "God, that's awful. How can you drink it?"

Max shrugged. "You get used to it around here. What's that line from Gilbert and Sullivan? A policeman's job is not a happy one?"

"It's 'lot,'" I said. "And quit flirting and tell us if you've made any progress finding Rudy."

Max shot me a wounded look. "I thought you wanted to tell me about the guys who tried to roll you?"

"I do, in good time. Any progress on finding Rudy?"

Max sighed and shook his head. "I'm sorry to say that nothing's turned up yet."

"How hard are you looking?" I asked.

That set him off a bit. His cheeks rose upward like someone had puppet strings attached to them. "Listen, for your information, we got beaucoup crime going on in this city."

"Really?" I reached in my pocket and held up the blackjack. "Are these things illegal?"

The raised cheeks drooped. "Of course. Where'd you get that?"

"From the two guys who tried to coldcock me with it."

"You know these guys?"

I shook my head. "No, but I introduced them to the city sidewalk."

"He was great too," Kali added. "Like I said, Chuck Norris–class."

"Lemme see that." He reached over and took the sap, tapping it lightly in his palm. "Hmmph. Spring-loaded too. That gives you more bang for your buck."

"Believe me, I know," I said.

"You didn't get hit with this, did you?" he asked. I could almost detect something close to a trace of real concern in his tone.

I shook my head. "No, but somebody else did."

"Who?"

"One of my assailants," I said. "Or would you prefer the word 'perp'?"

"Some of the dude's crooked teeth are probably still laying over there on the sidewalk," Kali said. "Along with some blood."

"And you'd never seen them before?" Max asked again.

"No," I said, "but I've got an idea. Maybe you can get Gary Sinise from *CSI: New York* to go process the scene and you can pick them up in a matter of minutes."

He frowned. "You, of all people, should know it don't work that way in real life. How come you didn't go by the Tenth Precinct to make out an assault report?"

"I didn't want to blow the mayor's new statistics regarding the drop in street crime," I said. "Besides, I did all the assaulting."

"But they're still out there?"

"Those two jokers belonged in a bad movie."

"I'll get a uniform in here to take their descriptions," he said. "Then we can put out a citywide—"

"Max," I said, "I'm not interested in pursuing charges against them."

"And why's that?"

"Because it all ties in to the case. Remember I told you about those two guys who jumped Rudy last week?"

"You saying these were the same dudes?" he asked.

"No, but it's got to be related somehow. Just like that letter I gave you. The one Rudy sent."

Max held up his open palm. "Hold on, Belz. I thought we went over all this before. First of all, you ain't sure it was him who sent it to you, right?"

"Come on, Max. Who else could it *have* been, dammit?" I felt myself getting angry and took a deep breath. I couldn't afford to lose it and alienate him just when I might have a good lead that needed following up on. "Remember the other half of the boxing ticket?"

"That was sent to the crime lab for forensic processing." He was starting to sound defensive.

"Well, we've been looking into things a bit on our own," I said. "For instance, those numbers in the letter—they're ME case numbers. Ones where Rudy did the autopsies."

"So?"

My creeping anger was overriding my desire to keep calm. "So, they were all relatively young men, and they all dropped dead."

"Shit like that happens. You got any idea how many people just drop on the street in a city this size?"

"Yeah, well, one of them was a Russian."

"A Russian?"

"And so is Rudy."

"No shit, Sherlock. Tell me something I don't know, why don't ya?"

"All right." I pointed at the blackjack. "Those two guys who jumped me today were Russians too."

He smirked. "The other day you told me they were Ukrainians."

"Well, those guys probably were. They were speaking Ukrainian."

"Belz, listen to yourself, for Christ's sake."

"Obviously, that's the only person who's going to listen to me around here."

He deliberately let his mouth gape and then held up an index finger. "You know, Holmes, I think you've got something. All we have to do is pull in every Ukrainian-speaking Russkie roving around the Big Apple and surrounding towns like Yonkers and such, and we'll have a bevy of suspects." Max frowned. "Look, getting mugged or almost mugged by two perps is standard procedure in certain neighborhoods. You ought to stay out of them. Both of you. This is New York, after all."

"Yeah, but one of these guys had a Russian accent. Don't you see? It's got to be all tied together somehow—"

"Hey, don't act like I'm some kind of fucking dummy." His face reddened. "I told you before, Belz, you ain't no cop. Now knock it off, and leave the investigating to us professionals. Who do you think you are, anyway? Dick fucking Tracy?"

His sudden burst of rage had an unexpectedly cooling effect on my own anger. "Actually, Rupert Cavell might be a better analogy."

This seemed to stun him. He considered saying something, pursed his lips, and stood up. "Stay right here. Don't move till I get back." He grabbed the blackjack and turned away.

We watched as he stormed out.

Kali leaned over to me after a moment and whispered, "I think he's kind of pissed off."

"Do you? Well, better pissed off than pissed on, I always say."

"I've been meaning to ask you." She was still whispering. "Who the hell is Rupert Cavell?"

"Jimmy Stewart's character in *Rope*," I whispered back.

After a solid fifteen minutes more of waiting, Kali looked at me and asked, "Where do you think he went?"

I shrugged. "Maybe to check on the progress of the case." Or maybe he went to check on the latest results from Alameda. He had been gone for what was beginning to seem like an awfully long time.

Five more minutes passed before a completely calm and sobered Max came back looking like he'd just been slapped across the face and given a whiff of ammonia. Almost placidly, like a patient father reprimanding an errant son, he pointed his finger at me and said, "Belz, I'm gonna give you one more admonishment. Quit nosing around and getting into trouble over this Markovich thing. Especially with a young lady with you." He cocked his head in Kali's direction.

"Then listen to what we've found out so far, dammit."

He shook his head. "I told you, we're looking into it."

"How hard?"

I figured my comment would make him blow his top again, but it didn't. It was like he was resigned to letting me vent.

"Hard enough. Just let us handle it. We're a lot better connected than you are."

"Which is why I keep coming to you with what we've found out."

He gave me a long, hard stare. "One more time: butt out. Let us do our jobs. You get the message?"

"Loud and clear," I said, standing up.

On the way out, Kali leaned close to me and said, "You're right. Something doesn't smell right here."

"And like I said before," I added, "it ain't wafting in from Staten Island."

# CHAPTER 12

We walked across Fifty-third Street toward the East River as I called Mickey to pick us up. It was now beginning to close in on late afternoon, and I had a night shoot to get to in less than three hours. I couldn't figure Max's indolence, or his idiocy. Every other time I'd seen him work a case, he was like a bulldog. A reasonably intelligent bulldog. My cell phone rang and I fished it out of my pocket, looking at the caller ID screen. Anna.

"I was wondering if you have found anything," she said.

What could I tell her? That I'd been going around asking a bunch of questions and had succeeded in pissing off the cops? I owed her an update. Plus, my stomach was growling a bit, but not for stuffed cabbage and beets.

"Are you at work?" I asked.

"I do not work today."

I suggested the Cub Room in SoHo, which was far enough away, but not too far from tonight's shoot. That way Kali and I could report in after our meet, and Vern Franker would be happy. Plus, I had no desire to make the long trek over to the seaside edge of Brooklyn. I was leery of the entire Russian ambiance tonight.

"I will meet you there," she said, and hung up.

"Feel like grabbing an early dinner?" I asked Kali as I shut the cell and slipped it back into my pocket.

"At this point I'll even grab a late lunch," she said with a smile.

I saw Mickey and waved my arm. If I added up all the taxi fares and limo fees I'd been doling out lately, it might be cheaper to buy myself a new Lexus. I opened the door for Kali and slid in the back beside her.

"Where to now, boss?" he asked.

"West Broadway and Houston," I said, using the proper New York pronunciation rather than the Texas one. I was in the mood for one of the Cub Room's juicy steaks, and after subsisting on bagels and McDonald's all day, I figured I deserved one.

As Mickey drove over to Second Avenue and then headed south toward downtown, I tried to picture myself in that Lexus battling the constant flow of traffic. Anybody who lives in Manhattan and owns a car has to be real rich and real stupid if they think they'll get a chance to drive it. Plus, I'd spend more time looking for a space to park than checking for Rudy. Or maybe I could do the Britt Reid Green Hornet thing in a big black limo and hire Sammo Lee to play an aging Kato. He'd probably drive me nuts the first day telling me about his old chop-sockies from his Hong Kong cinema days. On the other hand, I could lure Mickey Schlitz away from the limo service to drive me around town. It worked for Boston Blackie, but that was in the movies. The movies from the forties, at that.

I rotated my head and looked out the back window. "Hey, Mick. Make sure we're not being tailed, will you?"

He glanced in the rearview mirror. "Why? We trying to dodge somebody again?"

"You might say that."

He nodded. "I'll lose 'em, as long as it ain't the cops."

I should be so lucky, I thought. If I'd had some cops around, they could have collared those two Russkie creeps who tried to jump us at Crystal Imaging.

I'd blown off Mickey's earlier warning, but I had assumed it was Gustafson lingering around like a bad smell. With all the people who had been following me, and my degree of apparent obliviousness to them, one thing was certain: I was no Marlowe when it came to spotting tails. In fact, he would have called me a rank amateur.

But that's what I was, wasn't I? And being a Marlowe meant filling some big shoes. Rupert Cavell's were probably more my size. He was a nervous wreck at the end of *Rope* when he called the cops.

"You're awfully quiet," Kali said, interrupting my reverie.

"I was just thinking about how this little fracas today is going to sound to Vern in your daily report."

Her mouth tugged downward and the veins in her neck stood out. "Oh. You know about those, huh?"

"Big Brother Franker let it slip."

She looked down. "Sorry, Richard. He told me I had to do it or I'd be fired."

"I know. And I told him if he fired you, I'd personally help you file an EEOC complaint against him."

"You told him that?"

"I did. And I meant it too." I smiled at the memory of Franker walking away with his tail between his legs. Still, I'd gotten in another physical confrontation this afternoon. The second one in less than a week. Well, third if you count my minor wrist-twisting of Gustafson, but that had been more a lesson in manners. Plus, none of them was my fault. The other guys had started them.

Man, with so many excuses for getting into fights, I was beginning to sound like Mike Tyson's lawyer. "So what are you going to report to him today?"

"The truth, more or less."

"More less than more?"

"I'll just tell him that we were doing some research for the show, so we went to Staten Island, then came back and had dinner in Manhattan." She glanced at her watch. "And that I got you back in time for tonight's shoot."

I grinned. It just went to show that Big Brother was only as good as the sum of his parts.

As we got out on Sullivan, I kept stopping and turning around, looking for any telltale shadows. Things looked like business as usual with plenty of pedestrians crowding the narrow sidewalks between the shops and edging cobblestones. A couple of street peddlers held up some silver jewelry toward Kali. She ignored them in typical New Yorker fashion.

"Hey, buddy," a thin, bearded kid whispered to me. "You looking for a steal of a deal on a great new Von Tromp?"

Original name, I thought, as I shook my head. "But if you've got a genuine Markovich, I'll take it." He looked both stunned and mystified. One thing was for sure, with all this gentrified ambience, we'd be lost in the crowds like trees in the forest.

Kali tugged my sleeve. "Isn't that her?"

I looked and saw Anna standing in front of the restaurant, talking on her cell phone. I immediately wondered who she was talking to, then brushed the question away. She was an attractive young woman in one of the most vibrant cities in the world. And she didn't look like a nun. She probably got hit on constantly, and she had a right to a social life. Still, I felt a certain obligation to forewarn her that things were getting a bit rougher than I had originally anticipated. Plus, the last thing I wanted was my buddy Gustafson trying to get an exclusive with "the redhead."

As we walked up to her, she immediately told the person on the other end something in Russian and flipped her phone shut. Then she hugged me. "Richard, I'm so glad to see you." She smiled at Kali and said, "Hello again to you too."

Kali nodded.

"This is the place," I said, pointing to the front door. "I'm having a Cub steak, but their red snapper is excellent too, although I'll have to skip the *pâté de campagne*. It's made with pork."

Over appetizers I briefed Anna on our day's work.

"This man in the Island of Staten," she said, "are you sure he was Russian?"

"He seemed pretty excited when I greeted him with *Zdravstvujtye*," I said.

She compressed her lips. "Then perhaps I should go talk to him?"

I shook my head. "Let me figure out how things are tied together first. I asked you to talk to the people in Brighton Beach. Have you heard anything?"

"Many, many people, they say they know my father, but no one has seen him recently." Her gaze fell to the tabletop, then rose up to meet mine. "I don't even tell anybody I am his daughter. Just friend, I say. Old friend." It looked like her eyes were glazing over, and Kali reached out and touched Anna's hand.

"It's okay to feel bad," she said. "It can be hard sometimes."

Anna flashed a tight-lipped smile. "Thank you."

I pressed onward. "Anna, when you were talking with people, did you hear anything about any connections between Rudy and the four dead men?" I rattled off their names with rote precision. "Did you hear anyone saying names like that?"

She shook her head sadly. "Do you think this has something to do with my father being missing?"

I considered my answer carefully. The last thing I wanted to do was give her false hope, but there were too many coincidences for things not to be connected somehow. I just had to figure out the configuration. "I believe so," I said finally.

"But how? How does it all fit together?"

"That's the sixty-four-thousand-dollar question," I said.

Anna looked puzzled. "Sixty-four thousand dollars?"

"He's making an allusion to an old TV show," Kali said. "A very old show. My grandparents used to tell me about watching it back in the golden days of television."

"Yeah, when TV shows were TV shows," I said, frowning. "Before people knew they were going to be classics."

Our food came and we dug in. Kali had the snapper and Anna seemed to be enjoying the slices of pork in the *pâté de campagne*. We finished things off with small glasses of wine for the ladies and coffee for me. I still had a night's worth of shooting ahead of me, although I felt like I'd already run half of the New York Marathon. When we walked out, I started looking for the limo. "I'll have my car drop me by the shoot, then take each of you to your respective abodes."

"Oh, no, Richard," Anna said. "I have metro pass. I take subway back to Brooklyn."

"And I'm going back to the shoot with you," Kali said. "Aren't you forgetting my daily report?"

"I was trying pretty hard," I said. That's when I heard somebody behind me call out, "Hey, Belzer," in a way that made me feel like a pigeon had just crapped on my neck.

The voice had come from a nearby gangway. I recognized it even before I smelled the BO. Gustafson stepped out and gave us a leering grin. He was wearing the same black plaid sport jacket as yesterday. How I'd missed seeing or hearing him, I couldn't imagine. His irritating little strut set my teeth on edge.

"I thought we made it clear we didn't want to talk to you," I said.

"Yeah?" His upper lip curled into a sneer. "Ain't that a fucking shame?"

"Watch your language," I said. "There are ladies present."

"Ladies." He cocked his head in a smirk. "People probably think you're double-teaming a pair of hookers or something."

"That's it, pal," I said. "Either you turn your sorry ass around right now, or I'll finish what I started yesterday and this time you'll wake up in Bethesda. The hospital upstate, not the fountain."

He took a step back but the sneer didn't disappear. "Hey, just be glad I'm willing to overlook you assaulting me yesterday, pal."

"Actually I was effecting a citizen's arrest," I said. "What you were doing was assaulting a young lady at the time."

"Richard, who is this man?" Anna asked.

"He's nobody," I said. "An irritating gadfly who keeps buzzing around. But he's seasonal. And swatable too." I stepped in his direction, precipitating another backward step by him. He bumped into one of the street vendors selling miniature oil paintings.

"Hey, man, watch it," the vendor said.

Gustafson's head swiveled, and after assessing the guy as a minimal threat, he told the guy, "Blow it out your ass."

"So that's how you got here so fast," I said to Gustafson. I placed a hand on each of the women's elbows and started ushering them down the block. "I'm sure you can see why I suggested that taxi."

"Who is he?" Anna asked again.

Gustafson was running to catch up now, bumping into people and sending at least one person careening into a building.

I stopped. The idiot was a menace. Better to deal with him expediently and send him on his merry way. "You're about as pesky as an infected hemorrhoid, you know that?"

Gustafson must have taken it as a compliment. He stopped just beyond easy grabbing distance and flashed a phony smile. "So how's about we share what we found out about your missing buddy, Markovich?"

Anna perked up. "This man has information about my father?"

Then it was Gustafson's turn. His eyebrows arched upward. "Did you say 'father'?"

"Yes," Anna said. "Richard has been helping me find him."

Oh, shit, I thought, as I stepped between them.

"Belz," he said, drawing out my name like we were old drinking buddies, "you been holding out on me, haven't ya? This story gets more interesting by the minute." He leaned to his right and asked Anna what her name was.

"Don't answer that," I said to her. Then turning back to him, "I'm going to tell you one more time to get your greasy little ass out of here."

"Or what?" His sneer was back and as he looked up at me I could smell the foul odor of his breath. "You gonna beat me up again?"

I waited to give myself a few seconds for effect, then smiled with as much malevolence as I could muster. Looking down at Gustafson, it was easy. "I'm seriously considering it. Now beat it, *pal*. Before I ease up on my self-control."

It must have been the smile. Gustafson retreated a few steps. "Hey, I know you're working some angle on your friend Markovich's disappearance. And I know the cops ain't telling you shit. But like I said, I can help you. I been working this story too."

"Your kind of help I don't need, Gustafson." I turned and started to usher Anna and Kali away again. As luck would have it, I saw Mickey edging through traffic about ten feet behind us.

"Good timing," I said, as I grabbed the rear door and motioned for Anna and Kali to get inside. I turned back and waved. "Bye-bye, Cyrus. Don't call us, and we won't call you."

"Oh, yeah?" Gustafson took a step toward me. "Well, listen, Belzer. Someday soon you'll be begging me for help. I got information, pal. Hot stuff. More than you'll ever know. This is a big story, and I got the goods on it."

"Damn. Too bad nobody with any brains reads the *New York Inquirer*." I started to get in the limo.

"You want to know how I found you, Belzer?" he yelled.

The last thing I wanted at this point was him shouting my name all over SoHo. We were attracting enough stares from onlookers as it was. Plus, there was no way I could stop him from hailing a taxi and continuing to follow us. Vern Franker would absolutely love to see that. The thought that he'd apparently done so, despite my efforts to shake him, bothered me. But I wasn't about to let him know that. "All right, I'm listening."

He must have thought he'd gained the upper hand because his head lolled back and a cocky grin spread across his porcine face. "Sure, you shook me this morning, all right, for a while, but . . . I'm good."

Anna leaned over and stuck her head next to the doorpost. "Richard, I think this man followed me here. I remember now, I see him outside where I work."

Mystery solved. Gustafson hadn't tagged me, he'd just followed Anna. That bothered me even more.

"What breaking info have you got for me, Cyrus?" I asked.

Gustafson shook his head. "You want what I got? Uh-uh, you open up to me first or no deal."

"Yeah, right," I said. "That game is as old as the food stuck between your teeth. Get lost." I slid into the limo and shut the door.

Gustafson stepped in so close I thought he was going to press his face against the glass. He didn't, but he did let loose with a litany of swear words. He also tripped over something, probably his own feet, and fell into the door, accidentally clipping his nose. Gustafson reeled back, grabbing his bleeding proboscis. "You prick. You broke my fucking nose."

"Time wounds all heels," I said.

"Oh, yeah? You ain't heard the last from me, Belzer. I'll sue your fucking ass for this."

"Take a number." I tapped the screen and told Mickey to take off. I glanced back at Gustafson, still holding his face with one hand and giving me the finger with the other, and said to Anna and Kali, "Besides, it's probably going to be an improvement."

# CHAPTER 13

Much to my chagrin, Anna insisted that we drop her off after only half a block so she could take the subway to Brooklyn. "This car will be too slow." She looked back down the street. "And I must get to the restaurant."

"I thought you said you were off tonight," I said.

She shook her head. "No, phone call earlier. My boss. One girl call off sick. I must work now."

I craned my neck to look through the back window for any signs of the black plaid garbage container. When the coast looked clear, I told Mickey to pull over. I opened the door and got out, scanning the block again. Anna got out and stood next to me.

"Richard, I have one question of you."

"What is it?"

"That man back there. Why we didn't find out what information he had about my father?"

I blew out a slow breath. "I've dealt with him before, and I don't think he's credible." She looked a bit confused and I remembered she wasn't a native speaker. "I'm not sure we can believe what he tells us."

She nodded, but I saw a flash of doubt in her green eyes. "But should we not check more?"

"I'm sure he'll be back," I said. "Getting rid of him is harder than getting rid of gum on your shoe."

She nodded.

"Look," I said, "are you sure you won't ride with us?"

She shook her head. "Subway is faster. I know the trains."

It wasn't like I could keep her on a leash. She was a grown woman. "Okay, but if that guy Gustafson tries to contact you—"

"I will tell him nothing," she said, showing me her dazzling smile. "I am used to dealing with stupid, ignorant men. I grew up in Moscow, did I not?"

She had a point. With her looks, she was probably used to winding men around her little finger. Especially a schmuck like Gustafson.

Anna leaned in and gave me a quick hug before walking away, brushing her hair back as she took her cell phone out of her purse. No doubt to tell her inconsiderate boss that she was on the way back.

I gave Mickey the address of the set and turned to Kali. "I'm going to work and you're going home."

"What? I told you, I still have to report to Mr. Franker."

"You've already put in a full day," I said. "You can call in your report. Just tell him you spent the day keeping me out of trouble. More or less."

"Should I tell him about you beating up those two thugs? And what about Gustafson?"

I considered this. Most likely, the street encounter with Scarface and Rhino would go pretty much unnoticed. Gustafson had been following Anna instead of Kali and me, so chances were he wouldn't know about this confrontation. So unless a passing pedestrian had snapped a few pics with a cell phone, and I didn't recall anybody pointing any at me, there wasn't any documentation that it was me behind those photochromic Foster Grants. Besides, nobody seemed to be recognizing me lately anyway. They'd probably think George Clooney was having a bad day out on a bender.

"I don't think Gustabutt will be pitching any bitches to anybody, and the other one was over so quickly, with such little fanfare, I think it would be safe for you not to mention it."

"But what if Mr. Franker hears about it later?"

I scrunched up my face. "I don't like that 'Mr. Franker' thing. Sounds too respectful. Let's start referring to him as *el generalissimo*. Or just plain old Franco."

"General what?"

"*Generalissimo* Francisco Franco. He took over in Spain after the Spanish Civil War in the nineteen thirties. One of the most well-known dictators of the twentieth century. Vern would've loved the guy. Probably keeps Franco's picture by his bedside."

She smiled. "What is it about you and authority figures?"

"Let's just say I have an innate mistrust of all authority figures and anyone with the last name of Bush." I grinned. "Go ahead, call Franco."

As the tedium of waiting to be summoned for my scenes wore on into the night, I kept occupied by reviewing the day's activities and was amused by the memory of listening to Kali's report to Big Brother Franco via phone. She'd gone through a detailed but mostly fictitious recreation of our day for him. He seemed to have bought into it, because I hadn't seen him lurking around the edges of the set all night. Of course, I made sure I stayed on the right side of the red light door. I was beginning to like the sound of his new nickname too, and began to imagine his reaction when I addressed him by it.

But mostly I doodled on a piece of notebook paper. Circles on a flow chart. One containing Rudy, one containing me. Another with Anna, and four containing the names from the letter. I drew a couple of new ones for Rhino and Scarface, then two more for the thugs who'd tried to accost Rudy the last night I saw him. Something Russian was the common theme touching just about every one of them. Rudy and Anna were obviously Russian, and so were Buteyko and Odessa Imports. Sprinkle in some street punks for seasoning, and it was like a stuffed cabbage. But only one of the dead men, Ivan Peters, had a known Russian connection. The other two, Perry and Spaulding, didn't appear to have any.

One of the gaffers knocked on my dressing room door and said everybody was taking a break in the food tent—a cue that I'd be stepping up to the plate shortly. I folded the diagram and stuck it in my pants pocket as I walked to the tent.

"Hey, Belz," a voice behind me said. It was Jack Wilson, one of the cops attached to the Media and Public Relations Bureau, who served as technical adviser to the show. He also moonlighted as a security guard on the set, which was his capacity tonight.

"Jack, how you doing?"

"I'll be doing better once I see what they got for late supper." He had the physique of a man who appreciated a good meal. Lots of good meals.

"Richard," another voice called out, this time from off to my right. Friendly-sounding, but with an underlying smugness.

"Franco," I said, feigning as much cordiality as I could muster.

"It's Franker," he said.

"I was using the Spanish pronunciation," I answered back. "How goes the listening campaign? Kalisha give you the daily report on my activities yet?"

He tried to smile but looked prissy. Like he'd scored a goal, then realized it was for the other team.

"As a matter of fact, she did," he said. "And I was coming over to tell you that from all indications, you've been straightening your act up and have been a good trooper." The lips-only smile that punctuated his sentence had to rank up there among the most disingenuous I'd ever seen. "For one day."

He turned on the balls of his feet, like he was pivoting in a marching exercise, and walked away.

"Who's that asshole again?" Jack asked me after Franco had departed.

"Just some guy who thinks he's a general."

"He sounds like he's really full of shit."

"Believe me," I said as we walked, "if someone slipped a laxative in his drink, there'd be nothing left of him by morning."

After getting a full plate each, we sat at a table and began eating. Jack can eat faster than any man I've ever seen. He polished his off, looked longingly at mine, then, at my urging, went back for seconds.

"You don't think they'll mind, do you?" he asked. "I'm pulling some extra hours working the night shift here."

"Nah, they could feed a homeless shelter with what they toss every night," I said.

He grinned and went back to the buffet line. Of course, I failed to mention that they could also probably feed a homeless shelter with the amount he ate at any given sitting. The grin was still spread over his face as he plopped down across from me once again.

"So how you been, Belz?" He slipped off his jacket and draped it over the back of his chair. His snub-nosed thirty-eight rode along his belt in a pancake holster.

"Just ducky." I noticed the faded ink of his Marine Corps tattoo, visible just below his short sleeve, and it reminded me of Rhino's tattoo work.

"Does blue ink still mean jailhouse artwork?" I asked.

His mouth full of potato salad, he nodded between copious chews. "Yeah, usually. What kind you interested in? Gangs?"

"This guy I saw had some kind of spiderweb design here." I traced my finger around my Adam's apple. "I think he was a Russian."

"A Russkie? You sure?"

"Pretty sure."

"Where'd you see this guy at?"

"Over on Broadway."

"Oh, yeah? What was he doing?"

"Running away, actually," I said. "He and his partner tried to mug me."

"No shit? You okay?"

I nodded and sipped some now tepid coffee. "They got the worst of it."

He grunted an apparent approval and shifted some food to his cheek. "Probably a couple of Russian jailbirds from the mother country," he said. "Cheap muscle for some crime boss to import."

"We're allowing known criminals to immigrate nowadays? I thought we were only doing that with potential terrorists. I'm going to have to write my congressman and tell him to keep up the good work with those immigration bills."

He laughed. "Probably got their criminal histories erased before they left Russian soil, although it most likely cost them an arm and a leg over there to get new IDs."

"If they went to all that trouble, then why not get the tattoos lasered off too? Won't they make them more identifiable?"

"Oh, hell, those Russkies get tattooed all over their bodies when they're in the joint," Jack said, popping open a new bag of potato chips. "Gives a history of which prisons they've been in. Sort of like a road map. Probably worth more by way of job references to their prospective employer over here. They don't bring them punks over to sell Bibles and play canasta."

"Any idea about what prison the webbing might mean?" I asked. It might be an angle Max could pursue, if I got all the information and managed to light a fire under his ass.

Jack ran his tongue over his front teeth, sucking away the residuals. "You're kind of interested in this, aren't ya?"

"Let's just say my curiosity has been piqued."

He nodded and tossed in a few more chips. "Yeah, well, it's interesting, all right, but I just got kind of a general knowledge of that stuff. Been to a couple of training seminars to keep up on it." Shrugging, he added, "You know, you should talk to someone in the OCCB. They could give you a lot more info."

"The OCCB?"

"Organized Crime Control Bureau," he said. "You know how us law enforcement types love acronyms."

"Who should I talk to?"

Jack's eyes rolled to the right as he contemplated. "I'd say Howard Larkins. He's the guy who teaches all the classes on the Russkies. I think I got his number someplace." He leaned his head back and held the open bag over his gaping mouth, polishing off the remaining potato chip crumbs. After he finished, he crumpled the bag, took a drink of soda, and brushed his hands together vigorously. "Salt and grease. The staple of every healthy diet. Hand me one of them napkins, would ya?"

I gave him three of them, and he used them all in the process of removing the shininess from his fingertips.

"You mentioned you had Howard Larkins's number?" I said by way of a gentle reminder, before the residual grease could begin clogging the flow of blood to his brain.

"Yeah." He reached into his jacket pocket and took out his cell phone. "I think I got Howie's number in here somewhere," he said. "And don't call him that. He likes to be called Skip."

"I can't blame him with a name like that. Who would want to be known as Howie?"

"He likes doughnuts too." Jack smirked as he kept checking his cell phone number log. "And one other thing. Be careful what you ask for. Those Russkies are some dangerous dudes."

The next morning, after picking up two coffees, one generously spiked with extra espresso, and one box of assorted doughnuts, I sat on the side of Detective First Grade Howard "Skip" Larkins's incredibly cluttered desk, in an office at One Police Plaza. Larkins was a small guy with salt-and-pepper hair who was deceptively slim for someone with such a passion for strawberry-frosted and Bavarian doughnuts. He took a bite out of one of each and washed it down with a liberal dose of the coffee. I'd had them leave the espresso out of his. No sense both of us being wired, and besides, I'd only purchased one box of pastries.

What was it with cops and food? I wondered.

"You're that guy on TV, right?" he asked.

"I am." I didn't want to ask which guy he thought I was. The way my luck had been running, he might have mistaken me for the guy who used to host *The Mickey Mouse Club*. Or maybe Buffalo Bob.

Obviously pleased that he'd made a successful deduction this early in the morning, he took a bite from a new doughnut and asked, "So what brings you down here to the OCCB?"

We were getting into uncertain territory here. If I told him I was checking into a missing-person case and I'd been accosted by two fugitives from a Siberian gulag, he would very possibly clam up and not tell me squat. Or even worse, make a call to Max. So I decided to use the old tried-and-true MSU technique.

"I'm working on a script," I said. "About a tough New York cop who battles for truth, justice, and the American way." I held up my hands, as if framing his face in an imaginary camera lens. "There might be a part in it for his partner too. Ever done any acting?"

He smirked and grabbed a new doughnut from the box. Perhaps he was searching for that perfect-tasting one. "Who do I look like, old Eddie Egan?"

"That's a blast from the past," I said. Egan was the New York cop who'd jumped to the movies after making one of the biggest narcotics busts in NYPD history, earning him the nickname Popeye. Gene Hackman's Popeye Doyle character in *The French Connection* was based on Egan, and Eddie even had a small part in the film playing the division boss. Although he got eclipsed in both the film and real life by Hackman's masterful portrayal, Egan went on to have a fairly good career as an actor. But that's all ancient history. "I was thinking more like Dennis Farina. He made the transition from cop to actor too. He was a Chicago cop, you know."

"Oh, yeah? I thought he had the right moves when he was on that show—what's it called?" His attention was diverted as another dick walked by and reached inside the doughnut box to withdraw one with chocolate and sprinkles. "Hey, watch that. Those are spoken for."

"Share and share alike," the other detective said as he walked away with his prize.

I cleared my throat. "I'm in the process of writing it now, and I'd like to have him and his partner go up against the Russian mafia. Those guys have a lot of tattoos, don't they?"

"It's like a list of how many times they've been incarcerated."

"Like webbing on their neck and hands?"

Larkins gave the box a sideways glance, then turned back to me and nodded. "Yeah. They usually start out with a flowery design on their chests and branch out from there." He spread his hand out on his chest, then brought it slowly downward as if demonstrating a tapestry of illustrations on his stomach and legs. "Gives a clear indication of where they came from and what they did."

"Sort of like an employment history for when they get out and go looking for the new mafia kingpin, eh?"

"Right," he said. "But first of all, it's called the *mafiya*." He spelled it for me. Temptation got the better of him and he raised the cardboard lid, scrutinized the remaining contents, and decided on a French cruller. "You know anything about them?"

I shook my head. "My buddy Jack Wilson told me you were *the* man to see about stuff like that."

He nodded as he bit off half the cruller in one bite and set the rest back in the box. "Yeah, Wilson's been in a couple of the classes I taught on the subject. Good guy."

"Great guy."

He smiled as he chewed. "Well, I wouldn't go that far."

I was beginning to wonder if there were any whole doughnuts left in the box. "The *mafiya*, huh?"

"Their motto is *Vorovskoi mir*," he said. "Roughly translated, it means, 'It's a thieves' world.'"

"Impressive. There might be a gig for a technical adviser for this project too."

"Yeah?" His interest was definitely piqued. Either that or he was thinking about a steady supply of doughnuts. He felt around in the box until his hand emerged with an untouched chocolate. "You know," he told me, as he took his customary one bite and replaced it, "I watch your show all the time. It's pretty good. You guys go a long way toward getting it right."

After Larkins had wiped his fingers on a paper napkin, he leaned forward. I figured we were about ready to get down to brass tacks. But I was wrong. He still had one more matter to address. "If this thing comes through, you think you can introduce me to that one chick? What the hell's her name?" He held his cupped hands in front of his chest as he tried to recall. "The one with the big jugs? She's a real babe."

I told him who I thought he possibly meant.

"That's her." His grin was wide. "Is she married?"

"She is," I said, intentionally blowing his fantasy experience. His face fell a little as he went back to perusing the rest of the doughnuts.

"Does she . . . mess around?" He asked it in a half-assed joking manner.

"If she does, I pity the poor guy. Her husband's built like pro football lineman. Does that Ultimate Fighting stuff. Breaks arms like they were wishbones." That seemed to slap his libido back into place. I needed information, and for that he had to think with his big head, not his little one. Besides, there couldn't be more than four or five whole doughnuts left. To let him down easy, I promised to get him an autographed picture. Of her face, not her jugs. He selected a glazed honey-dip, took a bite, and, of course, set it back inside the box. I wondered if he was ever going to find one he wanted to completely devour.

"Well, regarding the Russians," he said, "they're here, they're smart, and they're totally ruthless. Wherever there's money to be made, they'll try to muscle in and get their cut. Their primary stomping ground's Brighton Beach. Little Odessa, they call it. That's named after the city of the same name in the mother country. But they're always looking to expand into new horizons. Believe me, nothing's off-limits to those guys."

"I've heard about Brighton Beach being referred to as Little Odessa," I said. It had been so named by the flood of immigrants in the last century who settled there and saw so many similarities between the area beyond the boardwalk and their hometown back in Russia. Yeah, only in Amerika: good old Brighton Beach now had more storefront signs spelled with the Cyrillic alphabet than with English. *No habla ingles* here, no problemo. Just know how to say *spasibo* and *nyet*.

"You know how organized crime works?" He reached around, slipped his hand under the flap, and withdrew another pristine doughnut. A blueberry one. He did the same single-bite thing and replaced it in the box.

I smiled and nodded, showing I was with him, glad that I hadn't brought another box. That would have made his lecture twice as long.

After licking his lips, then his fingers, he said, "Organized crime makes a hefty profit. What can you do with all that money?"

"Stuff it in your mattress?"

He laughed. "Sure, but there's two problems with that. One, you can only stuff so much inside before it starts to get lumpy. And two, mattresses don't give interest."

"But banks have a record of your deposits and tend to do things like notify the IRS, right?"

"Exactamundo. You have to have it washed clean, or laundered. And the only way to do that is to make it look like it came through a legitimate enterprise."

Another one of the detectives, a guy who looked wider than a city dump truck, sauntered over to Larkins's desk and said, "Hey, I heard you got doughnuts. Any chocolates left?" He raised the lid, then recoiled in disgust. "Jesus, man, these fuckers all have bites out of them."

Larkins grinned knowingly at me. "It's called marking your territory," he said to his colleague. "The man brought *me* the doughnuts, so why should I share? I could count on one hand the times you assholes brought me a fresh fucking coffee from the meat wagon."

The heavyset detective grabbed his crotch as he left. "Here's your meat wagon, Larkins."

Larkins maintained his self-satisfied look until the man had fully departed, then continued the lecture. "So certain subterfuges are developed to make it appear as though the money was legitimately earned. A phony business, or something similar that turns out to be a mailbox address. But on paper it looks as though it's raking in the bucks. Toss in a host of other scamaramas like identity theft, Medicaid rip-offs, bust-out businesses, and of course, the customary fifteen percent street tax they charge all the legit businesses for the privilege of unbroken limbs, intact windows, and fire-free storefronts."

"Intimidation and extortion, huh?"

He nodded. "Plus kidnapping and threats to your family. The *mafiya* operates by its own code of dishonor. Ain't nothing the least bit romantic about it. At least the old dago mobsters would keep their hands off the women and the kids, until they came of age."

I could almost hear a sped-up version of the *Godfather* theme being played to the tempo of a Rachmaninoff concerto.

Another detective walking by stopped when he saw the box and pointed. "Doughnuts?"

"Yeah, help yourself," Larkins said. "But they're just about all half-eaten already."

The other dick raised the lid, frowned, and let the cardboard flap fall back into place before walking away.

"But the cardinal rule," Larkins continued, "is you always protect the head man. The dirty money can never get traced back to its source."

"Or?" I asked.

"Or somebody's gonna die. And not from natural causes." He drew his index finger underneath his chin and made a slicing sound. "It's all about absolute loyalty, otherwise they'll kill you."

"Ruthless."

He nodded. "Totally. And not just you. They'll kill your mother back in Saint Petersburg, your uncle in Moscow, your ten-year-old daughter in Kiev . . ." He looked at me, then to the doughnut box, then back to me. I hoped he didn't think I was considering a run on it. "You know what the feds say?"

I shook my head.

"That when the Iron Curtain fell, it was the best thing that ever happened to Russian organized crime. They had this great spy network set up all over the place, and all of a sudden, there was this big vacuum. And a lot of these KGB and military guys realized they could make a hell of a lot more rubles acting as free agents. There ain't a heck of a lot left in Russia, or the former satellite countries that made up the Soviet Union, that hasn't grown legs and walked. And they had a lot of shit to sell."

"Isn't the Russian government controlling that?"

Larkins smirked. "In Russia today, it's all about making money, and I ain't talking rubles. Dollars. American."

"So you're saying the Russian government is turning a blind eye to its own country's organized crime?"

"You got that right." He raised the lid of the doughnut box, smiled, and let it fall, then reached for his coffee cup, shook it, and frowned. "Guess I got to go hit the reserves," he said, getting to his feet. I got up too, sensing that it was about that time. Larkins paused and looked at me. "Don't forget that autographed picture now."

"I won't. You can count on it." I thanked him and we shook hands.

"Listen," he said, "like I told you, the Russians are all about tightening up loose ends the expedient way."

"I'm sure our government's in dialogue with theirs to curb this lawless trend," I said. Larkins grinned, obviously catching my satirical lilt.

"Didn't George invite Vladimir over for beans and cabbage last year after that missile flap about Poland?" I added.

"That guy Putin," he snorted. "Just imagine what it would've been like if instead of getting shipped off to Alcatraz, Al Capone had been elected president."

"Well, I'm sure him and Dick Cheney got along great," I said.

# CHAPTER 14

I stood on the steps of One Police Plaza and called Kali. The sun was beating down and the fatigue that had started to seep over me as I'd watched Larkins's one-bite marathon began to evaporate. Still, I felt like I'd gained five pounds during the meeting. Kali answered on the third ring.

"Where you at?" she asked.

"Is that how you usually answer the phone? Or did you think it was Generalissimo Franco calling to check on me?"

"Get real. I knew it was you from the caller ID screen."

"You mean I'm in your Fave Five?"

"Will you stop?" she said. "I've been working hard this morning."

"Me too," I said. "What've you got?"

"A line on the place Joshua Spaulding used to work at." She ended with a triumphant up note. "It's over on Forty-second Street, and it's still in business."

When I got there, she was standing on Forty-second Street with two paper cups of coffee.

"Figured you could use the lift," she said.

"Thanks, as long as you didn't bring me a doughnut." I took a sip and found that it was actually almost warm. "Where are we bound for?"

She pointed across the street. The shop was sandwiched between two others, with *Splendid Things* above the door. In the window a smaller neon sign blinked, *We Buy and Sell*. Odessa Imports was two doors down and across the street.

"Look familiar?" Kali said, seeing where I was looking.

"Like déjà vu all over again," I said, sipping the coffee. "You find anything about our fourth victim?"

"Yeah." She drank from her cup. "I used a connection through one of my old professors at college. Gave me the number of Arnold Wassler's old editor at the newspaper. I talked to him this morning and he set up a meet with another reporter who was pretty close to Wassler. Name's Duncan Dropney. We got a meet set up for eleven at Marseille. You're buying him lunch."

"I am?"

"You wanted the meet, right?"

"I did, but that was before I found out his name was Duncan Dropney. What kind of a guy would have a name like that and keep it?"

"Your call, but it's probably as close to finding out about Wassler as we're gonna get."

"We'll always have Paris, I guess." I took one more swallow of the tepid java and tossed the cup into a trash can. "Whenever you're ready."

She drank some more and held up her hand. "Could we *please* go over our plan before we go in there? And don't say, 'Follow my lead,' okay?"

I compressed my lips and thought about it. What did we know about poor old Josh, and what could we learn from his old boss? And, more importantly, why would he tell us anything? Considering the warm reception I'd gotten from the Widow Spaulding, he probably wouldn't. It was one of those clear-cut situations.

"The situation is such that I think we should use the MSU approach," I said.

She looked askance. "MSU?"

"Just follow my lead," I said.

As we walked across the street, I explained that we were a couple who had a very large and recently acquired diamond that we wanted to have reset.

"A couple?" she said. "Like you're my sugar daddy?"

I did my Bogey imitation again as I said, "Here's looking at *you*, kid."

A real looker, clad in an elegant black dress, greeted us as we came in and asked if she could help us. The hint of a venal gleam in her eye as she assessed us told me that to her, the sugar daddy routine meant money. However, the gleam faded a bit as I gave her a thumbnail description of the very large diamond brooch that my dear, sainted aunt had bequeathed me and how I wanted the stone cut and reset into a ring for my fiancée. No new sales obviously meant less commission. The woman lifted an eyebrow ever so slightly as she shot a fractional glance in Kali's direction. She stood there beaming as she looked up at me.

"Very well, sir," the woman said. "Do you have the stone with you?"

I smiled, using my most patronizing look. "My dear young lady, you don't really think I'd be reckless enough to walk the streets of New York with a huge diamond in my pocket, do you?"

"Of course, sir," she said. "Perhaps you have a photo, then?"

I shook my head again, amping up the petulance in the smile. "No, no, no. You misunderstand me. I was referred here by one of your clientele. A Mr. Bloomberg. I'm sure you know who he is."

I was hoping she wouldn't ask if I was referring to the mayor. If she did, I was fully prepared to say I was. After all, I'd bumped into him a few times. But she didn't. The door behind us buzzed and we all glanced back. Another couple had come in, looking young, urban, professional, and rich.

"I'll be with you in a moment," the looker said to them. She turned back to me.

"As I was saying," I continued, "he had some work done here a few years ago and just raved about one of your jewelers. Spaulding, Joshua Spaulding."

The looker licked her lips. "Mr. Spaulding?"

"Yes, he wrote down the name. Said not to settle for anyone else."

"I'm afraid—"

"Aw, please don't tell me he no longer works here." I tried to tiptoe that fine line between shock and disappointment. "He was such a renowned craftsman." As if on cue, Kali turned her face toward me at the same moment I turned mine toward her. Peripherally, I saw the yuppies staring at us too. Synchronicity at its best. I love it when a plan comes together.

The looker's mouth was gaping slightly now. For whatever reason, our tag team had her rattled, just like a fighter who gets clocked with a straight right and ends up on Queer Street trying to survive the round. But before she could say another word, a door off to the side opened and an unctuous guy in a dark blue suit stepped into the room. I placed him in his early forties with broad shoulders and a swarthy look. His dark eyebrows went straight across his forehead like a strip of mowed grass.

"Vanessa, why don't you take care of those other guests?" He sounded like he was doing the Transylvania twist. Bela Lugosi from Leningrad? He directed his gaze to us. Suddenly I felt a chill, like Dracula's uncle had dropped in for a conversation. "May I be of service to you?"

I went through my spiel with practiced ease. No second takes for this one. When I was finished, he said, "We have several jewelers here who do excellent work. You're free to peruse our samples in the cases."

"But the diamond I have is"—I paused for effect—"very large, and will have to be reset."

He nodded. "As I told you, we have only the best here."

"I was told to ask for Joshua Spaulding," I said, raising my voice just a tiny bit over conversational tone. "Am I to understand that he's no longer with you?"

Bela nodded, then his face grew solemn. "He's no longer with any of us. He died."

"Died?" I affected an expression of total shock. "Why, when did this happen?"

He raised his shoulders in what passed for a shrug. "A little over a year ago."

"I'm sorry to hear that," I said. "Had he been sick long?"

Bela shook his head. "It was very unexpected, and very unfortunate."

"An accident?" I asked. "I'll bet it was one of these crazy New York drivers, right?" I turned my head toward the looker, who was now showing some very expensive-looking baubles to the other couple. "Now do you see why I never bring valuables into the city? You get run over and they rob you blind when they're taking you to the hospital."

Bela laid a commiserating hand on my forearm. "Sir, I assure you that if you return, your diamond will be in very good hands here."

"But he came highly recommended," I said.

"No one resets a gem with the care that we do," Bela said.

"Joshua Spaulding," I said, shaking my head. "Dead. It's hard to believe."

He nodded, his hand still on my arm, his body beginning to edge us toward the door. No hard sell here. Business must have been good. Or maybe they didn't need to worry that much about legitimate business.

"Say, you ever deal with a Russian guy named Nikolai Buteyko?" I asked.

The question clipped him like a left hook to the liver: no immediate effect, then a slowing of the legs. "Odessa Imports. Of course. He is one of our competitors, but a nice gentleman. Perhaps you should compare his services to ours for your own . . . edification?"

It wasn't a question so much as a dismissal.

"How about Ivan Peters?" I asked.

His face showed about as much reaction as a boiled clam.

"Of course," I said, "you might have known him as Ivan Petrovich. He changed it to Peters."

Bela just stared at me. Finally, he said, "Why are you asking me all these questions? I'm beginning to think you are really not so interested in diamonds."

It was crunch time, and I couldn't think of anything to ask except, "Hey, I'll bet you're from Transylvania, aren't you? I recognize your accent."

He shook his head and kept us moving toward the door. "Budapest."

"You're Hungarian? I thought you guys and the Russians didn't like each other much. Didn't you have a revolution there back in fifty-six?"

"More than one," he said. "But this is two thousand eight in America. And the Russians are our friends now. And also very much involved in the diamond market."

"Did Spaulding ever do any work for them?"

Bela shrugged as he lifted his hand from my arm and used it to open the door. "I'm sure it's possible that he did. But, as I said, we have the best jewelers here. Good day." He was pulling a cell phone out of his pocket.

I assured him we'd be back as the door closed behind us.

"Was it just me," Kali asked, "or did you feel like shoving the sign of the cross in that dude's face when he came in?"

"Sign of the cross?" I clucked as I looked at her. "I'd rather go with the Star of David. You know Elvis wore one of those."

My cell phone rang and I chuckled at the thought of Bela somehow calling me. But as I fished my phone out of my pocket, I saw a huge shape talking on his as he stood behind the full glass door of Odessa Imports across the street. Big old scary Wladimir. He was watching us. I leaned close to Kali and pointed at him. "We've seen Dracula and Frankenstein so far this trip. We'd better get out of here before the Wolfman shows up."

It had been Anna on the phone, inquiring about my progress that morning. I called her back as soon as we were safely ensconced in a taxi, gave her a brief summary of things we were checking out, and told her we were on the way to talk with a colleague of the dead reporter.

"Where are you meeting him?" she asked. "I would like very much to be there."

I put my hand over the phone and whispered, "She wants to tag along. Any objections?"

Kali pursed her lips momentarily, then shook her head. "It's her father we're looking for, right?"

"We'll meet you there," I said into the phone. "Do you know where the Marseille is on Ninth and Forty-fourth?"

"I will be on my way," she said and hung up.

"She's meeting us there," I said. "I hope this guy can give us some useful information. It's like we keep picking up bits and pieces of a jigsaw puzzle but can't figure how they all fit together."

"Yeah, it's not like a lot's adding up so far, but this reporter guy says he might be interested if there's a story in it for him."

"There's a story in it, all right," I said. "Finding it is another matter. All I know is we keep tripping over eastern Euros now making their fortunes in the good old U S of A, and four dead bodies."

"Don't forget the diamond angle," Kali said. "Two of them had that connection so far."

"But what about the other two?" I thought about the names as we drove north. In the old days this area had been called Hell's Kitchen, notorious as the neighborhood you didn't want to be in, even if you were a cop. In those days, the neighborhood was ruled by gangsters and immortalized by Damon Runyon. In recent decades, however, it had been undergoing a gentrification that made some residents long for the bygone days of the Jets and the Sharks dancing around snapping their fingers. It's also actor heaven, because it's right around the corner from Broadway and the Actors Studio. And my apartment, the address of which shall remain unspoken.

I always enjoy eating at the Marseille because it reminds me of my home in France. With the high ceilings and tiled floors sporting exotic designs, it lends itself to sort of a *Casablanca* motif. I can almost imagine I'm at Rick's Place and Dooley Wilson, aka Sam, will be accompanying himself on the piano singing "As Time Goes By" somewhere off in a corner. I resisted the temptation to say, "Play it again, Sam," as we walked up to the front doors, but then again, Bogey never really uttered those exact words in the movie.

"What's this reporter guy's name again?" I asked Kali.

"Duncan Dropney. Said he'll be here waiting. Supposed to be wearing a gray polo shirt and tan Dockers."

"Bingo." I pointed to a doughy-looking guy standing by the main door of the restaurant. He must have seen us at about the same time because he smiled and came walking over. Well, actually it was more of a waddle.

When he got closer, I saw he had a very unhealthy pallor. His head was shaved and his body looked bloated.

"Richard Belzer," he said. "This is a real pleasure. I watch your show all the time." We shook, and he said, "And you must be Kalisha." He shook hands with her too. I glanced around. No sign of Anna.

"I'm expecting another person," I said to the maitre d'. "A young lady with red hair. When she arrives, please show her to our table."

"Of course, sir," he said.

After we were seated at a table, we ordered, and I steered the conversation toward his relationship with the late Arnold Wassler.

"What kind of a guy was Arnold?" I asked.

Dropney leaned forward and took a sip of his coffee and gave his head an admiring little shake. The reflection of the overhead lights nearly blinded me. Leave it to Bruce Willis to start a fashion trend that's ultimately going to increase global warming.

"He was tops," Dropney said. "The best reporter I knew."

"You guys worked together a lot?"

"We did. But make no mistake about it, he was in a class of his own."

"You know, I used to be a reporter," I said. "Never for the *New York Times*, but I still have some of the old ink left under my fingernails."

Kali shot me the evil eye.

"And Kalisha here," I said, "studied journalism before she came to work for the show."

Dropney smiled. "No other job like it."

I leaned forward, figuring I'd set the stage and laid the right groundwork. "So I heard his death was kind of sudden."

"You got that right." Dropney picked up a croissant but fingered it instead of eating it, probably thinking about how badly it would clog his arteries. "Heart attack. Stressful work being a reporter, you know."

He *tsk*ed and shook his head. I did the same.

"Very unexpected, huh?" I asked.

He nodded and put the pastry down. "He always looked healthy as a horse. But I guess you never know what's going on inside."

"You guys ever share stories?" Kali asked. "Or work on them together?"

He shrugged. "Sometimes we would, but not usually." Dropney relented, picked up the croissant, and took a bite. "Mostly we had our own stories and our respective deadlines." I hate people who talk and chew at the same time.

"Do you know what he was working on when he died?" I asked.

He seemed almost offended. "Now how would I know that?"

It was my turn to shrug. "I don't know. I wondered if there was anything you had to close out for him."

"Your editor said you and he were pretty good friends," Kali added.

"Well, yeah, sure, Arnie and me both worked for the *Times*," he said, "but he did a lot more freelance work for magazines and stuff than me."

"Anything stand out?" I asked.

"His editor mentioned he was working on a book before he died," Kali said.

Dropney smiled. "He was. Lots of work writing a book."

"Tell me about it," I said. "I've written a couple myself."

"What was the book about?" Kali asked. "Diamonds, maybe?"

"Diamonds?" Dropney looked puzzled. "No, I think it was about the Russian navy, or something."

Kali frowned, momentarily puzzled.

Dropney laughed. "That was my reaction too. Who the hell wants to read about the freaking Russian navy these days? But Arnie was into all that esoteric kind of stuff."

"The Russian navy," I said, grinning broadly.

"The freaking Russian navy," he repeated, like we'd both just shared the punch line of a dirty joke.

"Say," I asked, "you wouldn't know if there's a copy of the manuscript lying around somewhere, would you?"

"You're joking, right?"

"No, I'm kind of curious about it."

"Wasn't on his hard drive at work. That I do know." Dropney looked from Kali to me. "Why all the questions?"

"I'm a patron of the arts," I said.

Dropney's face assumed what I guessed would be his attempt at a shrewd expression.

"My editor told me you two called him and were nosing around about Arnie," he said. "He also told me to find out why."

I shot a quick look toward Kali, who said, "We're writing a script."

Dropney pulled on his nose. "What are you two asking about diamonds for?"

I grinned. "She's the one asking about diamonds, and the rationale is easy. They're a girl's best friend."

The attempted shrewd expression lingered. "Come on, what's the real angle?"

"Who can I go to for some inside skinny on the diamond trade?" Kali asked.

"You tried Tiffany's?"

"Actually," she said, "we almost went there for breakfast the other day, but he took me to a bagel shop instead."

"Hey," I said, "nobody likes a smart-ass. But as far as the diamond trade goes, we're talking about details about the stuff that goes on under the tables."

"For a script?" The way he said it told me he didn't believe it.

"Among other things," I said.

"Come on. You invite me to lunch, pump me with questions about Arnie, and then won't tell me shit?"

He had a point, in a half-assed sort of way. I figured that merited a half-assed sort of answer. "What would you say if I told you the cops were looking into reexamining the circumstances surrounding Arnie's death?"

His face looked like someone had suddenly massaged it with horseradish. "No shit?"

I made a shushing gesture and did an exaggerated glance around. "That's just one of the things we're looking into."

"For a script?" he asked.

I nodded. "It would be the perfect role for me. Remember Jimmy Stewart in *Call Northside Seven-Seven-Seven*?"

"Yeah," Dropney said, "and that was based on a real case too, wasn't it?" His eyes were looking as big as the saucers on the table.

"And this one could read 'based on a series of articles by Duncan Dropney' too."

"Just tell me what you need me to do," he said.

I told him to make a few discreet inquiries about Wassler's last articles and book. "We'd really like to check out that manuscript too."

"He most likely kept that on his laptop," Dropney said. "Like I said, it wasn't on his work computer. I'll see if I can track it down."

We exchanged numbers and he promised to get back to us and left without even offering to leave part of the tip.

"I guess he thought there might be something in it for him," I said as I handed the waitress my credit card.

"You think he's any good?" Kali asked. "Seemed kind of underwhelming to me."

"At least we have someone else stirring the pot," I said. "Someone besides our buddy Gustafson, that is."

# CHAPTER 15

I was concerned that Anna never showed at the Marseille. We waited in front of the place while I tried to call her cell. No answer, just the voice mail service instructing me to leave a message. I did, telling her that we were leaving the restaurant and to call me when she got a chance. I was suddenly worried that maybe idiot Cyrus had accosted her somewhere en route to our meeting. An hour or so later, while we were at my dressing room going over the afternoon's script pages, she called me back.

"Richard, I am so sorry," she said.

"No problem," I said. "Are you okay? I was worried about you."

"Yes, yes, I am fine. Something came up. I could not make it."

I waited for her to explain further, and when she didn't, I asked, "That idiot reporter Gustafson didn't bother you, did he?"

"Who?" Then I heard her laugh. "No, of course not. It was a personal matter. With my work. Once again, I am so sorry."

*"Bis prabl'em,"* I said.

She laughed again. "Oh, Richard, your Russian is so good. You have hardly any accent of America at all."

I couldn't think of anything else to say but *"Spasibo."*

"If I didn't know better, I'd swear you were native speaker. Did that reporter friend tell you anything about my father?"

"Not much." I didn't want to get her hopes up, so I gave her a brief summary of the lunchtime conversation.

"So you think the dead man's manuscript will help us?"

I sighed. Things were unfolding, but at a pace that made an escargot look like a cheetah. "It might. But then again, I'm still trying to sort things out. In the meantime, keep listening for any news in Little Odessa. Call me if you hear anything."

"My ear will be," she said, "on the ground."

Kali and I went back to work on the script reading, with her taking all the parts except mine. I'd been slacking on learning the lines and had a substantial scene coming up. But still, Rudy's conundrum kept quietly rotating inside my head. What did it all mean? How did all these disparate parts fit together?

We didn't hear from Dropney for the rest of the afternoon, and when it came time for Kali and me to part company so I could report in at the set, she said she was going to go surfing for some of Wassler's old articles.

"Maybe we can get a feel for the guy by reading some of them," she said.

I agreed, although I wasn't sharing her optimism. I was still trying to assemble the pieces of the jigsaw puzzle inside a basic border for the picture.

"We do have one common thread," I said.

"The Russian navy?" she asked.

"Exactly. We're tripping over eastern Euro connections. Peters/ Petrovich, our buddy Buteyko, Spaulding working for Bela Lugosi the Second, and their proximity to Odessa Imports . . . and now, Wassler's missing manuscript about the Russian navy."

"Yeah, but what about Glenn Perry and Crystal Imaging?" she asked. "How does that fit into the big picture?"

"That's something we have to figure out," I said. "But when we do, we'll have solved our riddle wrapped in a mystery, inside of the enigma."

"You said that before."

"So did Winston Churchill."

When the ending wrap finally arrived in the wee hours, I was relieved to find that Kali had gone home, leaving me a note on my dressing room table that she was calling it a night and that she'd get hold of me in the morning. "Late morning," she'd written. I smiled. That sounded good.

I was equally relieved not to see Gustafson lurking about. For once, things seemed to be working out all right, and I was looking forward to catching a few extra hours on the pillow. But instead of my alarm, the phone woke me up. I glanced at my clock and saw it was a little after nine. Sunlight was already beginning to filter through the blinds, and I knew that even if I didn't answer the damn phone, I wouldn't be able to get back to sleep anyway.

"Richard?" Alexi's voice boomed in my ear. "I wake you up?"

It sounded more like a statement than a question. "Late night," I said. "What's up?"

"I am worry about Rudy. He no call, no home. You know anything?"

In all the configuring, I had assumed that Rudy's wife would reach out to all his friends and acquaintances. But apparently she hadn't thought to tell Alexi. The Russian-language newspapers always lagged behind the regular American editions, but the story had only been on page two of the metro section of the *Times*. Maybe Alexi didn't read the papers. Obviously he hadn't heard about Rudy's disappearance, and he needed to know.

"Yeah, I do," I said. "And we have to talk."

"I come your house?"

I rolled over and stared at the ceiling, calculating how long it would take me to shower and get dressed. "Let's meet for breakfast."

"Breakfast?" I heard him laugh. "Pretty soon lunchtime."

We agreed on Dimitri's in Brighton Beach. That way I could have the cook whip me up some scrambled eggs, and Alexi could grab a stuffed cabbage or something. Plus, he lived close by. On the long trip there, I thought about how to break the news about Rudy to him. Or at least what I knew about it.

When I'd arrived, Alexi and Dimitri were involved in a heated discussion over the latest copy of *Sports Illustrated*. Alexi kept smacking his palm down on the magazine and Dimitri kept nodding in agreement. As I walked up to them, Alexi saw me and picked it up.

"Richard, they do not give one page even to my fight from last week," he said.

"Not even half one page," Dimitri added. He gave me a quick wink. "I tell him he must become unified world champion first. Is that not so?"

I definitely didn't want to go there, so I simply said, "He looks like the champ to me. Now, what are the chances of getting some scrambled eggs with peppers and onions mixed in and some whole wheat toast?"

"Most certainly," Dimitri said. He turned and uttered something to Alexi in Russian before walking away.

"What did he say?" I asked, sliding into the booth across from Alexi.

"He say to ask you about Rudy."

After our food came I spent a few minutes drinking coffee and pushing the remnants of the scrambled eggs around my plate as I explained to Alexi that Rudy was officially listed as "missing." He hadn't touched his plate of food.

"Missing? He is gone?" Alexi said, his big jaw drooping in confusion. "Gone where?"

I shook my head. "I'm trying to find out. They found his car down by the East River last Saturday. His coat had blood on it too."

Alexi's jaw continued to hang open. The tracklike stitching along his left eyebrow, where Calvin Taylor had butted him, looked like it was barely holding back the angry red skin beneath it. "He is dead?"

"I don't know," I said, but my thoughts were that at this point, he probably was. Everything about this mess was pointing toward an unhappy ending.

"We must find him," Alexi said, starting to stand.

I put my hand on his wrist. It felt like I'd grabbed a baseball bat by the fat end. "The police are looking into it."

"The police." His tone told me how he felt.

"I know, I know, but I'm looking into it too. We'll find out something."

He slumped down into his chair, looking more despondent than I'd ever seen him. "I am set to go home two days after tomorrow."

"Home?"

"Kiev," he said. "Much business there."

"You going to set up a fight there?"

His smile was slight. "Yes, but different fighting. Fight for freedom."

"Freedom?"

He heaved a sigh. "You know I want to unify title."

I nodded. In order to be recognized as the universal heavyweight champ, he'd have to beat the other two or three titleholders, however many would step in the ring with him, in a series of elimination bouts. Although each boxing organization had its own champ, with his own belt, the last man standing at the end of the elimination would officially receive the ultimate recognition. Until one of the organizations stripped him of its particular title for not facing its choice of number one challenger. The trouble was, each group had its own list of top contenders and wanted the matchups that would make it the most money. Thus, once the title was unified, it would only stay that way for a short while. But at least it would be whole for a brief moment in time.

"Politics," I said. "The unification bouts, right?"

"Politics," he repeated. "That is why I am retire from boxing soon. I go back home. To Ukraine. Permanently."

"Retire?" I was stunned. "But you're at the top of your form. Even though you haven't got all the belts, everybody recognizes you as the true champ. So does *Ring Magazine*. And it don't get no better than that."

He smiled an acknowledging thanks. "The real fight is just beginning in Ukraine. I must go back."

My expression must have broadcast my confusion.

"We have a good government now," Alexi said. "The Orange Revolution.

Five years ago now. President Yushchenko poisoned. By old Soviets, KGB, Putin. Now his FSB." He pretended to spit.

"Yeah, Putin used to run the old KGB, didn't he?"

Alexi nodded, his face still grim. "They tried to steal it back from us. Poisoned Yushchenko, but still could not succeed."

I couldn't help but remember Rudy's description of his life before he came to America: *It was all secret police and terror.* "I remember reading about that."

Alexi took a deep breath and his frown transformed into a broad smile. "In Ukraine, freedom now reigns."

"Sounds like you're getting ready to run for office." I meant it as a joke, but his smile faded so quickly, I thought I'd insulted him.

"How do you know?" he asked.

"How do I know what?"

"I have announced that I will go back to Ukraine and serve on cabinet."

I raised my eyebrows. This was a surprise. "Actually, I didn't. I was making a bad joke. Something I've been getting better at lately."

Alexi smiled again. Seeing him like this, it was almost hard to imagine him in the ring, trying to separate an opponent from his senses. "Together, President Yushchenko, me, we will forge a new freedom for our people. And the people of Crimea, as well."

"That all sounds very Russian," I said.

His smile turned to a glare. "Not Russian. Ukrainian."

I realized I'd made another ethnocentric gaffe, but having grown up in the duck-and-cover Cold War era, I'd come to lump together all the countries of the old Soviet bloc as "Russian." Despite all the different nations that were asserting their independence since the meltdown of the Iron Curtain, old habits died hard. But then again, political correctness and ethnic sensitivities have never been my strong suit. "Please accept my apologies." I explained to him about the erroneous labeling.

He shrugged. "I understand. We used to do same thing when I was boy in school. Everything bad—American. Now I know that was wrong."

"I guess we're only the Great Satan to the Middle Eastern countries now," I said. "So tell me about Ukraine and your plans."

He did. And by the time they brought us another round of coffee warm-ups, I had a feeling that he was embarking on something that was very important to him. I wished him luck.

"You know, Rudy also was from Ukraine," he said. "People think he is Russian, but Markovich good Ukrainian name."

"I didn't know that," I said, wondering if it was something I should ask Anna about.

"He is like second father to me," he said. "I wonder if we ever know what happened to him."

"Like I said, both the police and I are looking into it." As if on cue, my cell phone rang. It was Dropney.

"I've got a contact on the shady side of the diamond trade, like you asked," he said.

"Great, who?"

"I'll get to that in a minute." His voice had taken on a sly overtone. "The guy's only going to talk if I'm sitting in on the interview."

"Is that a fact?"

"It is."

"His choice or yours?"

Dropney laughed. "I told you I wanted in on this thing, right?"

"You did," I said. "Okay, where and when?"

"Meet me on Sixth Avenue near Forty-seventh in thirty minutes," he said.

"Thirty minutes? Come on, I'm in fucking Brooklyn."

"Whenever you can get there, then." He hung up.

"Was that about Rudy?" Alexi asked, starting to stand up. "I go with you."

The last thing I wanted was the Incredible Hulk storming into the meeting and intimidating everybody. There was a time for muscle and a time for finesse. This was definitely the latter. "No, this has to do with something else."

Alexi slumped back down in his chair, like he'd just gotten through a losing round. "I need to know what happened to Rudy."

"As soon as I find out anything," I said, "I'll let you know."

• • •

Alexi left with the promise that he was going to start asking around Brighton Beach about rumors of Rudy. I thought about telling him to look up Anna, but hesitated, not sure if what I said would get back to Rudy's wife. And then to the cops. I wasn't ready to open that can of worms yet. Besides, Marlowe always kept things to himself.

I went to the washroom to toss some water on my face. These days of late nights and early mornings were beginning to take their toll. Something was gonna give, and I had a hunch it was gonna be me. I felt stiff and tired from lack of sleep, but I knew I had to keep pressing. I owed that much to Rudy. I was on my way out, calling Kali to give her an update about Dropney's call and to tell her to meet me there, when I saw a black Crown Vic pull up to the curb and park with the practiced audacity that only the driver of an unmarked squad car has. It didn't hurt that it had a spotlight on the driver's door either. Max Kaminsky got out of the passenger side. His expression was dour. Another cop in plainclothes got out of the driver's side.

Double-teamed, I thought. This must be serious.

"We need to talk," was all he said as he pointed to the car.

"You mind taking me to Manhattan, then?" I asked. "I'm late for an engagement."

Max's nostrils flared, a sure sign that he was really pissed. "Just get in the fucking car, goddammit."

I took out my cell phone and called Kali back. "Call that reporter and tell him I'm running late," I told her. "Looks like I'm on my way to Midtown North."

After getting comfortably ensconced in the rear seat next to Max, I asked, "Just how the hell did you know where I was?"

"Basic police work," he said. "Your doorman told us you took a cab, and the cab company was more than happy to tell us where to."

"Impressive," I said, but I had to stop myself from adding, You can find me so easily, so how come you haven't got a clue about Rudy? But that wouldn't get me anywhere, especially when I was effectively being "taken downtown." My mother always used to stress that lesson about drawing more flies with honey, so I asked nicely, "Any news about Rudy?"

Max shook his head. "No, but another acquaintance of yours has coincidentally turned up dead."

I felt like I'd bumped up against a live outlet. "Who?"

Max's grin had a hint of malevolence. "The guy was a big fan of yours. Even had an autographed copy of your book."

"I had a rough night and my bullshit meter's at full," I said. "Who the hell are you talking about?"

"His name was Cyrus Gustafson. A reporter for The *New York Inquirer.* Know him?"

"Yeah, more or less." I stalled, trying to figure the angle. "More less than more."

"His body was found in an alley."

"Murdered?"

Max nodded. "Yeah, the guy was a shitbird. He probably made enemies faster than he made friends. But somebody strangled him with a ligature. Not your usual method of choice for a street murder here in New York City. Very nasty, but very efficient. You know anything about it?"

"Other than what you just told me, no."

"Funny, one of Gustafson's buddies at the paper told me that you roughed the guy up yesterday."

"I'd hardly call it that," I said.

"What would you call it, then?"

I shrugged. "I don't know . . . How about a libelous scandal sheet trying to masquerade as a newspaper?"

Max frowned. "Listen, smart-ass. I was talking about you beating him up. Breaking his fucking nose."

"It was more of a lesson in manners after he assaulted my assistant," I said, "and he rammed his nose into the window of our taxi trying to yell at us." I almost added that I had two witnesses but thought better of it. I wasn't ready to tell him about Anna just yet. It would require too much explaining.

"So what was he working on?" Max asked.

"I'm not sure. Rudy's disappearance maybe."

"Come on." His voice had an edge to it.

"I'm serious. We weren't exactly friends."

"So why'd you rough him up, then?"

I blew out a slow breath. "The guy had all the tact and class of a well-bred New York rat. He hurled some nasty racial invectives at my personal assistant and grabbed her arm. I convinced him to let go."

"And?"

"And that's about it. Like I told you, we weren't exactly best buddies."

He frowned and settled back into the seat. We rode along in silence, broken only by the intermittent chatter of the police radio. I'd noticed we were taking an awfully roundabout way to the precinct after we crossed the Manhattan Bridge. I had a hunch where we were going when we stopped in front of the blue brick building at Thirtieth and First where the silver letters spelled out *City of New York Office of the Chief Medical Examiner*. The morgue. I was glad I'd already eaten. After this stop I probably wasn't going to have much of an appetite left.

Max got out and held the door open for me. The driver followed, bringing up the rear, as we entered the building. After conferring with the guard at the front desk and showing his tin, Max motioned for me to follow. We went down a corridor and past a viewing room. Large glass windows separated us from the bowels of the morgue, but Max kept right on walking. When he opened a solid metal door, and then another, the overwhelming smell hit me like an incoming wave. Sickeningly sweet, like stale garbage, but with more of a tangy bite. But I'd smelled death before.

We strolled through a refrigerated room with stacks of corpses, some in black bodybags, some lying naked on metal gurneys. Corpses of all ages and sexes, even babies. Oh, God, the babies. Death was nondiscriminatory. The ultimate equalizer. Now I was really wishing I hadn't met Alexi for late breakfast. Max kept glancing over his shoulder to make sure I was still behind him. Like I would consider stopping to lie down or something.

He paused at another door, which led into the autopsy room. It was large and painted that same sickening green that police stations and morgues all over the world are painted. They must have a certain brand name for it. Puke green, maybe.

Max stopped at a metal table with a naked corpse on it. It was a male. A wooden block, cut with a shallow U shape in the center, rested under the dead man's neck, looking like a hard wooden lounge pillow. A male attendant in green scrubs stood next to the body, blocking our view.

"You start yet?" Max asked.

The smell was twice as bad in here. If it bothered Max, he wasn't letting on.

"Waiting on the doc," the attendant said.

"Let my witness have a look at the guy," Max said, then snapped his fingers to motion me over. "Know him, Belz?"

I looked down. Cyrus Gustafson's bloated face and lifeless eyes stared vacantly upward. See no evil, hear no evil, I thought. But perhaps his body would speak about the evil that was done to him and offer some clues to his killer. As much as he had been an idiot in life, death had somehow made him almost sympathetic. He deserved a better end, that was for sure.

"It's him," I said. "Can I go now?"

Max's lower lip jutted out, like he thought he'd proved his point, but he pointed to Gustafson's throat. "Take a good fucking look first."

I did. A deep red slice ran completely around the neck, where something thin, strong, and unforgiving had dug into the flesh.

"Like I told you, he was strangled to death," Max said. "Garroted, probably with some kind of a fucking wire."

"Like a noose," his partner said.

"Yeah, well, I never have been much of a wire man," I said.

Max's face reddened. "You want to know the reason we brought you down here, smart-ass?"

"You thought I might break down and confess?"

That seemed to set him off more. Like I said, I'll never be asked to write the sequel to *How to Win Friends and Influence People*.

"No." His voice was close to a roar.

"I sense you're very mad now," I said. "No way to fake anger like that. Even the best actors like myself would be hard-pressed."

"Dammit, Belz." He stamped his foot. The attendant backed up a step. "I brought you down here because I wanted you to see firsthand the kind of people we're dealing with."

"These guys are killers, all right," the other detective said.

"You want to end up on a fucking slab here?" Max said, holding his hand above Gustafson and pointing downward. "You want to end up like him? In an alley somewhere with your throat cut?"

A female doctor, also clad in scrubs and rubber gloves, came in, flipping down the elongated plastic visor of her face mask. "Detectives," she said, pausing to look at each of us. "Am I to take it that we're going to have a big audience for this one?"

Max shook his head and motioned me toward the door. I was glad to get out of there, although the stench still lingered in my nostrils even in the hallway. He turned to his partner. "I got to get back in there. It's my case, but escort him out of the building for me, would you?"

The other detective nodded and motioned for me to accompany him. As I started to go, Max grabbed my sleeve and brought his face inches from mine.

"You got to back off this investigation shit." His voice was low, guttural, and full of emotion. "You think there's some kind of fucking script you're following here? This ain't one of your fucking TV shows, dammit. And you ain't no cop. Remember that."

# CHAPTER 16

I called Kali as soon as I'd waved down a taxi. She told me they'd been waiting for me in a small bar in the Theater District. "This guy with Dropney's kind of a creep, though," she said. "Hurry up."

"I hope he didn't hear you," I said.

"Not unless he's in the next stall. You picked a good time to call."

I had noticed an echo to her voice. I told her to take care of business and I'd be there shortly. The bar, not the restroom. The thought brought a smile to my face, despite the downer of paying a visit to the house of the dead. After I hung up, I sat back and watched the passing cityscape through the cab window. No need to worry about Gustafson following me this time. I suddenly felt a pang of regret about how I'd treated him. Had I given him a chance? If I had, would he still be alive? I hoped he'd have someone to grieve for him. Someone to stand over his grave and shed a tear. It had been a lot easier to dismiss him when he'd just been his obnoxious, insulting self, before I'd seen him lying on the metal table, ready to be sliced open. I'm glad I hadn't seen that part.

The bar was dark and redolent with the odor of booze, like most bars are. This one had the customary long mirror behind the counter, which reflected the drooping faces of some early afternoon regulars. If this had been a movie, I would have seen Gustafson's face staring back at me for an instant. As it was, the vision hung in my mind's eye all too clearly.

Kali waved from a rear booth. Two men sat opposite her. One of them was Duncan Dropney, and the other was a bulky guy who looked like the reincarnation of a slightly seedier version of Sidney Greenstreet from *The Maltese Falcon*. Kali got up and walked to meet me, whispering, "Glad you could make it. This dude's creeping me out."

I managed a fractional nod.

The space between her eyebrows creased slightly. "What's wrong? You okay?"

"Rough morning." I put my hand on her elbow and guided her back toward the booth. I noticed the bulky guy staring at Kali as she slid into place behind the table. I slid in next to her. Dropney extended his hand across the table.

"Rich," he said, "glad you could make it." Ordinarily I despise the nickname Rich, but in this case I let it slide. "This is Gilbert Moody. He's been telling us about the diamond business."

"Gilbert," I said, offering my hand.

He sat there like a big lizard. "I prefer you address me as Mr. Moody." I began to wonder if he'd even blink.

"Fine," I said, slowly bringing my hand back. Dropney's face had one of those frozen nervous grins stretched over it. Half a beer sat on the table in front of him.

After a few seconds of awkward silence, Kali took over. "Mr. Moody knew Joshua Spaulding, and he's familiar with Odessa Imports too."

Moody's eyes swept over her, settling on her breasts as she spoke. I almost wanted to reach over and smack his jowls.

Moody brought his eyes up to meet mine. "I was under the impression that you wanted information about the diamond business," he said.

"That's right."

He blinked, still milking the silence for effect. At least he didn't have a nictitating membrane instead of an eyelid, as some reptiles do. "I would be happy to enlighten you, but since I have wasted a good portion of my morning already, I should think some remuneration would be in order."

"I must have missed the first feature, huh?" I said, reaching into my pocket and taking out a twenty. I dropped the folded bill by his half-empty glass. The remainder of a highball, from the looks of it.

His eyes moved down toward the bill, his expression not changing. He still wasn't saying much either.

"Well . . . ," I said, trying to get him started.

He made a minimal gesture toward the twenty. "That's hardly worth my time."

"Whatever you have to say might not be worth mine," I said. "But how about if I agree to pick up the tab?"

His eyes fixed on mine, his mouth still drawn into a tight line.

"Fine," I said. "So far I've been having a real shitty day, and I'm glad to see this is shaping up to be more of the same. Because I don't have time to sit here and wait for you to shed your skin."

I started to get up and Moody said, "What is it you wish to know?" With a slick move he palmed the folded twenty, like he'd just captured an unlucky fly.

"You're in the diamond business?" I asked.

"Yes." He waited about four seconds before adding, "But I'd rather not discuss my personal business interests, unless you have something of value you wish appraised."

"What exactly is your line of work?"

"Let's just say that I am a wholesaler, of sorts." He picked up his now empty glass and shook it in front of me. I took the hint and ordered a new round for all four of us. Another highball for the lizard, another beer for Dropney, and club sodas for Kali and me. I still had a long day's shooting ahead. After the waitress brought the drinks, Moody seemed satisfied as he brought the glass up to his lips and took a copious sip.

I went down the list of our acquaintances thus far, starting with the four dead men and ending with my buddies Bela Lugosi II and Nikolai Buteyko, president of Odessa Imports.

"I already told this young lady that I knew Spaulding." His eyes swept over Kali again in a manner that made me shiver. "And I've dealt with Buteyko before. I told you, I am in the diamond business, as are the

Russians, Australians, Canadians . . . De Beers in London is at the helm of the price manipulation. The market is always in a delicate balance."

"Why's that?"

He went back to his fly-catching mode, sitting very still and just staring. I guessed he thought silence was indeed golden.

"You need to turn your hearing aid up?" I asked.

The thin lips twitched, and flies everywhere breathed a collective sigh of relief. "It's delicate because the aesthetic need for diamonds must be manufactured. They have only that value we have placed on them through the ages."

"The crown jewels are merely pretty baubles, eh?" I said.

"Precisely. Now, given that these baubles have been highly prized throughout most of our civilized history, in various cultures the world over, the law of supply and demand must dictate that they remain highly valued, expensive, and scarce."

"What about that movie with DiCaprio a couple of years ago? How does that kind of thing tie in?"

"*Blood Diamond,*" Kali said.

Her entry into the conversation sparked a lecherous glance. "There are stones called blood diamonds, or conflict diamonds," he said. "Just like in the movie, although I thought it was a ridiculous premise."

I felt like telling him I wasn't much interested in his pontifications as a movie critic, but I wanted to keep him talking in the hope that I'd get something for my twenty bucks.

"For the moment, all of the civil wars in the countries that coined the phrase have supposedly ceased," he said with an air of condescending superiority, "and although I don't see why, diamonds from these areas still cause problems for international markets."

"Yeah," I said. "Why worry about the specter of a young boy or girl with their arm hacked off hovering over your engagement ring?"

Moody nodded, oblivious to my sarcasm.

"We did a story on this," Dropney said. "What about that international registry?"

"The Kimberley Process," Moody said.

"Yeah, right," said Dropney. "They register the country of origin and a serial number of all diamonds now, right? To keep out the conflict diamonds."

Moody gave a one-shoulder shrug. "Many safeguards have been set up, but there are always ways to get around them, if you have the means."

I didn't think blood diamonds, as reprehensible as they were, played into our scenario. I mentally reviewed what we'd found out so far and kept coming back to what we'd been tripping over at almost every turn. The Russkies.

"You mentioned Russian diamonds before," I said. "What can you tell me about those?"

He stared at me and blinked. I didn't know whether to take this as a sign I'd be blessed with a prompt answer. Maybe my ignorance astounded him. Maybe he was thinking of asking for another double sawbuck.

"They account for perhaps twenty percent of the world market," he said. "The Kremlin was rumored to have a large reserve from Siberia in cold storage." He smiled at his own play on words. "Yeltsin used a large cache of gems to finance one of his reelection campaigns. Years later, Putin did the same thing when he needed money for his own political purposes."

"It must be nice to have that much ice," Dropney said. If he were thinking of trying his hand at rap, he needed to find some bigger pants.

Moody ignored the comment. "Putin allegedly threatened to flood the market and ruin the industry if he wasn't paid top dollar. Forced a deal with De Beers for a big payoff. Many were surprised that he was able to pull it off."

"Why's that?" I asked.

Moody shifted in his seat, probably considering how much speculating he wanted to do for twenty bucks and a couple of drinks. His enormous head rotated back to its stock position and his right eyebrow twitched ever so slightly. "There was a rumor that the big mines in Siberia were starting to get played out. The Mir mine, for instance, was over two thousand feet deep before they finally closed it. And they have to cut through a thousand feet of permafrost before they reach any prospects.

I've always felt the Russians weren't being entirely truthful about their resources."

"Meaning what?" I asked.

Moody shrugged. "Meaning whatever you want it to mean."

"Is the Russian mafia involved in diamond smuggling?" I asked.

Moody laughed. It wasn't a nice sound. Not joyous or rife with humor. Just like a hollow drum being tapped in a steady rhythm. "They are involved in nothing that I should care to know about."

"So if their mines are getting played out," I asked, trying to follow his elusive logic, "does that mean they're into selling conflict diamonds?"

Moody took a semideep breath. "The Soviets did a similar thing before, in the nineteen sixties. They started introducing a large number of diamonds into the world market, claiming their Siberian tundra had yielded a tremendous field." He paused and lifted his finger. "But it came to an abrupt halt when it was discovered that all of these diamonds had a greenish, rather than the customary bluish, glow, and they all had sharp, angular edges. And they were remarkably consistent in their size and shape. In fact, virtually the entire consignment consisted of melees." He stared at me intently, to see if I was following.

I wasn't, but I repeated "melees" and tried to look like I'd grabbed hold of the tail of his story.

He frowned. "Melees. Medium-grade diamonds of one-tenth to seven-tenths of a carat," he said. "The majority of these Soviet diamonds had a weight of approximately a quarter of a carat and were one to two millimeters wide."

"I never got that heavily into dope, so I'm not so skilled with the metric system," I said.

His frown deepened. "African diamonds come in a variety of sizes and shapes. Some are round, some are square, some flat, some twisted. These Siberian diamonds were virtually all octohedronal."

"Eight edges," I said, not wanting him to think it was all Greek to me.

"Their very consistency made them stand out, but De Beers continued to accept the consignments. They had no choice." This time his mouth tightened into a slight smile. Diamonds obviously were one of his life's major passions, his joy, the salt of his meat, and all that stuff. I wondered what else would bring a smile to his reptilian features. Maybe a helpless gerbil, ready to be swallowed whole? "Otherwise, the Soviets would have flooded the world market and the value would have collapsed." He sipped some of the remaining liquid in his glass. "Shortly thereafter, it was revealed that Soviet scientists had developed a new method of creating artificial diamonds. This, of course, could have ruined the international value system, so De Beers stepped in to investigate. In typical ham-fisted Communist fashion, the Soviets denied everything but quietly stopped their diamond flood. Now we have the technology to easily detect if a diamond is natural or artificial. Synthetic diamonds are not as highly valued as the ones Mother Nature provides."

Not that I couldn't grasp his mini economics lesson on the law of supply and demand, but how did all this tie into Rudy's disappearance? Still, the idea that maybe the Russian government might being doing something with diamonds that was under the table was like a shot of adrenaline to a conspiracy buff's heart. Maybe the pieces of the jigsaw puzzle finally were starting to come together.

"But"—Moody drained his drink and started to lift his considerable bulk from the seat—"I sense I've given you more than your paltry sum purchased."

"You've been a real jewel," I said.

He stopped and the edge of his mouth curled up in something akin to amusement. "I forgot to ask if you're armed."

I cocked my head back in a gesture that conveyed total self-assurance. Now it was my turn to milk the silent pause. Plus, I thought it best to keep the lizard guessing.

The thin lips twitched and he said, "If you aren't, perhaps you should be. The *mafiya* does not take kindly to people asking about their activities." He waved as he turned and waddled away.

"That guy was a real toad," Kali said. "Did you see the way he kept looking at my chest?"

"He reminded me more of a big salamander," I said. "Or maybe one of those Komodo dragons."

"Sorry, Rich," Dropney said, "but he's right about one thing. You ought to be packing heat or at least have someone around who is. Especially with such a charming companion." He nodded toward Kali.

I thought about her too, and about Cyrus Gustafson lying on that metal table at the morgue. Maybe I was drawing her into something I shouldn't. Maybe I was drawing myself in there too. But I knew the risks, especially after this morning. I didn't want to put her in harm's way. Or had I already done that?

"I know an excellent licensed private investigator we've used in the past," Dropney said. "Name's Al Giretti." He took out his wallet. "I might have his card in here somewhere." He began sorting through a bunch of business cards.

I gave him one of mine. "Here's my cell. If you find it, give me a call. We got to get going." I stood and waited for Kali to slide across the seat.

Dropney clucked. "Looks like I don't have it here, but I'll check at the office." He stood up too. "This helped you out any?"

"Yeah, sure," I said, shaking his hand. "Thanks for setting it up. You find that Wassler manuscript, by the way?"

"Still looking," he said, "but I'll call you when I get to the office."

I thanked him again and we left. I glanced at my watch. It was going on three, and I had to report in for the afternoon shoot shortly. I motioned to a passing cab with its light on.

Kali waved to the departing Dropney. "At least he's nicer than that creep Gustafson."

"Listen." I opened the taxi's rear door for her. "We have to talk."

"I'm listening."

I took a deep breath. Where to start . . . "I've been doing some thinking."

"Me too." Her smile was effervescent. "I've got some theories I want to check out while you're shooting this afternoon. Then we'll—"

"Wait a minute."

She looked at me, the little crease appearing between her eyebrows again. "What's wrong?"

I blew out a slow breath. "Look, this thing might start getting dangerous. It might be a good idea for you to take a few steps back for a while, okay?"

"Hey, I was assigned to keep you out of trouble, remember?" she said. "If you're in, I'm in."

I took off my glasses and rubbed the bridge of my nose with my forefinger and thumb. "I just came from the morgue. Max Kaminsky picked me up earlier."

"Uh-oh."

"Yeah," I said. "Cyrus Gustafson was murdered."

"Murdered? Oh, my God." She spread her hand on her chest, like she was trying to take a labored breath. "Who did it?"

"No idea," I said. "But Max made a point to show me the body."

She looked at me. "Stabbed, drive-by, what?"

"Strangled."

"Oh, my God, that's even worse. I mean, he was kind of a scumbag, racist jerk, but I hate to think of him getting murdered." Her fingers rubbed over the front of her neck. "Especially strangled. It's a bad way to go."

"Like there's a good way?" I inhaled deeply to summon up the courage to say it. "I'm afraid we might be getting in over our heads here."

"You got that right."

"So it's time for you to say *arrivederci*."

"Now you ain't gonna tell me you speak Italian too, are you?"

"A little. It's a lot like French. And Spanish."

"Yeah, yeah, sure, but answer me one question. In English."

I nodded.

"By saying *arrivederci*, you talking about both of us, or just me?"

I saw where this was heading. "Look, Kali, I don't want you to get hurt."

"Me either."

"You know what I mean. I can't take the responsibility for you."

"And I'm not asking you to." Her expression was stern. "But I was given the job of keeping you out of trouble. And that's what I intend to do. So, like I told you before, if you're in, I'm in."

"And that's all there is to it?" I asked.

She nodded emphatically, but I sensed a whisper of nervousness in her eyes. Maybe I should take Dropney up on his advice and hire a private detective. It was obvious that I couldn't depend on Max for backup when I needed it. And I certainly didn't want Kali or me ending up on a cold slab, like Gustafson. The search for Rudy was knocking over a lot of rocks. And something deadly had crawled out from underneath one of them.

# CHAPTER 17

I let Kali keep the cab and told her to check back with me later. They dropped me off in front of the entrance to the set, but I turned and strolled down to the corner Duane Reade for a bottle of water. A sip of the cool liquid did wonders for my parched throat. Although summer was past, and so far September had been relatively cool, today the air was so humid you could have stuffed it in a pillow. Maybe the coolness of the first part of the month was an anomaly, and now it was a return to global warming.

I took another sip and had just begun to think about Rudy, and Gustafson, and all the rest of it. Playing a cop on TV for the past fifteen or so years had taught me one thing, anyway. Try to look at the big picture, then see how all the little pieces fit in. Or maybe spread the pieces out on a table and connect the dots. So what did I have? A missing and presumed dead medical examiner and a murdered reporter from a New York scandal sheet. Plus four other dead men who apparently expired due to natural causes. One of them had been a reporter too, doing a book about the Russian navy. The fucking Russian navy. Everything I'd read since the Iron Curtain came down indicated that they were a shadow of what they'd once been, despite planting a metallic flag under the North Pole. What that had to do with the price of butter, or diamonds, in Poughkeepsie was anybody's guess. But one thing was for sure: If I tried to connect the goddamn dots on this one, I'd be dragging the pencil around the block. It was like trying to fit the slivers of glass back into a shattered mirror.

As I continued to walk, out of the corner of my eye I noticed a black Lincoln with smoked windows crawling along on the street like a big shadow, matching me step for step. Either someone was watching me, or Vern had taken to riding around in style.

A second or two later, the right rear window rolled down with electric smoothness, and I saw the round, craggy face of Nikolai Buteyko, smiling at me. It reminded me of one of those real ugly old jack-in-the-box toys that frighten kids and offend adults everywhere. I smiled back, nodding to him like I'd known he was going to pop out of the cake the whole time. I took another long swallow from my water bottle.

"Mr. Belzer," he called out, waiting for my reaction. I gave him none. "Yes, I know who you are now."

Well, so much for the William Petersen disguise. I lamented the passing of the modicum of anonymity that I'd enjoyed before. He must have looked up *CSI* on the Internet. Or maybe he caught one of the ubiquitous reruns on cable and realized that Grissom wasn't half as witty and debonair as I'd been when I'd visited him at Odessa Imports. But I couldn't let him see me sweat, so I answered with a hearty, "Nikolai. *Kakdela?*"

My asking him how he was in Russian seemed to delight him. His eyes closed with an accompanying simper. It was good to know that even on the way to the set, I still knew how to work a crowd.

"Your Russian is fabulous," he said. "You have hardly an accent at all."

"And if I believe that, I'll bet you have a real shiny rock of cubic zirconium you'd like to sell me, right?"

He canted his head and smiled in a way that had a hint of self-deprecation. "Why don't you let me give you a ride?" he asked.

*Three Days of the Condor* flashed through my mind. The guy telling Redford the CIA was going to hit him. "They'll pull up in a car and tell you to get in," the guy says, "but if you do, you'll never get out of it." And sure enough, at the movie's conclusion, the car pulls up, looking a lot like this one, but the old Sundance Kid is onto them. He refuses to get in and walks away.

I did too. "No, thanks. I'm right where I need to be." As I took my next drink, I shot a glance up and down the street. People were walking on both sides along the sidewalks, some walking dogs and carrying plastic bags. And I was glad to see them. The people, not the scoopers. I had more important things to think about than dog shit. Like staying out of strange cars and harm's way. At least on the street there were plenty of witnesses and I'd have a chance to move if I had to.

Buteyko's face crinkled and he heaved a complete but very theatrical sigh, mimicking the Good Samaritan who offers to help and gets his shoes pissed on.

"What?" he said. "You do not trust me?"

"You know," I said, "that's the same line Michael Jackson was fond of using to the parents of the kids on the sleepovers."

Being compared to the one-gloved wonder must have sparked something. Or maybe he thought I was insulting his manhood by comparing him to a pervert. He barked an order in Russian to the driver, who stopped the vehicle. Buteyko got out looking just as doughy as when I'd seen him in Odessa Imports. "Ah, yes," he said. "It is indeed a wonderful day for a walk."

He'd left the car door open, and a few seconds later I saw why. Another guy got out of the limo. At first I thought it was giant Wladimir, but it wasn't. This dude was about the same size but much more swarthy-looking. He looked like a big Georgian. In fact, he was almost as big as Alexi. But while the planes of Alexi's face have been brutalized by gloved fists in the boxing ring, this guy's visage showed an intrinsic ugliness. His expression said pure thug. If I could have patented and bottled it, I'd make a killing selling it to the rap artists. He moved with a fluid grace for a big guy too. Plus, I was willing to bet he had more than just a few tattoos on the parts of his body I didn't want to see.

Buteyko mumbled something in Russian to the big guy, who fixed me with a stare so cold-blooded that I didn't even need the water to cool me off anymore. I returned the favor by smiling and using the last of my Russian. *"Vsyego dobrogo."* It can be roughly translated as "Have a good day."

The big guy's face grew even more ugly and threatening. Who'da thunk it was possible?

"He doesn't seem to appreciate my Russian as much as you do," I said to Buteyko.

Buteyko smiled. "Vasili appreciates only beautiful women, true Russian vodka, and good weapons."

"I'll bet he's a delightful conversationalist at a dinner party." I continued to walk, and Buteyko fell in beside me. Vasili stayed about six feet behind us. For a moment I thought he was going to get within grabbing distance, but his boss said something in Russian and he backed off a few more feet.

"So, Mr. Belzer." Buteyko stressed my name. "As you see, it did not take me long to find out your true identity."

"At least you didn't catch me in a phone booth changing into my costume." I kept walking, turning my head toward him as I spoke. I cared less about politeness or communication than about keeping an eye on Vasili. The oversized mutt was still about twelve feet to the rear, walking slowly.

"Costume?" Buteyko looked slightly confused. Maybe the joke had lost something in the translation, so to speak. Or maybe it wasn't all that funny. Plus, phone booths are pretty scarce nowadays. But I found out a long time ago a comic is only as good as his audience.

"It was a joke," I said. "You know, secret identities, costumes, a strange visitor from another planet who came to Earth with powers and abilities far beyond those of mortal men."

He was still having trouble comprehending, so I pointed upward. "Look, up in the sky. It's a bird, it's a plane . . ."

His head rolled backward as he followed my finger. This was turning out to be more fun than a game of talking charades. I had about a block to go before I could cut these two jokers loose at the gate.

When Buteyko's face came level with mine again, his expression wasn't pretty. Not that it had ever been, but this time he'd puckered it into a very unflattering pose. It was so unflattering that if I had a dog that looked like he did, I'd shave his ass and walk him backward.

"Enough games," he said. "You have been causing problems for my business, and bothering other businesses in the Diamond District. Do not even try to deny it."

"I'm not sure what kinds of problems you're referring to," I said, "but I'll plead plausible deniability."

"I do not find your answers amusing."

"Really?" I affected a perplexed expression. "I've been told that most people think I'm hilarious. I used to do stand-up routines, you know."

If he did, he didn't let on. Instead he reached into his shirt pocket and pulled out a card. It was one of Max's. I glimpsed the writing on the back and surmised it was the same one I'd given him.

Buteyko held the card out as he spoke. "And I suppose you think this was funny also?"

I snatched the card from his fingers. "Where did you get this? I've been looking all over for it."

The shock of the snatch quickly gave way to a flood of anger. Big Vasili took a step closer, but Buteyko raised his hand and the big man stopped.

Buteyko's frown deepened. "It was not wise to give me the false card of a policeman."

"Actually," I said, "the card and the detective are real. I can introduce you to Max anytime if you want. In fact, he's probably waiting for me just down the block."

"You were being deceptive." His corpulent neck twitched. "As I said, you are causing a certain amount of embarrassment to my company, Mr. Belzer."

"Aw, shucks," I said, seeing how far we were from the gate. I still had about half a block to go. "Just doing what I do best."

Buteyko's nostrils flared outward. He took a few breaths and then something that I figured was supposed to resemble a smile brought up the ends of his lips.

"You enjoy playing the part of a policeman, do you not?"

"Yeah, I've been doing it for so long, it's almost become second nature." We were close enough to the gate now to be within sight of the security guard.

He looked around and took another deep breath. "It is a lovely day, is it not?"

I nodded. He'd obviously come here with the mistaken idea that if he let me know he had ID'd me, I would be intimidated. Still, it couldn't hurt to let him play out the rest of his little scene.

"Almost as lovely as your black female associate. Where is she, by the way? I hope she is aware of the dangers of the subway trains."

Another attempt at intimidation, this time letting me know that Kali was on his radar scope. It hit me like a punch to the liver. Did he know she sometimes took the subway, or was he just speculating? A lot of people who work in Manhattan take public transportation. Or had he actually been following her? I figured the best way to deal with this one was to ignore the question, so I kept walking.

"I see my mention of her upset you." His face took on a leer of triumph. I guess he figured he'd finally won a round.

"One of the great things about playing a cop on TV," I said, "is that I portray such a positive image, cops everywhere love me. The police commissioner, for instance. He and I are like that." I held up my hand with my index finger and middle finger crossed.

Buteyko's head rocked slowly up and down with little tiny movements. "That is good. But I have many friends too. And they do not like people who do things that hurt my business. I would not like to see things get ugly."

Touché, I thought. "Neither would I. But something tells me they already have for some people."

Buteyko winked and smiled. "And you could be right. But here's a little free lesson for you, Mr. TV Cop. If you and the black girl wish to continue enjoying such fine autumn days, I suggest you pay attention."

He stepped back and gestured to the big man behind us. With a smooth, fluid motion, Vasili drew something from his pocket and stepped forward, throwing it. The blur shot about three feet in front of my face and thunked into one of those thin sidewalk trees that the city plants in the huge cement plots for beautification purposes. As the blur vibrated in the wood, I saw it was a flat metal throwing knife. The shank was buried almost halfway into the bark.

Buteyko's smile was still plastered across his round, piglike face. He looked like a malevolent gingerbread man. "Vasili used to be with the Spetsnaz. As I said, he is very good with knives and with guns."

"It's great to see a guy with a hobby," I said.

The big man grinned and moved to the tree in three steps. He pulled the knife from the tree trunk with frightening ease.

"So keep in mind," Buteyko said, "you may find out more than what you want."

The Lincoln had been shadowing us all along; Buteyko turned and waved toward it. Like a trained gorilla, Vasili stepped over and opened the rear door. Buteyko moved toward the car but paused as he started to get in. "Mr. Belzer. I hope we will not have this conversation again. Good-bye, Mr. TV Man."

Vasili's smirk seemed to echo just the opposite sentiment. And he looked like a man who enjoyed his work. Beautiful women, Russian vodka, and weaponry. I wondered if he had a few more quirks that Buteyko had failed to mention. Like a sadistic streak, or maybe garroting fat, nosy reporters in alleys.

The creep's mention of Kali on the subway had sent a chill down my spine. As the long car drove away I wondered how long he'd had someone watching us. And why? Something we'd done must have struck a nerve somewhere along the way. But was it the right nerve? And did it have anything to do with Rudy? I was pretty much resigned to seeing this investigation through to the end. In fact, I was determined. And when I get determined, it takes an act of Congress to dissuade me. Well, those are usually pretty watered down by the time they get out of committee and have all the pork attached to them. Maybe I should change that to an executive order. Unless it came from someone with the last name of Bush.

But I was concerned about Kali's safety. And Anna's as well, since it seemed that she was getting drawn into the ever-expanding web.

I needed to do something. But what?

I took out my cell and tried calling Kali. Her voice mail kicked in, saying she was unavailable, but please leave a message.

"Kali, this is Belz," I said to the tape. "It's important. Call me when you get a chance to let me know you're all right. I just had a visit from Buteyko and his ex-Spetsnaz errand boy. Stay under the radar and watch yourself. And stay out of the damn subway."

After I hung up, it dawned on me that she probably wouldn't know what Spetsnaz was. They're the Russian army equivalent of our Special Forces, but I believe their berets are black instead of green. I didn't know much else about them, other than what I'd read, which was that they were supposed to be tough as hell, and not the kind of foe you wanted to go up against if you didn't have to.

Maybe that was why Buteyko had brought him along. The old organ grinder using a four-hundred-pound gorilla instead of a dancing monkey to extort larger donations.

I paused just outside the gate and tried the number Anna had given me for her cell. They might already know about her as well. Gustafson had. Her voice mail picked up as well. I left a less detailed message advising her to call me at her convenience and to not take any unnecessary chances asking around about Rudy.

I felt temporarily better, though I burned with anger that Buteyko's clumsy attempt to scare me had been reasonably effective.

Maybe Vasili wasn't really Spetsnaz at all, but just a big thug who was good with a knife. Either way, however, I needed to start honing a sharp edge of my own.

# CHAPTER 18

I kept checking my cell phone during breaks in rehearsal. Finally, I found a message from Kali saying she'd been incommunicado and to call her back. I went over to the side of the soundstage and hit her number. She answered on the third ring.

"I'm really glad you called," she said. "I found out some interesting new stuff and can't wait to run it all by you. You're not going to believe it."

"Where you at?" I asked.

"Home, why?"

I sighed, realizing I'd been projecting my uneasiness from my little street encounter with Buteyko and Vasili. I gave her a quick rundown.

"Wow, that must mean we've touched a nerve somewhere. You think he might be connected to the Russian mafia?"

"I don't know," I said. "It's certainly a possibility, which brings me to the reason I called you."

"What's up?"

I didn't know if I should tell her about Buteyko mentioning her specifically in his little strong-arm session with me earlier. The last thing I wanted to do was transfer more of my anxiety to her at this point. But on the other hand, I needed to let her know that the stakes had been ratcheted up a notch.

"I'm a little concerned about your well-being, with all this going on," I said.

"And I told you before, if you're in, I'm in." Her voice sounded strong and confident, but I thought I detected an ever-so-slight undercurrent of doubt swirling around the pillars of the pier.

"Just the same," I said, "I don't want you taking any unnecessary chances. So consider yourself grounded for the time being."

"Belz, listen to me. Franco assigned me to keep watch over you. If I fail to do that, and you go off and get yourself in trouble, I'll lose my job. He's already threatened to fire me, hasn't he?"

I sighed. "Speaking of old horseshit, did you report in to him for tonight yet?"

"Of course, using the best of your MSU techniques available." She laughed. "I told him I followed you around all day and made sure you didn't get in trouble."

I couldn't help but smile. "Looks like I've taught you well." An AD stepped up on the soundstage and announced that we'd be resuming rehearsal in five minutes. "Listen, I've got to go."

She laughed. "You mean back to work or answering the call of nature?"

"Both. Do me a favor and stay home tonight. I need to sort things out a bit. Figure out how to proceed." We had two days left of our eight-day shoot. Then we'd get a couple of days off and begin on the next episode. "Maybe I'll take that guy Dropney up on his offer and hire that private dick."

"Oh," she said. "I forgot to tell you that he called me. Gave me the guy's name and number. Want it?"

Should I or shouldn't I? I could always ask Max to recommend somebody. Or maybe one of the cops working security tonight. Yeah, right, after Max had made such a big production of taking me down to the morgue and showing me Gustafson's body as a way of emphasizing that I should back off. But I had gone too far to stop now. I couldn't very well go to him for any help until I had something more than some unusual circumstances and a couple of shady Russians throwing knives at trees.

"Sure," I said. "Give me the number."

• • •

We did a solid ninety minutes more of rehearsal and then went to wardrobe and hair and makeup. I kept my eyes peeled for Franco while I managed a quick call on my cell phone to the private dick Kali had gotten from Dropney. He answered with a crisp-sounding "Giretti Investigations."

"Yeah, I'm looking into hiring a private detective." I suddenly found myself in the rare situation of not knowing exactly what to say.

"Okay," he said. "What kind of matter is it?" His accent was pure Brooklyn.

"Sort of keeping an eye on me and a couple of other people while we ask a few questions."

He didn't reply right away. When he did, he asked, "And you got my name how?"

"From a reporter friend. His name's Dropney."

More silence. "What's his first name?"

"Duncan."

"All right. Now how about your name and a number where I can reach you?"

"My name is Richard Belzer." I rattled off my cell number for him.

"Belzer? The actor on that TV show?"

Finally, someone who didn't mistake me for someone else. I liked this Giretti guy already.

"One and the same," I said, wondering if I should have asked about his rates before I gave him my name.

"I'd certainly be interested in talking to you, Mr. Belzer. When would be the most convenient time?"

"We're doing a location shoot tonight." I gave him the address. "Could you meet me over there in, say, an hour?"

"I'll be there."

I told him I'd leave word at the gate for him to visit the set.

When I hung up I was already feeling better but figured I'd better reserve judgment until I'd had a chance to meet Mr. Giretti in person. I always like to know who I'm doing business with. Especially when that business is watching my back.

• • •

An hour later I was standing around waiting while the film crew completed their setups both on the street and inside the vacant building we were using. One of the techs came over and started to hook a remote mic onto my lapel. Since those things can throw a private conversation across a city street and be overheard by someone standing next to a sound monitor, I held up my hand and told him to wait. You never knew where Franco might be lurking on these night location shoots. Scanning the area that had been roped off farther down the block, I saw the security guard in conversation with someone. He was a big man, almost as wide as he was tall, wearing a sport jacket and porkpie hat. When was the last time anybody wore a porkpie hat?

I meandered over, wondering if Mr. Giretti had made it a point to arrive early. When I got within several yards, the security guard looked around and raised his eyebrows.

"Hey, Belz," he said. "I was just gonna send someone to find you." The big, rough-looking dude was standing next to him.

I gave the man a quick once-over as I walked up to them. The other guy looked to be in his midfifties, with a barrel chest and a square face. At first glance he looked pretty impressive, like an Abrams tank in a tan sport coat. His expression was all business, the corners of his mouth and eyes devoid of any laugh lines.

I extended my hand. "You must be Mr. Giretti."

We shook. He had big hands and a strong grip. "And you must be Mr. Belzer. Unless, that is, you've had someone else playing your part on the show these past few years."

After he secured a visitor's pass, I escorted him to our temporary refreshments tent and got two coffees. The food would come later. They don't like you to eat too much before you get at least a few scenes under your belt. Too much lethargy otherwise. They didn't mind your being wired on caffeine, though.

"You're earlier than I expected," I said, silently reflecting on the fact that I hadn't had time to get hold of Dropney to verify this guy's references.

"I've worked for celebrities before," he said. "I know with you people time is at a premium."

"I appreciate that." I handed him one of the cups of java. What I didn't appreciate was someone trying to blow smoke up my ass before I even gave him a preliminary explanation.

Giretti accepted the coffee and declined any additives. We sat down in a relatively isolated section.

"I like it black," he said. "My motto is to keep things as simple as possible." He reached in his pocket and removed a business card, shoving it across the table. It read *Alphonse Giretti, Private Investigator, Licensed, Bonded, and Insured in the State of New York*. His address and phone number followed.

"Your office is in Brooklyn?" I asked.

He nodded. "That's home base, but I go all over, as needed." He drank some coffee. "Now suppose you give me a rundown of your specific situation."

This was moving pretty fast, and I still wasn't sure I was making the right move.

"Before we get to that," I said, "what are your rates?"

"That depends on the type of job." He took a sip of his coffee. "My standard fee is two hundred fifty dollars an hour, plus expenses, with a guarantee of at least five days. Half in advance."

I gave a low whistle. "That's a lot more than Jim Rockford used to charge."

The corner of his lip turned upward into a crooked smile. "Yeah, I used to watch that show too, when I was a kid. But that was back in the seventies, and it was just on TV. That can be a far cry from real life sometimes." He took another sip from his cup, then added, "No offense intended."

"None taken," I said, wondering if he'd jacked up his rates just because he'd pegged me for some rich celebrity. Mentally calculating: two fifty an hour, at eight hours a day, times five days . . . A cool ten grand. That was a lot just for being a glorified babysitter.

"What I had in mind was more of a straight bodyguarding gig," I said. "You do that kind of stuff?"

"Sure." He set the cup down and used his right hand to pull open the lapel of his jacket. I could see the butt of a semiauto hanging under his left arm. "Beretta nine mil. Full mag with fifteen, plus one in the chamber. I'm ready for anything."

At least I was getting to see what I'd be paying for, if I hired him.

"So who's bothering you, Mr. Belzer?"

I had to figure out how much to tell him. I decided to play it close to the vest for the time being.

"I'm looking into a matter for a friend," I said. "A missing person."

His head cocked back slightly. "A missing person?"

I gave him a thumbnail sketch of the situation with Rudy, mentioning that I'd been interviewing a few people about his disappearance but leaving out certain pertinent details, like the letter and the list of four dead men. I added, "My questions seem to be making certain people a bit nervous. I'd prefer to have a professional watching my back as well as my personal assistant's."

"Yeah, I heard about Dr. Markovich disappearing," Giretti said. "I had it pegged for a carjacking gone sour. But you're making it sound more complicated."

"It is."

He considered this, looking down at his half-drained coffee on the table. "You know, I get the feeling there's more here that you're not telling me."

"There is. I still haven't made up my mind if I want to hire you yet."

"Well, let me tell you this," Giretti said, leaning forward. "I'm based in Brooklyn, so I know the Brighton Beach area like the back of my hand. And what you're describing is exactly the type of work I do for a living. For your two fifty an hour, I could be looking into this exclusively for you, and reporting back."

The offer sounded tempting. Why not let someone who knew what they were doing check into it? Plus it would take me and Kali out of the line of fire. And away from any flying knives.

Giretti picked up his cup and drained it. "Think about it. Total exclusivity, and complete privacy about what I find out. Plus, you don't have to worry if things get kind of rough. It's what I do." He set the cup down and gave me an askance look. "So, are we in business?"

"I thought the proper line was 'Trouble is my business.'"

"Like I said, it's what I do." He crushed the Styrofoam cup in his big fist.

"When can you start?"

"I can start tomorrow. Ask around, check with some of my street contacts and see what I can find out."

"I need to be involved in this," I said. Time was a precious commodity, and there was too much Kali and I had discovered to drop in favor of letting someone else start from scratch, regardless of how many street contacts he had. Plus, I still had to figure out the riddle. Rudy'd sent it to me, and I owed him that much. "However, all I'm looking for are some solid leads so we can go to the cops."

He pursed his lips and nodded with foregone assurance. "Absolutely. I used to be on the force. How about I call you in the morning and we meet for a late breakfast? I'll bring one of my standard contracts."

As we shook hands, I couldn't help thinking that maybe, just maybe, I'd finally made the right move. Perhaps we should have done this in the first place. Let a pro handle things. I wanted to call Kali and tell her, but that could wait till the morning. She'd approve, I was sure. This way, even if my buddy Buteyko came back, we'd at least have an armed backup standing there with us. So, I couldn't resist the temptation to do my Bogey to Claude Raines imitation from the end of *Casablanca* by saying, "Al, I think this is the beginning of a beautiful friendship."

# CHAPTER 19

Night shoots have a way of lasting a lot longer than everyone intends. This particular one had been due to wrap up by midnight, but we found ourselves doing take after take until three fifteen. How many times I repeated the same four or five lines of dialogue with the poignant gallows-humor punch line, I have no idea. But I was good at delivering those kind. Guess it's the Lenny Bruce in me. When Giretti's phone call woke me up at nine, I realized I'd been so tired I'd shut off the eight o'clock alarm and dozed off again. It had been a long time since I'd felt this worn-out and tired.

"You sound beat," Giretti said. "Don't tell me I woke you up. I thought we agreed on nine."

"Okay, I won't tell you," I said. "And we did agree on nine. My REM sleep just got in the way. Late night last night."

"We can make it later if you want."

As tempted as I was to hit the pillow again, I told him I'd meet him in ninety minutes at a place of his choosing. Depending on where he was and crosstown traffic patterns, that is.

"Right now I'm in my office in Brooklyn," he said.

Kali lived in Brooklyn. So did a lot of Russkies who lived in Brighton

Beach. We agreed on a little place called Henry's near Prospect Park. I called Kali's cell and told her to meet us there.

"You hired that dude?" she asked.

"Yeah, why?"

"I kind of figured we were doing pretty good ourselves, is all."

"Well, there's more to it than that. Another set of eyes and ears, another person asking the right questions. Plus, this guy does this for a living."

"But," she asked, "is his strength the strength of ten, because his heart is pure?"

"What the hell are you talking about?" It was too early in the morning for another riddle.

"I got bored last night and watched this old movie about the Knights of the Round Table."

"The guy's name is Giretti, not Lancelot," I said, wishing I had a cup of hot coffee.

"Actually, the line refers to Galahad."

"I don't care if it's about Sir Thanksalot." I struggled to my feet and stretched. "See you in Brooklyn."

After a quick shower and that much-anticipated cup of java, I got dressed. In my haste to get the hell out of there last night, I'd worn the sport jacket from wardrobe home. As I picked it up, I felt a trace of metal graze my fingers.

The damn remote mic. I'd worn that home too.

I smirked as I slipped on the jacket. It actually didn't look too much different than my regular wardrobe, except it was less expensive. For the show, I had to dress like a cop. I thought about unfastening the mic and leaving it on my dresser, but I left it in place. No sense taking a chance on forgetting it, and the probabilities of sending any residual electronic frequencies out to all the laptops around me was practically zero. I could return it later.

What would Franco say if he knew of my flagrant disregard for studio property? The mere thought of that brought a smile to my face.

But still, my forgetting I had the remote on bothered me slightly. It had been a long time since I'd done anything so remiss.

Perhaps I was more on edge than I thought.

I went down to meet my taxi. The driver looked totally preoccupied with his cell phone until I waved a fresh twenty under his nose. I imagine his reaction would have been about the same even if it had been a stale one.

"Yes, sir," he said, his white teeth looking like a commercial for Listerine Whitening Strips in contrast to his caramel skin.

I told him it was his tip if he got me to Prospect Park in time for my meet. He nodded and we took off like we'd been on a pit stop at a NASCAR track.

I figured Brooklyn was a good choice. This way I could introduce Giretti to Kali and possibly Anna, if the situation warranted it. Since I wanted him to be watching over them, he'd have to know what they looked like. He'd also have to know the whole story.

Where could I start?

He knew the search was basically for Rudy. Or what had happened to him. I'd have to bring him up to speed on the rest of it, including what had happened to Gustafson. He had a right to know that. Then, if he still wanted to put his ass on the line for two fifty an hour, plus expenses, I'd let him.


Giretti was waiting for me at the restaurant. When I walked in, he gave a small wave and we went to a booth near the back. It looked cozy and well away from the rest of the patrons. Not a bad spot. He motioned for me to sit across from him, evidently so he could face the door. But then, he'd said he was an ex-cop, so it was probably a habit born of necessity.

"Figured this would give us a modicum of privacy," he said.

I had to admit, the man seemed cautious and competent. The waitress came by and filled my cup with some heavenly-smelling coffee. I told her I was expecting someone and described Kali. She nodded, and left after filling Giretti's cup.

"I guess we'd better get business out of the way first," he said, reaching into his pocket. He withdrew some folded sheets of paper and set them on the table in front of me. "As I told you last night, this is one of my standard business contracts. I'll need you to look it over and sign it before I can officially start."

I unfolded the papers and began reading. It said pretty much everything we'd discussed last night, along with a very vague description of security and bodyguarding duties and hours. "This is pretty nonspecific."

"It's designed to be," he said. "Specific enough to delineate that I'm working for you in this matter, but vague enough to ensure we're not intruding on an official police investigation."

"Is that a no-no?"

He shrugged. "It depends. If I'm working for a lawyer, no. Or even a family member. But if I'm not mistaken, your relationship with Dr. Markovich is one of friendship only, correct?"

"It is."

He grunted and drank some coffee. "Then it's better for both of us not to mention specifics. And even though I wasn't actually under contract, I did some nosing around this morning down by Coney."

"And?"

"Basically, all I did was put the word out a little." He shrugged. "Maybe it'll turn up something solid I can look into further."

I felt a twinge of guilt. I should have mentioned all the risks last night. But I hadn't counted on his early morning start. "Look, Al, there's a little more to this than you know." I was about to say more when he pointed toward the door.

"Is that your friend?" he asked.

I turned around and saw Kali standing inside the front door scanning the crowd. She was dressed in a black skirt and jacket, with a white blouse. A delicate gold chain with a charm gleamed at the juncture of her neck. She looked about as comfortable as a baby lamb in a Greek meat market. I stood and waved. A smile lit up her face as she made her way toward us and slid in next to me. I noticed Giretti's eyes appraising her as she sat down.

"I was worried I'd missed you. Sorry I'm late," she said. "The traffic was murder."

"You drove?" Giretti asked.

"No, but the bus driver hit a couple of minor traffic jams."

"It's good to see someone making use of our public transportation system here in the Big Apple," Giretti said.

Buteyko's comment about Kali taking the subway came back to me like an elbow to the kidneys. I was going to have to lay things out for both of them, the sooner the better.

After brief introductions, I held my hand toward Kali and ended with, "This is one of the people I want you to protect."

"Protect?" Kali said. Her tone was as skeptical as she looked.

"That's one of the things I'm hiring him for," I said. "Plus, he's probably a lot more adept at asking the right people the right questions than we are."

Her eyes held mine for a moment, then looked away. "Okay, but I grew up here, in public housing, so I know a thing or two about being careful and protecting myself."

I remembered the rush of air by my face as Vasili's flat-bladed knife whisked by my nose, the rapid, trilling sound as it vibrated in the split wood. I needed to do my best to shelter her from that. Anna too.

I took out my pen and signed Giretti's contract, then shoved it back at him. He folded it and stuck it in his inside jacket pocket.

"Don't I get a copy of that?" I asked.

"Yeah, as soon as I get it notarized. I'll run one off later on today for you."

Kali frowned. "Doesn't the notary have to witness the signature?"

He smirked. Oil and water, these two. "Only when it's done strictly by the book," he said. "But you're hiring me to operate by a different book, right? The book of fast results?"

"Fast and loose?" Kali asked.

Like I said, oil and water.

Giretti sighed. "Okay, ordinarily that is how it works, but she'll witness mine. It saves time. And that's what we want, right? Less money for you that way."

It bothered me a little bit but not enough to make an issue out of it.

We needed to move on this thing, and having Giretti to run interference put somebody professional between Kali, me, and Buteyko. "Okay, both of you need to listen while I give you my take on the big picture."

Over a nice breakfast of scrambled eggs and toast all around, I went into a quick but thorough summation of just about everything that had happened in the past week, up to and including my little tête-à-tête with the two rejects from a bad James Bond movie. "Plus," I added, "Buteyko mentioned that his buddy Vasili was ex-Spetsnaz. And he had the knife to prove it."

"Spetsnaz?" Giretti said. "Shit, those guys are like our Green Berets."

"I think theirs are black," I said, and regretted the way it sounded. The last thing I wanted to do now was to come off as flip and have this guy back out because he felt I wasn't taking things seriously. The risks probably outweighed the benefits, that was for sure.

"They are black." His nostrils flared slightly and he took another long drink of coffee, as if contemplating something.

"Is that going to be a problem?" I asked.

He smirked and shook his head. "No, not at all. I appreciate your concern, and your honesty. But like I said, I spent quite a few years on the job, so I'm used to risky situations."

"You were a cop?" Kali asked.

"I was."

"Where'd you work when you were on the force?" I asked.

"The one-eight mostly. I started out in patrol, then went to vice and narcotics."

"Oh, really?" Kali smiled and leaned forward. "How long were you on the force?"

Giretti scrunched his lips. "About seventeen years."

"Didn't you want to retire with your twenty?" she asked.

Giretti shrugged. "Let's just say I got tired of working in the asshole of the city, giving it, pardon the expression, a periodic NYPD blue enema. I figured I could make better money working for myself."

"Plus," I said, "you don't have to worry about getting an asshole for a boss, right?"

That brought a laugh all around. I was going to have to think about getting the stand-up routine back in shape.

"All right," he said. "Let's figure out our next move, shall we?" He placed his elbows on the table and leaned forward. It creaked under the bulk of his massive upper body. "Give me what you got on this Buteyko guy and I'll do some checking."

I wrote down the info on the sheet of paper he gave me.

"Okay," he said, looking it over when I'd finished. "Now, when's the next time you two have to report in to work?"

"I've actually got a day off," I said. "We were burning the midnight oil pretty late last night."

"If he's off, I'm off," Kali said. She was trying to sound nonchalant, but her tone told me something was bothering her.

"Good," Giretti said. "That'll give me a little time to do some follow-up questioning in Brighton Beach."

Before we could discuss any further plans, my cell phone rang. I glanced at the screen. New York area code, unfamiliar number. Looked like a cell. I pressed the button and answered it.

"Rich?"

I recognized the voice right away. "How goes the reporting business?"

"Depends on who you ask," he said, then laughed. I guess it was his cue to let me know he'd made a joke. I shot him a quick chuckle as a reward.

"Sorry to bother you," he said, "but I was just checking to see if you got hold of that PI I recommended."

"I did. And I'm with him now."

"Great. Uh, make sure you tell him I recommended him, okay?"

I looked over at Giretti. "Duncan Dropney recommended you to me."

Giretti's eyes narrowed. He nodded and picked up his coffee cup.

"Mission accomplished," I said. "You have something else you wanted to talk about?"

"Yeah, I'm up in Albany covering that train wreck," he said. "Looks like it might turn into a haz-mat situation."

"All right," I said slowly, but resisted the temptation to ask what that had to do with the price of butter in Poughkeepsie.

"I guess that's more than you need to know. Kind of dumb telling you, huh?"

I grinned and remained silent. Never overlook an opportunity to keep your mouth shut, I always say. Of course, I seldom follow my own advice.

"Anyway," Dropney continued, "I didn't want you to think I forgot about what you asked me."

So much had happened, I had actually forgotten exactly what I'd asked Dropney to check on. "I know better than that. What did you find out?"

"Well, I managed to get hold of Arnie's editor and asked a few questions about exactly what he was working on when he died."

"Great." I took out my pen and spread a napkin on the table to take notes.

"It turns out he wasn't doing too much," Dropney said. "He was actually on a sabbatical trying to finish this book he was working on."

"The one about the Russian navy?"

"That's what's confusing," Dropney said. "His editor told me it was about the Black Sea."

"The Black Sea? Don't the Russians have a fleet there?" I asked.

"I don't know. Maybe. I mean, it's over by Russia, ain't it?"

I made a mental note to check on that.

"Regardless," Dropney said, "I also asked about the whereabouts of his manuscript."

It was obvious this guy wasn't the fastest keyboard in the East. No wonder his editor had sent him upstate to cover a train wreck. He probably caused enough of them around here on his own. "And what did he say about the manuscript?"

"Seems Arnie mentioned he had the whole thing on the hard drive of his laptop."

Ah, I thought. A bright spot on a fog-draped shore. "Any chance of finding it?"

"Slim and none," Dropney said. "And slim left town. It was stolen."

"When?"

"When he died. Somebody took it off him right there on the damn street." His laugh was bitter. "You got to love New York, don't ya?"

I thanked him and promised to keep him in the loop. The loop of what, I didn't say, but he had other things occupying his one-track mind at the moment.

"So what's new with Dropney?" Giretti asked. "Off on an assignment, I take it?"

"Not much of one. They've got him exiled temporarily to upstate."

"What was all that talk about the Russian navy and the Black Sea? Am I going to have to take them on, in addition to the Spetsnaz?" He grinned.

It was time to get back to the basics. I smoothed out another napkin and began to chart the things we'd found out so far. "My old high school algebra teacher, Miss Forester, used to tell us, always look for the common denominator. Only in this case, I'm not even sure what the equation is."

I started writing on the napkin: Four disparate deaths, all listed as natural but now highly suspect. Russian *mafiya*, diamonds, a laser company, a gemologist, and a dead diamond company executive.

"Plus," I said, putting the final touches on my scribblings, "a very shady Russkie named Nikolai Buteyko, and a very huge ex-Spetsnaz thug."

"You know," Giretti said, "the more I hear about this Russian Special Forces dude, the less I like it."

I suddenly got worried that he was going to back out after all. But now we'd signed a contract. "Meaning?"

"Meaning, you two better be real careful," he said. "I'll handle things from here. I get paid to take the risks and to protect you two."

"That's reassuring," I said. "And I appreciate it. There's also another person I'd like you to keep an eye on."

Giretti raised his eyebrows.

I told him about Anna, and where she worked. "So far, she's been keeping a low profile, and I don't think she's been threatened at all. But I want to make sure she stays out of harm's way."

Giretti compressed his lips, like he was suppressing a bad case of flatulence. "Okay, I'll need to get a look at her, so call her and find out when she's due in at the restaurant. I'll stop by there." He paused and ran his big fingers over the brackets of his mouth. "This is getting a little bigger than just a simple bodyguarding job, you know."

I grinned. "Which is why you're getting paid the big bucks."

"Big bucks or no," he said, "I might need to call in some other operatives to assure coverage of all the different parties."

I saw where he was going. "And that'll be extra?"

"If it is, it'll come under the heading of related expenses," he said. "Let me check things out first and I'll let you know on that."

I considered this. I had hit the man with a lot this morning. "Okay. Sounds fair."

"Plus, the more you tell me about this," he said, "the more I have to believe that maybe Dr. Markovich was involved in something that wasn't aboveboard."

His words hit me like rabbit punches. Rudy involved with the *mafiya*? Still, it wasn't something that I hadn't already thought of. I had just conveniently forgotten for a while.

Giretti looked at me. "You still want me to see what I can find out?"

I glanced downward momentarily, then met his gaze. "I do. This is something that I have to follow to its conclusion, whether it's pretty or not."

"One more thing." Giretti held up an open hand, flailing it for emphasis with each word when he started talking. "Just let me make it clear that if you want me to handle this, nobody is to do any further investigating unless I'm with them. *Capisce*?"

"Sounds good." Out of the corner of my eye, I saw Kali stiffen slightly.

Giretti's cell phone rang, and he answered it. "Yeah, hold on, you're breaking up." He looked at us. "I'll be back in a minute."

He stood and began walking toward the front door, talking as he went.

Kali watched him go, then turned to me and asked, "You already hired the dude, right?"

I nodded.

She shook her head.

"What?" I asked.

She did an abbreviated version of her irritated-black-girl head waggle. "I just don't like him much, that's all."

I threw my hands up. "Why?"

"You see the way he kept looking down at my ti—my breasts?"

After she said that, I couldn't help but steal a glance downward myself, before I grinned. "Well, that probably makes him a card-carrying member of the heterosexual male population of New York City, and perhaps a bit of a chauvinist, but remember, I'm hiring him to watch our backs as well as our fronts." Actually, while Moody the lizard's surreptitious glances had the air of creeping perversion, for some reason Giretti's darting eyes hadn't set off any alarm bells for me.

"Ha ha," she said. "I'm not saying to fire him, but I just wish we could keep looking into things ourselves, without some big guinea muscling his way in and taking everything over."

Oh, my God, I thought. She's jealous.

I laughed. "Don't worry, I still value all the investigative work you've done and everything you've found out."

"Good," she said, " 'cause I found out something else. I was holding back telling you in front of the Godfather."

"Tell me now," I said, imitating Brando's husky yet nasal Don Corleone voice, "or I'll have to make you an offer you can't refuse."

"That's another reason why I don't like Giretti much. The way he dresses, it's like he's been watching that movie way too much."

"You wouldn't say that if he looked more like Al Pacino."

"Whatever. Now you ready for something really good?"

"Absolutely."

She looked around and leaned her head closer. "I did some checking on that Crystal Imaging joint, Glenn Perry's last place of employment. Went out of business right after his death. You remember what it used to specialize in?"

"Yeah, etching photographic images in blocks of crystal."

Her lips rose upward in a triumphant Mona Lisa smile. "With a laser."

"Right. With a laser."

"Well, lasers have to be registered with the government."

"I wonder if James Bond knows about that."

"And," she said, "they're also used to etch serial numbers and countries of origin on diamonds. See the connection?"

"Hot damn." Suddenly the puzzle was taking shape. I still didn't have all of it, but this was a major chunk. It tightened the string tying the four dead men together. "If the Russian *mafiya* were involved in some sort of diamond-smuggling scheme, and they were using the laser to put false ID numbers on blood diamonds, it would explain a lot."

"You got that right."

But as I pulled the string tighter with my extrapolations, it began to sag instead. "But what the hell did a reporter writing about the Russian navy in the Black Sea have to do with it?"

Kali bit her lower lip thoughtfully.

"And the damn fight ticket Rudy sent me," I said. "What else did Rudy have to do with all of it?"

I felt Kali's slight kick under the table as Giretti walked back and sat down.

"Sorry about that," he said. "Reception is lousy in here for me."

I thought about withholding what Kali had just told me but couldn't see how that would help. If I wanted this guy to do the work, I had to lay it all out for him. Otherwise, I'd be paying him to uncover things we already knew. I gave Giretti a quick rundown about our laser theory, giving Kali the credit for coming up with it.

"Interesting," he said, but his expression said anything but. "I'll have to check into that as well." He asked if we needed an escort anywhere.

"I think we're good right now." I could almost feel Kali's disapproving aura hovering next to me. Giretti stood and shook our hands. I noticed that his eyes once again strayed downward as he stood over her, but hell, her blouse was open one too many buttons. Besides, this was New York, and ogling pretty girls never went out of style. After admonishing us one more time not to try investigating on our own, he left. I asked if she wanted anything else to eat and she shook her head. Her glum expression made me feel bad.

"So we're cool with Giretti, then?"

She scrunched her lips together but nodded. "Yeah, I guess so, but I wish you wouldn't have told him what I found out about the lasers."

"Look, if he's going to be investigating for us, we can't very well leave him out of the equation, can we?"

"I guess not. But he mentioned he used to be a cop in the Eighteenth Precinct, right? I'm going to ask my brother-in-law about him."

"Good," I said. "Come on. We've got a couple of places to go."

"Where's that?"

"The nearest Duane Reade, for one," I said. "So you can get what you need to take a shower."

"Huh? You saying I need one?"

"No, but you will," I said. "I'm going to take you for some martial arts lessons."

"Martial what?" Her dark eyes rolled, like she was making a calculation. "That kung fu stuff you know?"

"Right. The place specializes in a very eclectic curriculum. You'll love it."

"Like, am I going to have to take out some big, badass black beret dude?" she asked.

"Let's just say," I said, picking up the check as I urged her out of the booth, "that fortune favors the prepared mind."

# CHAPTER 20

We took a cab over to Jimmy Lee's *dojang* and I introduced him to Kali. Jimmy smiled and called his assistant, a very pretty Chinese girl named Soon Li, to help Kali pick out a *gi*. "The styles are pretty much variations on basic white or black," Soon Li said as they walked away. I figured the clothes excursion would buy me at least fifteen extra minutes, but rather than use it to get changed myself, I let my mind continue to ruminate over the puzzle and what Giretti had said about Rudy. It was as if I could almost see it now, like looking at an emerging island through a blanket of fog. I just hoped it didn't turn out to be an iceberg.

After putting Kali in a beginner's class with Soon Li showing her some of the basics, Jimmy came sauntering over to the striking board. It was your basic two-by-four, secured and braced perpendicular to the floor, and wrapped with heavy ropes at the top end. It toughens the hell out of your hands, when it doesn't cut the shit out of them. Even though I was still in street clothes, I was practicing my ridge hand against it.

"Conditioning your hands, I see?" he said.

"Working on it." I sent another ridge hand smacking into the heavy coil of rope.

"I appreciate you bringing me another student." There was something about his demeanor that looked a bit askew. First Kali and now Jimmy. It seemed like I couldn't make a move today without pissing somebody off.

"Don't mention it," I said. "What's bugging you?"

"Your friend, Kali," he said. "She mentioned that you'd hired a bodyguard. Some dude named Giretti."

I nodded. "Just temporarily."

"Aw, come on, Belz. A bodyguard?" He canted his head and shot me a perplexed expression. "Are you saying I'm not teaching you the right techniques?"

"Not at all, but there's this big, mean guy with a throwing knife," I said. "And I still haven't mastered that technique where you catch it with both palms as it's flying through the air."

Jimmy laughed. "You been watching too many reruns of that old *Kung Fu* TV show."

"Rumor has it," I said, "that David Carradine used to catch them in his teeth."

"Rumor also has it that he didn't know squat about kung fu. Plus, they say Chuck Norris kicked his ass on the set of *Lone Wolf McQuade* too."

"Ah, yes, one of my all-time favorite flicks," I said. I hit the board again. "Look, I'm a bit concerned about some local badasses and wanted Kali to get some of the basics."

"Okay." Jimmy nodded thoughtfully. "That settles it. Today we're doing some knife defenses." He went to the equipment cabinet and removed a rubber knife and a green water pistol. "Plus more squirt gun techniques. Get ready."

Sammo Lee, who'd apparently been listening, walked over and looked at the water pistol. He was carrying a foot-high stack of VHS tapes, which he carefully set down by the side of the mat.

"Remember, those who study the past will know the future," he said.

Jimmy and I exchanged glances. "I give up," I said. "Which movie is that from?"

The old man smiled. "From one of my greatest, *Shaolin Assassin*. I have brought copy for you. Remind me later." He walked toward the locker room.

We both looked down at the stack he'd left behind. "I guess it wasn't one of these, then?" I asked.

Jimmy laughed. "Just what we need. More of my grandfather's Bushido wisdom."

"Bushido?" I said. "Isn't that Japanese?"

Jimmy shrugged. "Yeah, but what the hell do I know. I was born in Brooklyn. Besides, you know me. I borrow from all the arts, as long as it works."

I went to my regular locker in the men's dressing room. As I slipped out of my jacket, I heard the clunk of metal hitting the locker. Anna's pendant. I was carrying that one around as faithfully as Elvis wearing a cross and the Star of David. Apparently he didn't want to take any chances if the angels came calling. Stacking the odds, just like my keeping the remote fastened to my collar so I wouldn't keep forgetting it. I realized I needed to call Anna and let her know about Giretti, in case he stopped by her restaurant. I took out my cell and dialed her number. I needed to tell her about Gustafson too.

Her voice sounded breathy and warm when she answered, "Hello, Richard." Sort of like a Russian version of Marilyn Monroe.

That caller ID was taking the surprise out of everything. After a quick exchange of amenities, I told her about Giretti.

"I do not understand," she said. "Who is this man?"

"He's what we call a private detective. He's like a cop but works only for his client. In this case, me."

"And he is going to find my father?"

"Among other things," I said. "He's based in Brooklyn, and he's got a lot of experience. I also want him to keep an eye on you and Kali in case this thing turns ugly."

"Ugly? I do not understand."

I told her about Gustafson's untimely demise. She was silent for a time, then asked, "And this is related to my father being gone?"

"I don't know," I said. "Maybe."

"But this Gustafson, he was an awful man, no?"

"That's a pretty accurate description, but just in case, this guy will be watching over us." I sighed, thinking I should have waited to explain this in person. "Look, Anna, I have to go. If Mr. Giretti shows up at your restaurant, you can call me if you have any questions or need me to verify anything. But like I said, he works for us."

I heard her laugh. "Trust, but verify. An old American saying, yes?"

"Right," I said. After a few more reassurances, I hung up and put the phone into the locker.

When I turned around, I saw Sammo standing a few feet away, watching me with his customary mixture of serenity and amusement. He bowed and I instinctively bowed back. It's hard not to.

"*Sifu,*" I said. "I didn't hear you come up."

He immediately retracted into a modified horse stance and waved his left hand out in front of him with a theatrical exaggeration that let me know he was joking.

"A Shaolin monk can walk through walls," he said. "Looked for, he cannot be seen, listened for, he cannot be heard, touched, he cannot be felt." After straightening up, he squinted as he looked at me. "You know what that from?"

"If I had to venture a guess," I said, "I'd say from one of your movies."

He shook his head with a disgusted expression. "*Kung Fu* TV show. David Carradine." Another disgusted shake. "My friend Bruce Lee, Little Dragon, come up with idea for that show. Then, just like Charlie Chan, your Hollywood friends steal it and give role of Chinese Shaolin to another round-eye."

"Those weren't my friends," I said, "and sometimes things don't turn out the way they should."

Sammo grinned. "That's okay. Bruce went back to Hong Kong and started making kung fu movies. Gave me and Jackie Chan small parts and pretty soon we stars too." He laughed. "Broke Jackie's nose when we all making *Enter the Dragon*. Lots of good time." He held up a cardboard box with an old VHS tape inside. The outer portion of the carton was brightly colored with Chinese characters and wicked-looking paintings of Sammo engaged in mortal combat with a host of foes. "*Shaolin Assassin*. My best, best movie. You got VHS machine?"

I said I did, and he thrust the tape toward me.

"Put it in locker. Take home. Watch." He kept nodding in agreement with what he was telling me. I accepted the tape with another bow and said I'd return it to him shortly. I silently figured I could probably fast-forward through a portion of it just to say I watched it. I thought about his last aphorism. "*Sifu,* I didn't understand the significance of what you said before."

"Before? When?"

"A little while ago. About looking to the past to know the future. Why were you telling me that?"

The old man studied me and asked if I was still on my quest.

"Yes," I said, "in a manner of speaking."

He nodded. "It will soon be over. Your chi is gathering strength." His hand shot out and his index finger began pecking the picture on the back of the VHS package, which pictured a formidable young Sammo in a business suit. "You watch this one, you understand. And give it back, okay?"

"Is it in Chinese?"

"Yeah, and it's got some great lines." Sammo flashed his familiar mock grin as he did his John Wayne imitation again. "Sometimes the answer come when you least expect it, pahdiner."

I smiled and placed the tape inside the locker before closing it and twisting the key in the lock. When I turned, he was still there, this time his expression serious. The epicanthic folds over his brown eyes made them look almost hooded. "You look troubled."

He was right. When Giretti had said that Rudy had to be "involved" in the whole mess, it had slapped me in the face. It wasn't something I hadn't considered myself, on some level, but it wasn't something I wanted to hear either. But deep down I already knew it. An inconvenient truth, as Al Gore was fond of reminding us. Like hearing your parents argue for the first time when you were a kid. Your first clue that maybe all wasn't idyllic in the world.

But I also remembered what Larkins had said about the Russian *ma-fiya: The mafiya operates by its own code of dishonor. Ain't nothing the least bit romantic about it.* Suppose they threatened his family. Could he be blamed for going along with whatever they wanted? And the way things were looking, with the four unrelated, relatively young men who'd all died of natural causes on different days, at different times, that most likely meant falsifying the autopsy reports. But if that was the case, how had they really died? And why?

Sammo placed a calming hand on my shoulder. "Belzer-*san*, remember what I said about seeking enlightenment."

I thought for a moment, then silently thanked my photographic, or in this case, phonographic, memory. "Sometimes you have to steal the fortune out of the other guy's cookie?"

He laughed. "Exactly." He gave my shoulder two quick pats and was gone, leaving me to banish my own ghosts before I went out to the *dojang* floor.

Kali threw a punch and then a snapping front kick into the big curved pad that Soon Li was holding. Her kick looked pretty good for her first workout. I walked over and saw Soon Li urging her to do it again. Kali did, with such force it knocked the smaller girl back a step.

"Very good," I said. "You must have done this before."

"Reminds me of a guy I used to go out with." The breathless quality of the words told me she was working hard.

"Oh, really? Was he into the martial arts?"

"No," she said, delivering another kick. "But he pissed me off once too often."

"Belz," Jimmy called from the other side of the mat. He held up the plastic weapons. "Which one you want to work on first?"

I thought of Vasili throwing the knife and asked what defense he could show me for that.

Jimmy scratched his head. "Maybe get out of the way?"

"Cogent advice. I'll keep it in mind."

"No, seriously, Belz, the main thing to remember when confronting somebody with a knife is distance." He assumed a crouched stance with the knife in front of him. "Okay, now we're about ten feet away, right?"

"Give or take an inch or two."

"So, would you say you're at a safe range for avoiding an attack?"

"Not really." My police friends had shown me their knife attack tape so many times that I knew the distance was at least twenty feet, and that was only if you had a gun to draw.

"Right," Jimmy said. He reiterated that there was no safe distance if you weren't armed. "But, in case you find yourself in close quarters, with no place to run, I have a few techniques."

He tossed me the knife and told me to hold it in a threatening manner and advance on him. I did, holding the knife like a street thug, ready to slice and cut. When I got almost within arm's reach, Jimmy's right leg swung up, catching my forearm. The knife went flying from my hand.

"Crescent kick," he said. "It's a great movie technique from one of my grandfather's old movies, but dangerous in real life because you run the risk of getting your leg sliced open."

"You're not giving me much to look forward to," I said.

"This one's a little better."

Next he showed me a scissoring move with his hands, catching my outstretched knife hand with a simultaneous crisscrossing blow to my inner wrist and the back of my hand. Once again, the knife went flying. He showed me a few more and let me try them, reiterating how they were only to be used as a last resort.

"And once you disarm your opponent, make sure you follow up with another striking technique." He brought the heel of his hand up toward my face, stopping just short of my chin, stepped to the side, and simulated a low front kick to my groin. "See what I mean?"

I looked down at his foot, still hovering dangerously close. "I appreciate your restraint."

"When you're at close quarters against a knife, unless you can act fast, it's almost a certainty you're going to get cut."

"I usually like to avoid that," I said. "Even when I'm shaving."

"Okay, now we'll use the squirt gun." He picked it up and held it out toward my chest. "You remember that wrist double-back technique I showed you last time?"

I nodded and he told me to do it. It's basically using your left hand to push the assailant's gun hand (usually the right) away as you twist your body out of the line of fire. You then bring your right hand upward, grabbing the bottom of the assailant's gun hand and pivot, forcing the weapon back toward him and ultimately out of his grip. Jimmy told me to execute it again, only in slow motion. When I got to the last part, he said, "Freeze."

I did.

"Now," he said, "look down where the gun is pointing."

I did and saw it was right under my head. He punctuated his lesson by squirting me in the face. Apparently Kali and Soon Li had ceased their workout to watch, because I heard a chorus of feminine laughter.

"And for my next trick," I said, wiping off my wet cheeks, "I'll expel the colored water out through my nostrils."

"What I wanted to show you, Belz, is that you have to make sure you bear down enough on the wristlock to make sure it points back at your opponent's head, not yours."

I snorted like a frustrated horse. Some of the water had actually gone up my nose and I would have killed for a tissue at that moment.

"Good thing these things don't carry a lethal load," I said. "Like acid."

"You need to watch my grandfather's movie." He pointed to the stack of tapes still sitting by the edge of the mat. "He give you *Shaolin Assassin?*"

"It's in my locker."

"Good. It was made during the seventies, you know, back when the spy craze and the Cold War were hip."

"Back when all we had to worry about were the godless Commies trying to take over the world to liberate the proletariat," I said. He handed me a paper towel and I blew my nose. "Compared to these al-Qaida assholes, the Soviets were a bunch of pussycats."

"Actually," Jimmy said, "they could be kind of ingenious too. Just like in my grandfather's movie where they use squirt guns for assassinations."

"Lethal squirt guns? Isn't that what I was worried about before?"

Jimmy laughed. "My grandfather will tell you it's all based on fact."

"Assassinations? What did they have in them?"

"Some kind of poison," Jimmy said. "Made it look like a heart attack. They wouldn't have discovered them at all if this one dude hadn't defected with one of the squirt guns."

A heart attack. The lightbulb went off over my head. Four relatively young men, all collapsing on the streets of New York, all of their deaths apparent heart attacks.

Jimmy looked perplexed. He must have noticed the look of enlightenment spreading across my face. "What's up? You look like you just figured out the secret of how to win the lottery."

"Maybe I have," I said. "I think the Russian mobsters used that same technique to murder at least four people here in New York."

"Good for the movies or your TV show, maybe," Jimmy said, his face scrunching into a skeptical expression. "But wouldn't the poison show up in an autopsy? I mean, this ain't exactly nineteen-seventies Europe."

Not if they coerced the medical examiner into signing death certificates listing natural causes, I thought. I let Jimmy's question go unanswered.

Once again, I hated to think that Rudy had falsified the cause of death on his reports, but who knew what pressures they must have exerted on him. Family wasn't off limits to these *mafiya* creeps. Maybe that was why he'd been reticent to openly acknowledge Anna as his daughter. Why give them another target? It also could explain his abrupt resignation from his post. He must have gotten tired of being forced to do their dirty work. Or maybe they ordered him to do something he absolutely wouldn't do—a line he would not cross. With the pieces of the big picture almost all in place now, the riddle wrapped in the mystery and stuffed inside the enigma had mostly come unraveled.

All except for the torn fight ticket and the cryptic message, *Tried and true, Four of a kind. Nyet five.*

When I had the answer to that one, I'd have the puzzle solved.

# CHAPTER 21

There's nothing like a good kung fu workout to get the mental juices flowing. After I'd been shot in the face by the squirt gun at least half a dozen more times, to the delight of Kali and Soon Li, I finally started to get the timing down and was able to rip or twist the gun out of Jimmy's hand with the aplomb of an Israeli commando. Upon my accomplishing it the last time, he asked if I thought I had it down now.

"Not quite," I said, and raised the gun and squirted him in the face. Payback.

He laughed as he wiped his face and said, "I was wondering when you were going to figure that out. Actually, it makes good street combat sense. Use your opponent's weapon against him if you have the chance."

"In that case—" I squirted him again.

Since I figured that Kali would naturally take twice as long as I would showering and getting dressed, I skipped my usual turn in the sauna and limited my time under the shower to a quick eight and a half minutes. When I was done, I asked Soon Li if I could use the computer in their office.

"Sure thing, Belz," she said, leaning close and whispering, "the password is *Jeet Kune Do*."

Way of the intercepting fist, I thought. Hopefully, I could get a few cyber punches in. I thanked her and made a beeline for the office. Jimmy was busy teaching his early-afternoon class, so the room was empty. I sat down behind his desk and flipped on his computer. After a few deft keystrokes, I was on the Internet and Googling "Soviet assassination techniques of the seventies." The search engine gave me a whole list of sites. I was going to have to thank Al Gore someday for inventing all this.

The first thing I did was to verify that the Soviets did, in fact, use lethal squirt guns filled with a combination of cyanide and sodium nitrate. Sprayed in the victim's face, the liquid would evaporate, leaving the doctors to conclude it was a heart attack. Very effective. Very low-key. Especially now, with all the attention from the messy and totally traceable poisonings in London using dioxin and polonium-210. Who was going to take notice of one more nice, quiet, sodium-cyanide-induced heart attack in the Big Apple? Plus, it was bound to be overlooked in Manhattan, so long as they had Rudy to cover for them.

Poor Rudy. But why the hell didn't he tell me? And why send me the letter?

I blew out a slow breath and tried to put it together one more time.

What was it Larkins had said about the Cold War ending? *A lot of these KGB and military guys realized they could make a hell of a lot more rubles acting as free agents.* So suppose the former head of the KGB, who happened to be president and now super prime minister of the new Russia, needed an increase in his cash flow for some political reasons . . . The old prez, Boris Yeltsin, had supposedly cashed in some diamonds to finance his reelection bid.

With the big mines in Siberia like Mir maybe getting played out, and the artificially produced diamonds now more easily identified, they couldn't use that trick again. But they had plenty of AK-47s to trade in Sierra Leone or Angola or one of the other African hotbeds for some quick conflict diamonds when their president needed some extra money. And the Russkie mobsters found a way to get around the Kimberley Process by putting on false labeling with their "registered laser," which satisfied the KPCS (Kimberley Process Certification Scheme). And once the dirty deeds were done under the expert eye of craftsman Joshua Spaulding, it was best to tidy up. Dead men tell no tales, in English or Russian. So good old Wladimir has his KGB, or the FSB now, reach into their retro bag of tricks and give the Russian mobsters in New York an old tried-and-true squirt gun weapon to accomplish their task. And as insurance, they revisit their old friend Rudy Markovich, Russian immigrant from the Soviet days and dedicated public servant working for the City of New York in the ME's office.

I heard a knock on the door and turned to see Kali standing there holding the black gym bag I'd bought her.

"Hi," she said. "Soon Li told me you were in here."

"I think I've peeled away most of the conundrum. Almost got it all." I gave her a quick rundown of my theory. When I was finished, she raised her eyebrows.

"It does sound plausible. I wish I were writing this up for the *Times*."

"Maybe you will," I said.

"One thing, though. Putin was reelected in what, two thousand four, same as Bush, right?"

"And Dubya promised him Florida too. He probably gave him more tips on stealing elections when he had him over to Kenne*bum*port last year."

She smiled. "But didn't the first deaths on our list happen in two thousand five?"

"Oh-five through oh-seven," I said, "the last of which was Arnie Wassler, the reporter."

"Working on his book about the Russian navy."

"Or the Black Sea, depending on whom you ask."

I think we both thought of it at the same time. I swiveled back to the computer and typed "Russian Navy (Black Sea)" into the slot and hit the search button. The site came back with a bunch of listings, which after a minute gave me the information we were looking for. The Russian navy did have a base on the Black Sea, but it wasn't in Russia. It was in Crimea.

It suddenly felt like cold fingers were dancing up the back of my neck.

Alexi's words about going back to his homeland, Ukraine, and running for office. *They tried to steal it back from us. Poisoned Yushchenko, but still could not succeed.*

He'd said something else too. Something about *freedom for the people of Crimea.* Crimea, on the southern edge of Ukraine, bordering the Black Sea.

Dropney's mention of the Black Sea fleet tiptoed along the edge of my memory.

"I've got a hunch about that Black Sea connection," I said, pointing to the screen.

After a bit more reading, I found mention of a movement in Ukraine to grant independence to Crimea, where the largest seaport on the Black Sea is located. The Putin administration had been threatening that it would not tolerate the loss of such an important strategic port. Sort of like Reagan woofing back in the midseventies about giving up the Panama Canal.

My guess was that base would be very important to the new Russian navy. Without it, they'd pretty much be cut off from easy access to the Aegean and Mediterranean seas. A bunch of orange Ukrainians running around spreading talk about freedom and democracy would be enough to make an old ex-KGB Communist shudder. Maybe that's why Putin or the Russian government needed the cash—to try to buy the Ukrainian parliamentary elections. Putin had already tried that with the presidential one back in '04 and had even given the rightful winner an acid-based facial. The attack had caused a lot of notoriety, so this time they'd want to go more low-key. And they'd also want to put away a nosy reporter who was calling attention to the issue right around the time of the next election. Or maybe Wassler had caught on to the diamond connection and was going to put that inference in his new book. Either way, instead of a Pulitzer, all he got was a sodium cyanide cocktail. Then they leaned on Rudy to once again mark it down as a heart attack. That made four . . . *Tried and true, Four of a kind. Nyet five.* And maybe they told him who number five was going to be . . .

The line Rudy wouldn't cross. And suddenly I knew what that was.

Poor Gustafson, I thought, finding myself almost feeling sorry for the dead schmuck. He was sitting on the biggest conspiracy case of his deluded little career, and he didn't even know it. I scrawled Rudy's name down on a piece of notebook paper beside Jimmy's computer.

"I think we've found the common denominator," I said, pointing to it.

"Your friend Rudy," Kali said. "But the note said something about not wanting it to become five, right? Who was the next intended victim?"

"Somebody that Rudy didn't want to see die," I said. "Somebody who'd been making rumbles about quitting his boxing career and serving the freedom movement in his native Ukraine—the same Ukraine that was talking about granting independence to Crimea, the host site of the Russians' Black Sea fleet, and their main port and gateway to the Atlantic via the Mediterranean Sea. And maybe that's what he was trying to tell me with the torn fight ticket . . ."

"That big boxer guy you know?" she asked.

"Yeah," I said. "Prospective Ukrainian political candidate Alexi Zotkin."

Just then my cell phone rang. I glanced at it but didn't recognize the number.

"Hello," I said, keeping my voice low and cautious.

"Belz? It's Giretti. I'm in Brighton Beach." I could sense the tension in his voice.

"You got something?"

"Maybe," he said. "I might have a line on your pal Markovich. Some guy's claiming he knows where he's being held."

"You mean Rudy's still alive?"

"Maybe. I want to go talk to this informant and see if he's real or just blowing smoke up my ass," Giretti said. "Then I'm going to the cops."

I felt a shiver of anticipation. "How will you know if he's telling the truth?"

"That's the tricky part. I know next to nothing about Markovich. What I need is your expertise to decipher if what he's saying is bullshit or the real deal. You up for that?"

"Count me in," I said.

"This also could run into another expense, depending on how much he wants for the info. I figured I'd be up front with you on that."

"Not a problem."

"I was hoping you'd say that." Giretti's voice sounded supremely confident. "I got a hunch this might pan out. Where you at? I'll swing by and pick you up."

# CHAPTER 22

After giving him my location, I hung up and briefed Kali.

"So where we going?" she asked.

"I'm going with Giretti. You're going home."

"No way," she said. "Like I told you before, you're in, I'm in. That's the deal."

"Kali, look—"

"No, Belz, you look." Her head began the waggle again. "I've been with you in this from the beginning. My job depends on keeping you out of trouble, and I can't very well do that if I'm sitting at home while you're traipsing around the city alone, can I?"

"I won't be alone. I'll have Giretti with me."

"Mr. Godfather himself?" she said. "I thought the reason you hired him was to take the risks for us."

"It was."

"Well, then, if he's gonna be taking them, it won't hurt if I tag along, will it? And there'll be two of us to evaluate this snitch's story. I'm real good at separating the cream from the bullshit."

I threw up my hands. "I'm just worried about you getting hurt, that's all."

"And I'm worried about the same thing. For both of us. Besides, if you say no, I'll just hop in a taxi and follow you."

I blew out a slow breath and snuck a look around for Jimmy. He was still engrossed in teaching the class, so I took that as carte blanche for peeking in his desk drawer to see if he had any gum or mints. I needed something to sink my teeth into. I found an open package of Tic Tacs and shook a few out, then offered them to Kali.

She shook her head, giving me the hard stare.

"All right," I said. "You can come. But we follow Giretti's lead, and if it looks dangerous, you boogie, understood?"

Once again she smiled that familiar triumphant Mona Lisa smile that women the world over are so fond of showing when they've won. "I knew you wouldn't be letting all these fine kung fu lessons go to waste."

While we were waiting, I called Anna just to prepare her that I might have some news for her soon.

"What do you mean?" she asked. "You have found my father, yes?"

"No," I said, trying to keep my words vague, not wanting to get her hopes up. I still had to figure out how to broach the whole subject of her father's being forced to play ball with the *mafiya*. Of course, being from the mother country, perhaps she'd understand totally. "I'm just meeting someone who might have some information. I'll get back to you."

"Information? What kind of information?"

"Information about . . ." I hesitated. What exactly could I tell her? Oh, what the hell, I thought. "He claims to have information about the whereabouts of your father. I'm not at all sure it's true."

"Where are you?" she asked. "I want to come along."

"Sorry, that's not possible. I'm at my martial arts school, and Kali and I are waiting on that private detective I told you about. He's going to take us somewhere to follow up on a lead."

"Take you where?"

"I'm not sure." I really wasn't at this point, but I certainly didn't want her nosing around trying to find me. "Look, if it appears to be a decent lead, I'll get back to you. I promise."

After a moment of silence, she said, "All right, but please, be careful."

• • •

Giretti picked us up about thirty minutes later in a big black SUV with windows smoked so dark I didn't even know it was him until he honked and lowered one of them.

I held the rear door for Kali, who seemed a bit perturbed about being relegated to the backseat. But I needed the leg room more than she did, and Giretti was driving.

"Nice wheels," I said. "What is this, an Escalade?"

"Yeah." He grinned. "It's also a rental. Comes under the heading of expenses."

I frowned and said, "It's nice to go first class on my dime, huh?"

"Hey, I'm a big guy and I need the space. Besides, it's only for one, two days max. Costs about the same as a Chevy Impala."

"Bet it gets great gas mileage too," Kali said. Her sarcasm was obvious, but if it bothered Giretti, he didn't show it.

"I didn't recognize your phone number when you called," I said.

"Yeah, it was a disposable. I use them all the time when I'm working a case. Keeps my number from popping up. That way nobody knows it's a private dick calling them."

"Disposable? I've heard of those," I said. "Didn't think many people used them, though."

"Except drug dealers," Kali said from the backseat.

Giretti frowned slightly. "So what were you two doing in Chinatown, anyway?"

"Kung fu lessons," Kali said. "So we're totally ready to kick some ass."

Rather than let things escalate in the Escalade, I broke in, asking Giretti about this guy we were going to see. "What's his name?"

He shrugged. "Goes by Yuri, or some shit like that. Most likely it's not his real moniker anyway. Which brings us to another question."

"Shoot."

He glanced over at me and curled his lip back in what I guess must have been something akin to a smile. "How much you willing to pay for this info? Provided it's legit, of course."

"Of course." I thought about this. I had no idea what the going rate for information on the street was in a case like this. But if it could lead us to Rudy, and if he was still alive, the last thing I wanted to do was quibble. "I'm good for what it takes, as long as it's reliable. How are we going to figure that out?"

Giretti wiped at his nose as he changed lanes. "Best way is to hear him out, then question him as to how he's privy to this stuff. We can ask him to take us there, which I wouldn't recommend, since we don't know if it's going to be dangerous. Better to sound him out, see if you think it's valid, and then let me check it out."

"And if it is, you'll do what?" I asked. "Notify the police?"

"Sure. If he's alive and being held against his will, then it's a job for the ESU cowboys."

I nodded. We were coming up to the bridge's first set of Gothic pylons, which had inspired everybody from Walt Whitman to Teddy Roosevelt. It was hard to believe the structure was moving through its second hundred years. We rode in silence under the network of cables and I wondered how this one was going to play out. If this guy was legit, and Giretti was giving every indication that he thought he was, then we might have enough to go back to Max and throw it in his face. That alone could be worth the price, I thought.

We got on the freeway and headed east.

"Where we going, anyway?" Kali asked.

"Brighton Beach," Giretti said. "Where else?"

About fifteen minutes more and we were exiting onto Ocean Parkway. In the distance, I could see some of the high brownstones and the metallic superstructure of the el tracks silhouetted against the blue sky.

"Too bad we don't have time to stop for some frozen custard in Coney," Giretti said. He grinned, but I noticed his face was covered with sweat. Nervous? My own mouth felt a bit dry with anticipation. We cut over into Brighton and down a few streets that I didn't know the names of. Giretti obviously knew his way around, but he'd said this was his stomping grounds. As long as he knew, I figured that was all that mattered.

"I been meaning to ask you," he said, "what's the name of that cop friend of yours again?"

"Max Kaminsky," I said. "He's a dick out of Midtown North. Why?"

"Just wondering if you'd told him about me. For when we eventually go to him with the goods."

"Not yet. Why? Are you worried I checked you out?"

He grinned. "Sometimes the guys still on the job take a dim view of those of us who have gone on to greener pastures in the private sector. You tell him we were tagging up to see this guy?"

"No, I figured I'd wait till I evaluated what he has to say. Max hasn't been real supportive of me nosing around in this matter, so when I do go to him, it'll have to be with something good."

Giretti held up his hand, making a circle with his thumb and index finger. "Gotcha."

We'd turned onto a street of warehouses. Exactly where, I didn't have a clue, except that we were close enough to smell the ocean when we stopped and Giretti lowered the window. I got a sudden whiff of his BO. The guy was sweating like a racehorse after a derby run.

"Know where we are?" he asked.

In the distance I could see the elevated train tracks and luxury co-ops of Brighton Beach. "More or less. Where's this guy at?"

"Hiding." Giretti gestured toward a row of buildings. The windows were pockmarked with jagged holes, and the whole block looked like a candidate for urban renewal. "He was a bit paranoid I'd bring the cops with me. I assured him I wouldn't."

We rode around the block once, then down an alley. Judging from the midsized weeds that had begun to spring up through the gaps in the asphalt, it wasn't a well-traveled one. Giretti pulled into what looked like an old loading zone area and put the vehicle in park. "Another good reason to use a rental."

"Just so I don't get billed for your deductible in case it's not here when we come back," I said.

"Ready?" he asked.

I nodded and got out. I started to open the back door for Kali but she popped it herself and jumped out, giving me a look I knew meant she didn't like this at all. I was beginning to have some misgivings myself, but I didn't want to appear like Caspar Milquetoast. Still, we were on unfamiliar ground here.

"Hey," I said to Giretti, "you strapped?"

He held open his coat, showing me the Beretta hanging down under his left arm in a shoulder holster, and smiled. But it was a nervous smile. And if he was nervous, where did that leave us? The hairs on the back of my neck were beginning to stand up and I was seriously wishing I hadn't let Kali talk me into letting her come along.

"Look, why don't you give Kali the keys and let her wait in the car?"

Giretti shook his head, motioning us forward. "That'll attract the wrong kind of attention. Come on. It's just over here."

I glanced at her, and she shrugged. We followed as he walked down to the mouth of the alley and looked both ways. He waved his arm at us and then disappeared around the corner. We followed. We came to the boarded-up entrance to one of the factories. The glass windows on either side had so much sludge buildup, I felt like I was looking through a lens covered with bacon grease. The inside looked dark and foreboding.

"Don't worry," Giretti said. "I got a flashlight." He pulled out a big metallic cylinder that looked like it was police issue and depressed the soft button on top. The brightness of the beam cut through the smudges on the window, lighting the interior. I could see a paneled wall with some kind of information desk in front of it. Giretti snapped off the light and took out his cell phone. It did look like a cheap disposable. He pressed a button and held it to his ear.

"Yeah, we're outside." He listened, then said, "Of course we're alone, just like we agreed." More listening, then, "Okay. We're on our way." He hung up, stuck the phone back into his pocket, and motioned toward another entrance about fifty feet away. "Down this way."

I glanced at Kali and we followed him again. He was walking fast and we had to do some quick stepping to keep up. The sidewalk, which had that old city cement look, seemed to make sounds like the grinding of glass under our soles. I tried not to catch my foot on any of the copious cracks. Giretti stopped at an inset doorway, this one apparently boarded up too. But as he stepped into the recess, he pulled slightly on the graffiti-covered plywood and it popped open. He shone the flashlight inside, exposing a barren hallway, and cocked his head for us to go in. I stepped through the opening, followed by Kali. Giretti came in behind us and pulled the plywood back into place, plunging the inside into near darkness again. Several shafts of bright sunlight filtered down from gaps in the roof, and as we moved, we were accompanied by the sudden rapid flapping of frightened wings. I hoped they were pigeons, not bats. Giretti held his light out, illuminating things. Cobwebs and dust motes floated everywhere. Giretti stepped in front of us and said, "Follow me."

Like we had much of a choice.

He walked with a purposefulness, like he was comfortable in the place. Had he been here before? Somebody had. As his beam swept over the floor in front of him, I saw two sets of footprints ahead of us leading down the corridor.

The flapping had ceased, giving way to an eerie silence. We came to a juncture and Giretti flashed his light down the intersecting corridor. "This way."

Just follow the footprints, I thought. I glanced back to try to see if Kali was all right, but the roof of the current section must have been intact, or covered by a second floor. Seeing anything other than what was illuminated by Giretti's light was virtually impossible.

"Are there rats in here?" Kali asked, her voice sounding nervous.

"Probably," Giretti said. "Just stay close to me."

"Hey," I said, "how much farther?" This was not playing out the way I wanted.

Giretti stopped and held up his hand, holding the flashlight up toward the ceiling to spread an umbrella of light and canting his head, as if to listen.

Then I heard it too.

A rhythmic tapping. Several knocks, then silence. A signal?

Giretti raised his hand to the wall and tapped back. His face glistened with sweat. He waited until he heard his tap repeated, then reached inside his coat and withdrew his Beretta. This immediately made me feel better.

Until he pointed it at me.

"What the hell are you doing?" I asked.

"Earning my money," Giretti said. "Now don't fucking move, either of you." He lowered the beam, focusing on us and making us feel like we were caught in a freight train's headlight. His left hand reached into my pocket and removed my cell phone. He pocketed it and pushed me back, then ripped Kali's purse out of her hands. "Okay, I got them," he yelled out.

A pair of flashlight beams snapped on and I could see two figures moving behind them. One was shorter and fat-looking. The other was just plain massive. As they got closer, I recognized them, first one, then the other. Buteyko and Vasili. Why the fuck hadn't I seen this coming?

I turned my head to prevent the bright light from shining in my eyes, and said to Giretti, "You dirty son of a bitch."

"Yeah." I heard his low chuckle. "But I'm gonna be one rich SOB too, with what they're paying me."

# CHAPTER 23

"Bring them down here," Buteyko said in his fractured English.

Giretti stepped back against the wall and waved his gun at us, indicating we should walk past him. He fell in behind and shined the light between us. Buteyko and Vasili walked ahead, leading us deeper into the bowels of the building.

A fucking double cross. A trap. Something I hadn't even imagined, and with no one knowing where we were . . . I felt the panic begin to sweep over me. But I had to stay calm. I had to figure a way out. It was dark. Maybe we could make a break for it and hide. But they had the only lights. And the only guns. They'd simply hunt us down, if they didn't shoot us as we ran. Plus, I had to communicate the break with Kali. Make sure we moved together. Otherwise I'd be abandoning her to these wolves.

No, Giretti wasn't a wolf. He was a fucking jackal.

So maybe I could reason with him.

"Whatever they're paying you, I'll double it," I whispered to him as we walked.

"Fat chance," he muttered. "Just shut up."

He was bringing up the rear, maintaining the tactical advantage if we tried to run. But that was the only chance we had. In another few minutes, we'd be totally at their mercy.

He reached out and shoved Kali's shoulder. "Move it, bitch. Either of you try anything, I'll shoot you both."

She stumbled a bit and regained her footing. "I knew you were a pig from the start, motherfucker."

God, she was tough.

I tried another tactic. "Giretti, you think they're going to leave a loose end like you around? Wise up." I was talking low but fast. If I could reason with him, we might have a chance. "That's what they've been doing. Eliminating all the fucking loose ends. These guys don't leave anyone alive who can trace things back to them."

Giretti snorted like he was enjoying the ramblings of a kid being taken to the principal's office. Or maybe of a condemned man taking that final stroll. An already dead man muttering as he walked that last mile . . .

Ahead I noticed Buteyko glance back at us and then whisper something to the gorilla.

"Giretti," I said, "don't be party to this. People know I hired you."

"So fucking what? I'll be long gone before they find you and the bitch. With what they're paying me, I'll be retired in a nice warm climate."

He shoved my shoulder. We turned another corner, opening into what must have been the large product assembly floor of the factory. Buteyko stopped and went to an old counter. He reached out and switched on a large portable lamp, walked down and switched on another, and then a third and fourth one. When he cut his flashlight, the room glowed with a weak light, but it was enough to illuminate all of us. We were in a cleared-out section surrounded by piles of metallic junk and garbage. The musty smell curdled inside my nose. Kali sneezed.

"God bless you," Buteyko said. In the dim light his accompanying smile looked even more sinister. Pure evil personified.

"We wish to assure you, Mr. TV Star, that we will be as"—he searched for the right word—"expedient as possible." The grin widened. "You made fun of my English before, didn't you?" Now the smile faded completely. "But I don't hear you laughing now."

My smart-ass comeback got caught in my throat.

Buteyko's fat face nodded up and down slightly, like he was agreeing with himself on something. "Know this, Mr. Belzer and friend." He spat out the last word. I suddenly grew even more fearful for Kali. "You are going to tell us everything you know, and everyone who you have told what you know. Then we are going to go over it, and over it, until we are certain you are not hiding anything from us."

"Sounds like we could work something out," I said. Even I could hear the tremor of desperation in my words. "Say the word and we close up shop."

"That is not an option any longer!" Buteyko yelled. "You had your chance before, and you persisted. Now you will pay."

"I think this is where I bow out," Giretti said, still holding the Beretta. For a brief second I thought he was going to shoot them and save us, then I saw the gleam in his eye. "We agreed on five hundred thousand for the delivery, the rest when the deed was done?"

Buteyko said something in Russian to Vasili, who began to move off.

"Hey, where's the big guy going?" Giretti said.

"He's getting the suitcase, with your money," Buteyko said. He smiled, but it looked about as benign as the bear who's about to have you for dinner.

Vasili reappeared with a small suitcase. He held it toward Giretti. It was zippered shut.

"Go ahead," Buteyko said. "Count it, if you like. We have time. Plenty of time."

Giretti licked his lips and reached out, taking the suitcase. The idiot set it down and knelt beside it, holding the edge with his right hand, which also held his pistol, and using his left to pull at the zipper. As soon as the Beretta wasn't pointed in a lethal direction anymore, Vasili reached down and grabbed Giretti's gun hand.

"Hey!" Giretti said, trying to rise up, but Vasili was too strong. He pulled him up, still controlling Giretti's right hand with his own, and circled the man's neck with his left, actually lifting Giretti's feet off the floor.

"Do not try to interfere," Buteyko said. He was holding a gun of his own now, a lethal-looking semiauto that reflected the ambient lighting off its blue steel slide.

"*Do svidaniya,*" Vasili said, the effort distorting his voice as Giretti continued to gurgle for a few moments more. The Beretta slipped from the detective's limp fingers and hit the floor with a sharp thud. Buteyko walked around us and picked it up, smiling.

"Don't worry, Mr. Belzer," he said, smiling. "Such an ignominious end would not be suitable for a man of your stature. We have something different in mind for you. And for the young lady too."

Vasili let Giretti's slack form drop to the floor, stirring up a small cloud of dust. I couldn't say I was sorry to see the prick buy it, but I wondered what terrible thing was in store for us.

"Not as messy as a garrote, huh?" I said. "Like the one you used on Gustafson?"

Buteyko's lips stretched into a simper. "Ah, yes. But you have only yourself to blame for your friend's death in that case. If you would have only left well enough alone, as I told you . . ." He fluttered his hands. "If only you would have."

I thought about trying to shove Kali one way and make a break in the opposite direction, but there was no way I was going to leave her. With Giretti dead, there was one fewer of them now, and I might be able to disarm Buteyko in a one-on-one. But that would still leave Vasili after her. Could I get a gun away from the fat man and get off a shot to stop the Spetsnaz giant?

Vasili lifted up the black bag he'd given to Giretti.

"Ah," Buteyko said, obviously relishing the moment. "Let us see what treasures really awaited Mr. Giretti, shall we?" He nodded and Vasili began to pull open the zipper. "You really should choose your friends more carefully, Mr. Belzer. Your man Giretti came to me with a proposal of betrayal yesterday. I had only to offer him money and he became your Judas."

"And you offered him a lot more than thirty pieces of silver too," I said, trying to buy time. But I knew it was running out. Too quickly. I had to do something, or we'd both be lying next to Judas on the dirty cement floor. I thought of Harlee. When was the last time I'd talked to her? When was the last time I'd told her how much I loved her?

Vasili had the bag open and removed something that looked like a gun, but even in the dim lighting I could see that it wasn't real. He held it gingerly by the barrel, and I saw the trigger had a short but thick round cylinder behind it. Suddenly I knew what it was. One of their lethal squirt guns.

"As I said . . ." Buteyko smiled. "Your deaths will be from something more . . . natural."

A couple of squirts and we'd be going into convulsions, looking like we both just had twin heart attacks. It wasn't the way I wanted to make my exit, and I certainly didn't want that for Kali.

"Now, Mr. Belzer," Buteyko said. His voice was slow, his tone deliberate. "I want you to know this gun is filled with a very special and extremely poisonous substance composed of cyanide—"

"And sodium nitrate," I finished for him. I raised my hands.

Buteyko seemed as delighted as when I'd addressed him in Russian before on the street. "Excellent. You have done well. Now you are going to tell me, in detail, everything you know. Everyone you have told, every step you have taken. Or else . . ."

Vasili raised his arm with the squirt gun and held it about a foot in front of my face.

If I could move a bit closer, I thought, I might be able to try that disarming move I'd practiced.

But I remembered getting shot repeatedly by Jimmy, especially until I'd gotten warmed up and in sync enough to get the distance and timing down exactly right. This would be a one-shot deal. Literally. No second chances. And if the spray hit me or Kali . . .

I needed some kind of diversion.

Looking over to Buteyko, and still keeping my hands elevated, I hoped I looked like I was in total surrender. In reality, it would allow me a smoother grabbing gesture.

"Look, Buteyko," I said. My chin brushed against something metallic. The remote. I still had it pinned to my lapel. I swallowed. I wanted a diversion, didn't I? And this was a job for an actor.

I spoke to my lapel and said in a loud voice, "You guys get all that?"

Buteyko's brow wrinkled like a puckered asshole. "What? Who are you speaking to?"

I held up the lapel, showing him the clipped-on mic. "I'm wired, asshole." I couldn't see Kali, but I hoped she was following my lead, knowing that we'd have to make a break soon. Very fucking soon.

"Are the snipers set with the infrareds?" I said into my lapel. I nodded, just like I was listening to an earpiece. "Good. We're being covered by—Oh, you already see that." I raised my eyebrows and grinned. "Better have the SWAT teams move in now."

"Who are you talking to?" Buteyko demanded. "NYPD?"

"NYPD, FBI, CIA," I said. It was a desperate bluff. "This whole fucking place is surrounded. Both of you better give up now, while you still can."

"Give up?" Vasili said. I was glad to hear that he was developing a command of English. I was gladder still when his big head rotated to the side to glance around for those mythical snipers. I used it to seize the moment, lashing out with my left hand and twisting my body to the side, narrowing the target surface. I yelled for Kali to run, figuring that was the only chance she had, then brought my right hand up and gripped the gun, trying for the wrist double-back.

"Run!" I yelled again. In a peripheral flash I saw her move, but everything suddenly tunneled down to my hands on Vasili's, both of us struggling for control.

Handling Jimmy's small, ladylike hand was vastly different from the gigantic paw I found myself gripping now. I bore down with all my weight, trying to force the squirt gun up and out of his grasp, but he slammed his left fist into my face, almost knocking off my glasses. I shook off the blow and knew I couldn't release my grip on the squirt gun. If I did, I'd die. I pivoted again and remembered Jimmy's sage advice: *Use a follow-up technique. Don't depend on just one.* I brought my foot up and snapped it into the general area of his balls, hoping to connect. Seconds later, with the delayed reaction every male who's been hit there knows, I heard him grunt and weaken slightly.

I forced my weight forward, trying to wrench the squirt gun away from him, but his recovery was amazing. I felt his enormous power pulling my hands away, and then I remembered the other thing Jimmy had taught me today. I leaned my head back and held my breath as I squeezed, hearing the wet squeak as the trigger depressed. Vasili expelled a horrified breath, then released his hold on the squirt gun and staggered backward, doing the dead man's dance. His big hand pawed at his face as he fell, and he screamed for a good five seconds, before that sound was replaced by a grotesque gurgling.

I saw Buteyko hold the gun out, straightening his arm and aiming. The semidarkness exploded with a piercing yellow light that flashed by me with a thunderous sound. Seconds later Kali, who'd taken a few running steps off to my left, screamed and fell forward, clutching her left side as she smacked hard against the floor.

"No!" I screamed, although the ringing in my ears made my voice sound like it was coming through a tunnel from far away.

Buteyko stood, holding the pistol, which had a wisp of smoke trailing from the barrel. He stepped backward, putting more space between us. I held the squirt gun now, I but doubted its spray could reach him where he was. He shifted slightly and pointed the gun directly at me.

"Too late, Mr. TV Star," he said.

A bright beam of red light dotted the dust motes and centered on the whiteness of Buteyko's dress shirt. Milliseconds later, a sharp, vicious, whipping sound cracked the stillness. But it wasn't his gun exploding with the yellow fire like before. Buteyko's mouth turned downward at the ends, a thin stream of blood forced its way from inside his mouth and another one began winding down the front of his white shirt. The arm holding the gun seemed to go slack and fell to his side. He looked down at his shirt, dumbly, as the whipping crack tore another hole in him, close to the first entry wound. His body collapsed in sections, like a set of folding blocks, the pistol skittering on the floor a few feet from his leg.

I looked around, feeling as dumb as a box of rocks, following the red laser beam back toward its source. The laser went out, and I saw some movement behind me, off to the left. Then Anna stepped out of the shadows holding a pistol with a barrel so long I knew it must have had a sound suppressor. Her strawberry blond hair was pulled back into a ponytail, and she had on a dark jacket and tight leather gloves.

She went to Buteyko and kicked the gun away, then she bent over him, lowering her own weapon toward his face, and stuck it against his eye.

He didn't flinch. She straightened up and walked over to Vasili. Instead of bending down, she pressed something and the bright laser light zoomed downward. She centered the red dot on his face and fired. His big head recoiled only slightly from the impact of the pop. It sounded sweet to me. There's nothing like insurance.

"Anna?" I started to ask. "What . . . ?"

"I suggest you check on her," she said, pointing toward Kali. "But first, please set that squirting gun down very carefully on the floor and kick it to the side. Do not kick it hard and do not drop it. Do you understand?"

She spoke slowly, like she was addressing a recalcitrant child, her voice as calm and flat as a glass of warm beer. I did as I was told, wiping my hands on my shirt as I rushed over to Kali. Thank God she was still breathing.

"Can I have some light over here?" I yelled.

Anna stepped forward, switching on a flashlight as bright as the one Giretti had had. She shined it down on Kali's back. I saw a frothy redness bubbling from her side.

"Kali," I said, touching her face. She still felt reasonably warm, which I took as a good sign. I stripped off my jacket, rolled it into a ball, and slid it as gently as I could under her head. "Call an ambulance for her. Please."

"I'll let you do that. Here is your cell phone." She held it up, then handed it to me. I scrambled to dial 911, then realized I didn't know where we were. When the emergency operator asked me, I said, "We're in an abandoned building in Brighton Beach somewhere. Hurry. A woman's been shot here."

Anna snapped her fingers. I looked up at her and she rattled off the building's address. I repeated it into the phone.

"You get that?" I asked. My ears were still ringing like I was trapped under a school bell.

"We've got it, sir," the operator said. "Help's on the way. Now please, stay on the line with me. Is there anyone else with you besides the injured person?"

I started to answer but saw the laser light center on my arm. It worked its way over to my chest. I looked up at Anna.

She shook her head and said, "Hang up the phone now, Richard, and place it on the floor."

I hesitated, and she said, "Do it now."

I did.

Anna swept the beam over Kali's back. More blood bubbled out of the wound.

"Place your hand over the wound to seal it," Anna said. "The bubbles mean she has been hit in the lung. If you have a laminated card, you can use it instead of your hand. Then roll her on her left side."

Remembering my old army training for a sucking chest wound, I grabbed my plastic SAG card out of my wallet and pressed it against Kali's back. Oh, God, please let her live, I thought.

"As long as the ambulance is on the way, she should be all right," Anna said. Her calmness was like someone dipping my privates in fucking ice water.

"Who the hell are you?"

Anna shrugged. "Let us just say I work for the government. My government."

"You're KGB?"

She smiled. "We say FSB since the Revolution failed."

"Where's Rudy? Did you kill him too?"

"I was actually hoping you would eventually lead us to him. I was sent here to eliminate loose ends. But now, he does not matter."

"Loose ends . . ." I nodded toward Kali. "Does that include us?"

Something halfway between amusement and admiration flickered in her eyes. "If I wanted that, I could have let them kill you. I must say, I was impressed by how you disarmed Vasili. He was always boasting about being Spetsnaz, you know."

"So I've heard."

"Now, Richard, I need my pendant back, please." She tucked the flashlight under her arm, focusing the beam on me, and held out her hand.

"What?"

"My pendant." Her voice rose slightly, growing firmer. "Give it to me now. I know you have it."

I was totally perplexed, but I reached into my pocket and handed it over to her.

Her beautiful face smiled. "It contains a powerful GPS locator. One of our most advanced." She lowered the gun. "It's how I tracked you."

"Tracked me?"

She gave a slight nod as she placed the pendant in her pocket. "I'm glad you believed the story of it belonging to my mother. You Americans are such sentimentalists."

"Just like you Russians."

The smile flickered again.

"So what happens now?" I asked.

Anna shrugged again. "With those two incompetent idiots dead, any legal case against my government will be impossible now to prove, even if Markovich does show up. His death, like yours and the death of your female friend, would serve no purpose for us at this time. Thus, the matter is now closed." She canted her head as the distant wail of sirens started to become audible.

"Ah, I must be going," she said. "If I leave you Giretti's flashlight, will you be able to carry your friend and find your way out of here?"

I nodded.

She reached into her pocket and set the long flashlight on the floor. Then she straightened up and began to walk away.

"I guess I should say something like thanks," I called after her. "Or *spasibo*."

"You're welcome." Anna paused, then turned. "It was never in my hope to have to kill you, Richard, but I must tell you, what I told you before about your Russian sounding so good—I was lying."

There was still enough ambient lighting for me to see her seductive smile. Except now I knew it was on the face of Lucifer's handmaiden.

"Besides," she said, "I really do like your show. *Do svidaniya*."

But then again, maybe she wasn't Lucifer's handmaiden. Maybe she was just a real hot angel of death.

"You're not such a bad actress yourself," I called after her. But she'd already disappeared into the darkness.

# CHAPTER 24

The sight of Max's contrite expression as the Brooklyn dicks escorted him into that emergency room was almost as pretty a sight as the doctor's when he came out to tell us Kali was going to be okay.

"The wound was a through-and-through," he said. "Nine millimeter, most likely. Collapsed her lung but practically sealed itself due to the high velocity. That makeshift field dressing with the card you put on there helped save her life, Mr. Belzer."

Thank God for that, I thought. And for modern medicine and the emergency room crews of New York City and their expertise at treating gunshot wounds. Of course, they get plenty of practice.

"When can I see her?" I asked.

"She's sedated now," he said. "In a few hours. In the meantime, do you know how to notify her immediate family?"

I took out my cell phone and went to work, calling the right numbers until I finally got hold of Vern and told him I wanted the studio limo service to go pick up Kali's mom and bring her to the ER. Luckily, he didn't even try to argue with me.

Max and I walked to her room and I peered inside. She lay in quiet repose, tubes attached to her nostrils and a bunch of telemetry screens flashing static lines. I zeroed in on the one I figured was her heart and watched as the blips rose and fell with a regular cadence.

Thank God, I thought. Thank God. I should have trusted your instincts all along, kid.


Two days and countless interviews and debriefings later, I walked into Midtown North and told the desk jockey that Detective Kaminsky was expecting me.

He stared at me for several seconds after making the call.

"Say, anybody ever tell you you look like that actor guy . . . what's his name?"

"Detective John Munch?"

"No." He shook his head, then snapped his fingers and grinned. "Billy Bob Thornton."

Before I could refuse to dignify that one with an answer, Max opened the hallway door and motioned me inside.

"Okay, Belz," he said, when we stood alone, "what you're about to see practically cost me an arm and a leg, but I figured you'd earned the right."

"I'm glad you won't have to grow some new ones," I said.

He frowned and nodded. "Yeah, I know I had that coming, but you got to understand, I was under orders almost from the start."

"Just following orders. That has a familiar ring to it. You ought to register as a Republican and run for office."

I was following him down the hall now, and he was talking over his shoulder about how right I'd been: the Russian mob had been threatening Rudy's family and forcing him to falsify the true causes of death on the four autopsies by listing them as heart attacks and suppressing the toxicity screenings.

"No shit?" I asked, as sarcastically as I could.

"He balked when they told him to do the same for your buddy, the boxer, Alexi Zotkin." Max placed his hand on the knob and twisted it, still holding the door closed. "And I just want you to know that the NYPD and yours truly were kept in the dark about a lot of this until just recently."

"Nice of you to let me know," I said. "I'm sure I'll sleep easier."

He blew out a heavy breath and opened the door. "What I'm saying is, Rudy's death was faked by the Feds so he and his family could go into the witness protection program."

As the door opened fully, I saw Rudy standing in the center of the room, his head cocked half to the side, his face a model of penitence.

"Richard, my friend," he said. Even his voice sounded weak. "Will you ever forgive me for drawing you into my web of deceit?"

I went over to him and he embraced me, giving me the customary two kisses on my cheeks.

"I can work on the forgiveness part," I said, "but don't go thinking we're engaged or anything."

A guy in a blue suit who had Fed written all over him stood off to the side watching us. Max ushered Rudy and me over to a beat-up old table and chairs. We sat, and Rudy went into confession mode, telling me about how the *mafiya* had first approached him with a picture of his young daughter outside her day care school.

"When they told me what they wanted me to do," he said, his face draining of color, "I thought I was back in the Soviet Union. I realized I had no choice. Even here, after all these years, I could not escape them. Suddenly, how little things had changed for me. I thought about telling you, my friend, but did not wish to draw you in. Then, as we were leaving, when those thugs attacked us that night, I knew I had to give you some clue. In case things went bad."

"So you mailed me a riddle, wrapped in a mystery, inside an enigma," I said.

He listened, then smiled. "Ah, yes. Winston Churchill's quote. I mailed you the letter. I knew, with your inquisitive mind, that you would figure things out and go to the police if I did not survive." His eyes misted over and centered on the floor. "My stupidity was unforgivable. I am so sorry."

I placed my hand on top of his and patted it slightly. "It's all right. I understand."

"He finally went to the Feds and admitted everything," Max said. "They figured the best thing was to fake his death. Hell, even I didn't know what was going on at first."

I shot him a sour look. "Yeah, at first."

"Hey, I was told to clam up by the upstairs brass." Max shrugged apologetically. "Anyway, how's your partner doing? What's her name? Kalisha?"

I gave him a hard stare for a few moments before answering. "Kali. She's going to make it. She's tough."

"Good," Max said, scratching his head. "You know, maybe we should send her flowers or something."

"Oh, I already did," I said. "Several times. And speaking of women, did you ever track down Anna Katrina?"

"Miss Diplomatic Immunity?" Max shook his head. "She disappeared quicker than a Coney Island custard on a summer day. Best we can figure, she retreated to her embassy and they fixed her up with another name and gave her a plane ride back to mother Russia. This case was what they call a real confundrum, wasn't it?"

"That's conundrum," I said. "And yes, it was."

"I never could have imagined that the FSB would send a woman to pose as my daughter," Rudy said. "She was no doubt an assassin whose assignment was to kill me."

"And when she couldn't find you," I said, "she iced the two *mafiya* goons so they couldn't flip on her ex-boss, Vladimir. Two for the price of one."

Rudy nodded. "Thanks to you, my good friend. But I can never forgive myself for putting you at risk." As he started his second round of profuse apologies, I held up my hand to cut him off.

"Like I said, it's all right."

But he continued anyway. "You see, Richard, I was not sure I was going to survive, that this witness protection program was the right thing. I have a mistrust of police, especially those who work directly for the government, since my days under the Soviet oppression." He looked straight at me, his eyes still glistening. "But I knew you, my friend, would never rest until you knew the truth. But never did I assume you would do this investigation yourself. Not with all your police friends."

"Yeah, I sure have a lot of those, don't I?" I said, still giving Max the hard stare. "But not to worry. Next time I probably won't."

"Next time?" Max said. "For Christ's sake, Belz. You ain't gonna go stirring up more shit again, are you?"

"A man does what he does best." I grinned. "After all, I am not a cop. Not even in Brighton Beach."

# EPILOGUE

## And now, a few words from the Belz . . .

Just like they're so fond of saying on TV, the preceding story is a work of fiction, and any similarities to any real person (with the possible exception of yours truly) is totally unintentional.

That's another way of saying it's a novel. Phony locations, businesses, addresses, characters. In other words, total fiction. Well, almost total.

I made the decision to include myself as a character in this one to make sure things came off right. I'm the author of two nonfiction books, so I figured playing a more active role in my first novel was a natural extension of self. To prepare for this role of character/author, I engaged in a rigorous training regimen consisting of heavy thinking and even heavier drinking. Now ain't that a very Marlowe thing to say?

But really. I mean, although I'm basically a red wine kind of guy, with an occasional sidetrack into tequila, I believe in moderation, for the most part. It's too easy to forget the important things when you're blasted.

I envisioned the novel to be a combination of the stuff I've enjoyed all my life. A potent mix of Dashiell Hammett with a twist of Oscar Wilde and a dash of Lenny Bruce. Toss in the iconoclasm of Robert Altman, as well as a few other influences like James Dickey, Norman Mailer (who was always fond of putting himself in his "semi-fictions"), and of course, Truman

Capote, whose *In Cold Blood* sent chills down my spine when I read it as a teenager, and you have a partial list of my literary aspirations. Sprinkle in some Belzerian seasoning, and the wry, raucous worlds of make-believe and reality begin to converge. Thus, in a sense, this is the first reality novel of the new millennium that explores a unique universe and poses the eternal question: what is reality?

The question has been often asked but seldom answered satisfactorily.

So perhaps it's appropriate that as I started writing, a Chandleresque voice kept echoing inside my head. It was like Philip Marlowe telling the literary version of myself how to proceed. (I figured that since Altman cast Elliott Gould as Marlowe in his movie version of *The Long Goodbye*, I was in good company.) And as Chandler said in *The Simple Art of Murder*, down those mean streets I had to go, not mean and certainly neither tarnished nor afraid (this was fiction, after all, and I hope to star in the movie when it comes out). I cast myself as a knight errant in this fictional world, and strove to make it a better place, even though it was a slight variation of the real world I live in.

So I ask you again, what is reality?

I know I haven't answered that question, and you know what? I ain't even gonna try.

One more time, this is a novel, not autobiography. In some ways, writing it was like stepping into one of those virtual reality training rooms that my friends on the NYPD have been gracious enough to let me participate in from time to time. In other ways, it was like looking in a mirror and having the reflection smart off to you and give you the finger.

The uniqueness of the experience has been nothing short of fascinating. But like any good actor, I played my role to the best of my ability, this time not only as a character but also as an author.

How well I've accomplished what I set out to do remains to be seen, but I can tell you that it's been one hell of a ride. And I'm very glad that you, Dear Reader, are along for it. I hope you have enjoyed it as much as I did.

All the best,
Richard Belzer

# ACKNOWLEDGMENT

I am not a cop but I play one on television. . . .

For over a decade and a half I have had the good fortune to play the same character, Detective Sergeant John Munch, on *Homicide: Life on the Street*; and *Law and Order: SVU*, not to mention (although I will) as many as ten guest appearances on other prime-time shows.

Even with that extensive fictional experience, there's nothing like the real thing. That's where Mike Black comes in. A twenty-eight-year veteran police officer in the south suburbs of Chicago who has worked in various capacities, including patrol supervisor, tactical squad investigator, raid team member, and SWAT team leader, he also holds a black belt in tae kwon do and, perhaps best of all, has five cats.

The combination of his real-life experiences and being a gifted writer of three novels and two nonfiction books was invaluable in crafting *I Am Not a Cop!*. Quite simply, the book could not have been created without his insight, diligence, talent, and graciousness of spirit. I will be forever grateful to Mike for our collaboration and look forward to a continuing creative relationship.